You, Kwaznievski, You Piss Me Off

Rumours abound that John Lavery resulted from the shattered test tubes of Flann O'Brien, Janwillem van de Wetering, and Arrabal. I just think he writes the freshest sentences in Canada. The stories in *You, Kwaz16ievski, You Piss Me Off* are brooding, musical, deeply human, and loaded with the beautifully unexpected.
— Stuart Ross

Lavery's use of language and characterization is incredible.
— *Scene Magazine*

Impishly intellectual, gorgeously repulsive, fractiously knit, earthily out of this world: the only paradox *You, Kwaznievski . . .* doesn't encompass is that of John Lavery (mad genius? compulsive crafts-man?) himself. Rarely has language been so inventively precise, and such mind-mulching fun. Read this collection and you will wake from the slumber those other books have been lulling you into.
— Melanie Little

You, Kwaznievski, You Piss Me Off

John Lavery

MISFIT

ECW PRESS

Published by ECW PRESS
2120 Queen Street East, Suite 200, Toronto, Ontario, Canada M4E 1E2

NATIONAL LIBRARY OF CANADA CATALOGUING IN PUBLICATION

Lavery, John, 1949 Dec. 31–
You, Kwaznievski, you piss me off / John Lavery.

Fiction.
ISBN 1-55022-674-6

I. Title.

PS8573.A845Y69 2004   C813'.6   C2004-902605-4

Editor: Michael Holmes/a misFit book
Cover and Text Design: Darren Holmes
Production and Typesetting: Mary Bowness
Printing: Marc Veilleux Impremeur

This book is set in Bembo.

The publication of *You, Kwaznievski, You Piss Me Off* has been generously supported by the Canada Council, the Ontario Arts Council, the Ontario Media Development Corporation, and the Government of Canada through the Book Publishing Industry Development Program. Canadä

DISTRIBUTION
CANADA: Jaguar Book Group, 100 Armstrong Avenue, Georgetown, ON, L7G 5S4

PRINTED AND BOUND IN CANADA

ECW PRESS
ecwpress.com

Contents

Acknowledgements

Earlier versions of some of the stories in this book have been previously published: "The Man on the Stamp" in *Arts and Opinion*, "Two Bass Birds" in *The Canadian Forum*; "The October Tree" in *This Magazine*; "The Chocolate Dick" in *Grain*. I would like to thank the editors of these publications, Robert J. Lewis, Maggie Helwig, Alana Wilcox, and especially, Elizabeth Philips, whose perceptiveness was particularly helpful.

"Collector's Item," the essay referred to in "The Man on the Stamp," may be found in Joseph Brodsky, *On Grief and Reason*, Farrar Straus Giroux.

Thanks to Darren Holmes for his cover design, to Emily Schultz for her copyediting, to Sergeant André Filiatrault for his expertise, to James Moran and the Tree Reading Series regulars for their close attention, and to Catso, who not surprisingly tried to escape after reading this book. Thanks also to the Canada Council.

Thanks to siblings, in-laws, outlaws, cousins, nephews and nieces spread out over the planet, and thanks to the agèd p's, whom we all now miss.

I'm particularly grateful to those who so graciously agreed to read the manuscript: Sean Wilson, Lee Henderson, Stuart Ross, Mark Jarman, and Melanie Little. Melanie is the best antidote I know to the self-administered poisons of doubt and uncertainty.

Sincere thanks to Jack David and Michael Holmes at ECW for, as Gil Adamson puts it, bringing me in off the street.

Bon, et je ne peux pas passer sous silence l'appui constant des chefs du bataillon, à savoir, Claire Dionne, chef, Charles-Éric et Madeleine, assistants du chef, et Coco, assistante-chef des assistants du chef.

Merci à vous tous. Merci à mort.

for Rocket Ron

SNORT

My mother died before I was born. Not long before. Twenty-two minutes. My father's brain was so eaten with grief he couldn't even come up with a name to give me. Except my mother's name, Olivia.

I never knew my father with both arms. He strapped the right one to his body so he wouldn't forget my mother, stuffed his empty coat sleeve into his pocket, taught mathematics left-handed at Las Palmas de Oro High School. Writing was easy one-armed. He said. Even with the wrong hand. What was hard was getting the chalk off his fingers.

Why are you writing with your left hand? He yelled at me. Write with your right! He was off-balance trying to hit me with his right arm tied to his side. I could jump away easily. Bitch, he called me.

Why are you working so hard at your mathematics? I don't want you to. Oh no, you're not going to be a teacher. I forbid it. I'm not going to pay. Get away from me. Do something else.

I taught math left-handed for twenty-three years. Not at Las Palmas de Oro.

Bitch.

My brother's hair was made of candied wheat, his eyes were crystalline, semi-precious. At their best when he was lying.

He was always in my room, my brother was, in his undershorts, giving me presents, drawing me with colored pencils, to look like himself. Telling me about the girls who wanted him to do this with them, or to wear that, or to move like this other. I'm myself with you. He said. Just you.

When he was with me, my brother's eyes were always at their best.

Police Sergeant Paul-François Bastarache, 11th precinct, Montreal, marvelled at how the buttery California sun transformed the flat aluminum of the San Buenaventura police station into brushed gold, the raspy stucco into thickening caramel. He monitored his gait closely, not wanting the delight he felt to translate itself into an inappropriate, an un-American lilt, looked Clint-eyed across the street and was struck by a still more Californian apparition:

A small, municipal park with roaring plants whose leaves were so spiked and green they looked almost as real as plastic. With Parisian benches. On one of which, directly opposite, was seated a woman of indeterminate age, weathered, over-bundled. Reading a thin book. Beside her a coffee-maker, through which the morning sun ricocheted in sudden sparks.

Police Sergeant PF, who was nearing the end of a 12-week training stint intended principally to perfect his English, could not prevent himself from grinning, or from striding exuberantly into the station and bounding up the reverberant central stairway to the glassed-in front corridor from which he could just see the Pacific Ocean.

Lieutenant Hrbek was there, gazing out and down towards the park, his potatoey hands pushing lightly on his buttocks to ease the strain the American-standard dimensions of his body placed on his lower back.

"Canada," Hrbek said, PF's country of origin being, in this context, of greater significance and easier to pronounce than his name, "why don't you go down and tell that woman to kiss off."

"But," said Police Sergeant PF, "who's she bothering?" The note of petulance in his voice caused Hrbek to look at him sideways.

"Me. Obviously."

Captain Chernoff stepped out of his office then into the corridor, holding what appeared to be a greeting card close to his chest. His lower lip was so thick and purplish it seemed inflamed, sore, the air wheezed through the lampblack tufts obstructing his nostrils, the skin under his eyes was mushroom-coloured, folded into deep, convoluted wrinkles into which were wedged small growths, like bits of breakfast cereal. The initial impression he gave of solitary, hound-like drowsiness yielded gradually to a more restless impression of struggling, of hounded perhaps, misgiving.

"Gentlemen," he said quietly by way of greeting. "Our lady of the joe-maker with us again today?"

"I do not," said Hrbek, "understand how you can tolerate her watching the station."

"Why not?" said Chernoff. "Police officers watch soup kitchens."

Police Sergeant PF looked at the captain, intrigued by how much the mild irony of his remark was overmatched by the intense sparkle in his eyes.

Hrbek removed his hands from his buttocks, put his thumbs in his ears, and waved at the woman on the bench below.

"What, gentlemen," said Chernoff more quietly still, "do you make of this? It was in my mail." Casually, triumphantly, he lowered the card he had been holding against his chest. On the outside of the card, luridly coloured photographs of the Almendros Golf Course overlapped each other, fighting for attention. There was a message on the inside, composed of words and letters cut out from a magazine:

"Captain Crunch, how is your golf? In case you're interested, I killed someone."

Hrbek fluttered his lips scoffingly. "You have to get used to the captain, Canada. He hasn't had a murder in what, eight months? He's getting antsy."

Chernoff angled the card towards PF. "What do you say?"

"I don't know," said PF, crinkling his forehead. "Maybe just some thirteen-years-old who wants attention."

Chernoff raised his eyebrows briefly in a gesture of theoretic concurrence. "He wants attention, certainly. He's young, yes, brash. He's done his grubby little thing, very likely by accident, discovered it hasn't changed his life after all, and decided he deserves a little recognition for it."

Hrbek spun on his heels with surprising gracefulness for the semi-giant he was, took several steps down the corridor, spun around again.

"No, I . . ." He did not want to flatly disagree.

"In any case," said Chernoff, "there's nothing we can do. Maybe his needy little ego will be satisfied with this. Maybe not. He knows he's got to give us more if he wants to be taken for real. Which is risky. If he is for real. It's up to him."

"And that," said Hrbek, "irritates Captain Crunch."

Chernoff smiled slightly to disguise his pique, closed his eyes. "Yes lieutenant, that irritates Captain Crunch."

Police Sergeant PF could think of nothing he would rather do than sit in the California sun, so pervasive he felt sure it was tanning his Nordic skin under his clothes. On a Parisian park bench. Next to a burbling, redolent coffee-maker.

"To wet my whistle with, of course," she said. She was wearing a bulky, V-necked sweater that might have been white, flecked with black, or black, flecked with white. Over this, a cloth, turquoise raincoat so eroded by time and the sun it appeared to have been chiselled from a quartziferous formation with a naturally greenish mud-blue hue. "For company. A woman alone looks undignified, as though she wished she had something to hide. So I like my coffee-maker. It keeps my dignity up."

"Where do you plug it . . . ?" An extension cord was just visible under the bushes, leading towards a small storage shed. "Oh I see. And you enjoy to sit across from the police station?"

Her hair seemed older than she was, the colour of dead leaves, kinked, floating, so fine her rosy, visible scalp revealed the lunar curve of her head. Her nose might have stopped growing when she was eight.

"I do. The comings and goings. The sounds especially. I've noticed that you, for example, when you run up the steps, you imitate the sound of a car engine. Vrrrmmmm."

PF reddened. He could think of nothing he would rather do than sit in the California sun and be told he imitated the sound of a car engine. "It's an old habit," he said. "I don't even know I do it. You can hear me from here?"

"And the big one," said the woman, perhaps to attenuate PF's embarrassment, or perhaps simply following her own train of thought, "if *he* made a sound going up the steps, what would it be?"

"Hrbek? The noise of chains raising an anchor."

"He punches through the air, very logical, convincing. Whack, smack." Her eyes were perched on her pudgy cheeks. "And the shorter one with the black, curly hair?"

"Chernoff."

"Chernoff?"

"*Cap*tain Chernoff."

"He's difficult to hear."

"Yes, I agree."

"He leaves at noon everyday, by himself. Comes back by himself. It must be while he's gone that he makes his sound." She narrowed her eyes, as though to sharpen her hearing. "Flip-flops," she said, "walking over crushed glass."

PF was struck by this. He turned his face to the sun, fitted the sound as he imagined it to Chernoff, Chernoff to the sound, thought the union tellingly apt. So much so he could not help wondering if he was not being beguiled by the woman's evocative foreignness, if he was not, as an outsider, mistaking as truly meaningful what was merely unaccustomed. He stood up grudgingly.

"On your way?"

"Have to work on my engine. Vrrmm." Again he reddened, less out of self-consciousness than in acknowledgement of the woman's keen sense of observation. "Maybe I will stop by tomorrow."

"I'll show you how to snort."

"Snort?"

"Tomorrow."

Captain Chernoff upbraided himself for the eagerness with which he collected his mail each day. He reproached himself further, as no new anonymous card arrived, for allowing his disappointment to degenerate into an absurd sense of betrayal. Further still for seeking his pouting revenge by not collecting his mail at all, by qualifying as purely tentative his interest in the original card.

During this period, he found the presence of the joe-maker lady strangely soothing. Was it the steadfastness with which she endured her colourless, sun-filled days? His days being busier of course, less sunny, but equally colourless. Was it the mystery that surrounded her? Was it the lack of mystery? He did not know.

Chernoff was, in fact, a man who did not know. He had the impression of caroming from impulse to instinct, was perplexed, haunted by an inability to discern, except regressively, after they had translated themselves into action, the forces directing his personality. "Of course," he might say, "even then, at the outset, I knew. I did. But I did not know I knew. How much better I would be at this if I — if I were more present inside my own skull."

He was respected by his colleagues, deeply, admired for an assumed philosophical braininess, due in large part to his habit of disappearing on long thinking sessions, alone, on foot, in any weather. But only Chernoff knew that during these walks, which were as necessary to him as sleep, he did not think, not about anything. Except walking.

He stood in the glassed-in front corridor, ready to slip into his office should he hear Hrbek's heavy, pigeon-toed step, and observed the joe-maker lady talking to Canada on the bench below. He was gently envious of the Canadian's evocative foreignness, so different from his own, which was a denizen's foreignness, a skin-tight mask under which he itched relentlessly. He watched them with an odd, a not unpleasant exasperation, as though he were looking at a close-up of the moon, unable to perceive the rounded hillocks as the craters he knew they were.

"So," said Police Sergeant PF, "how do you snort?"

"Snort?" she said. "Oh. Right. Snort is a game. It requires a piece of paper and a differently coloured pencil for each player."

"Want me to go get that?"

"If you want to play."

PF returned with the required material.

"Alright," said the woman. "To play snort, you begin by drawing a map. That is, you cover the paper with a continuous line, letting it cross itself as often as you like." She did this. "Right. The points of intersection are vertices, the lines joining the vertices, edges, the areas within the edges, regions. Each player in turn colours a region. The region thus coloured must either be independent, or share a vertex with an opponent's region. It must not share an edge. The loser is the first player who cannot colour a region according to the rule. I'll start."

"Is it an advantage to start?"

The woman studied PF for a moment, as though considering whether or not the tone of his question cast a shadow on her competitive integrity.

"Yes," she said, "it is. I'll give you the choice of colour."

Captain Chernoff was sitting, perfectly naked, on the cool surface of the table in his friend's kitchen. The only illumination in the kitchen came from the nocturnal, exploratory glow of a nearby streetlight.

"Now," he muttered, "I need a drink, alcoholic in nature, after the heavy lectures involving quantum mechanics."

The friend herself was sitting beside him, her somnolent breasts hanging sloth-like, upside-down, her navel deeply sunk into the creases of her midriff. Their nakedness was the sort of nakedness appropriate to an unsleeping, stifling summer night.

"Quantum mechanics?" said the friend quizzically.

It was now two weeks since Chernoff had received the card. He was willing to accept that there would not now be another, to grant

Hrbek his minor victory. He was less willing to face another bland summer of water-use violations, kite festivals, sweat-stained domestic infighting, the odd newborn dropped into a garbage can.

"Now I need," he repeated, ". . . alcoholic in nature, after the heavy lectures . . ."

"Explain yourself, young man."

He sawed his legs back and forth gently under the table, causing the table to creak.

"For the last two, two and a bit weeks," he said, "a woman has been sitting in the park directly opposite the station. She brings a coffee-maker with her." He talked about the woman's mystery, about her lack of mystery, about Canada, the Frenchman from Montreal, who spent his noon hours sitting on the bench with her playing mathematical games.

"I find myself watching them, every day. At first, I was simply intrigued. I thought, if the woman's there for a reason, we won't find out if we chase her away. I didn't say it in so many words maybe, but that was, that must have been, my thinking. But now, frankly, I envy them. They . . ."

The friend sawed her legs in inverse rhythm, steadying the table. "They what?" she said encouragingly.

"They have a great time!" Chernoff turned his face away from his friend. He stopped sawing his legs, the table began to creak again, but on a different note. "They're like children together. They play hackenbush, sun cattle, snort. Canada shows me how to play, but I have no talent for that kind of thing. I just don't catch on."

He looked mournfully at the ceiling. His eyes had the polished quality of eyes that do not weep, although they might wish to. He could not bring himself to mention the anonymous card.

"I can't say as I'm catching on to much these days. My instincts are stumbling around like . . ."

The friend adopted a furrowed expression so as not to smile, hearing, as she did, a distinctly childlike quality in Chernoff's own voice.

"And then," he said, suddenly vigorous, "there's this *fuck*ing sentence that Canada got from the coffee lady and that has lodged itself in my brain." His voice turned shrill, priggish. "Now I need a drink, alcoholic in nature, after the heavy lectures involving quantum mechanics." His voice relaxed. "It's for remembering the value of pi-fucking-eye."

"The value of pi? Three point one four? One five nine two six, and so on."

"How do *you* know that?" snapped Chernoff, outraged at discovering his friend in flagrant collusion with Canada and the joe-maker lady.

The friend shrugged loosely. "But I don't see the connec . . . oh yes, it's the number of letters in each word."

"Good for you," he said with loud, accusatory sarcasm. "You catch on."

"Shhh," said the friend, "shhh. Isn't it of the nature of instincts, true ones, sometimes, to stumble around like . . . ?"

"Have you done your homework?" said the coffee lady to Police Sergeant PF. "You've had well over a week now."

"Sort of," hemmed PF.

"The question was: what is the maximum number of players that can play snort without redundancy? Or, conversely, what is the minimum number of colours required to colour a map without two adjacent countries being the same colour?"

"That was the question."

"And the answer?"

"Four?" said PF delicately.

"Can you prove it?"

PF shook his head, baffled. "No, I can't."

"Hrbek!" Chernoff stood, in the glassed-in front corridor, outside his door. He inched forward in order to get a glimpse of the park below, discovered the empty bench staring up at him coldly, menacingly, as though protecting its not-yet-arrived occupant. He drew back quickly. He was very agitated.

"Hrbek!"

He heard Hrbek scuffing up the reverberant central stairway, saw Hrbek himself round the corner, wiping his hands on a dish towel.

"Ah-hah," said Chernoff. "What's for breakfast?"

"Latkes Acapulco. Want some?" Hrbek not infrequently used the station's well-equipped kitchen to prepare polychromic, seething food.

"Definitely," said Chernoff. His lower lip was so deeply purple as to seem about to split, his eyes smouldered with a victorious intensity. He held a greeting card close to his chest.

"Oh-oh," said Hrbek, "another card after all. Crunchy's happy now. Let's have a look."

It was a get-well card, meant to offer encouragement to someone recovering from a life-threatening illness. On the outside, "I hear there's a golf course in heaven . . ." On the inside, ". . . but they won't give you a starting time!"

"Captain Crunch, only kidding about the golf. I know you're interested, just helpless. I thought I might kill someone else to prove it."

"Prick," muttered Hrbek, the colour in his cheeks less an indication of anger than an admission of misjudgement.

"Notice," said Chernoff quietly, "the card is somewhat bent. I'd be willing to bet it has been sitting in his pocket for some time. He hesitated before sending it. But now he has, he's got on the carousel. There will be more cards now. Curious. Why so grammatical? 'I thought I might . . .' Doesn't seem to mind clipping out and gluing, does he? Painstaking, wouldn't you say? He must have been good at kindergarten."

He held the card at arm's length, not unlike a couturier regarding a silk maillot, weighing his admiration against his disdain.

"So where do we go from here?" said Hrbek.

"Nowhere. We wait." His disdain outweighed his admiration apparently.

"Wait. Fuck that. Somebody, somewhere, may be in danger."

"Is in danger. But not today."

"Well then. We can start by sending the card to the lab."

"We can. I sent the first one. They told me the words were cut out from at least two magazines. One was *Sports Illustrated*. Wow."

"No prints?"

"Sure. Mine."

The third card arrived two days later. There was a drawing on the cover of a golfer with geriatric knees and semi-circular wrinkles under his eyes not unlike Chernoff's own. "Old golfers never die," it read, "they just lose . . ." The last two words had been whited over.

"Captain Crunch, the police exist because criminals exist. You exist because I exist. If you can't find me, how do you find yourself? I will give you a hint. At midnight on the 28th, I will kill again. Another hint, why not. Melrose overpass, also on the 28th."

"Canada," said Captain Chernoff, "you're working on a degree in criminology are you not?"

"Yes I am. And in business administration."

Chernoff's restrained smile seemed to indicate that his admiration for PF outweighed his disdain for himself. "What," he said, "do you make of this card?"

Police sergeant PF studied the message for a long moment before offering his opinion with disarming solemnity.

"I believe this person wants to commit the perfect crime."

Captain Chernoff cocked his head in order to observe PF from a slightly different angle. "Explain yourself, young man," he said. Something about the words struck him as odd, but he did not know what.

"First of all, someone should tell to this person that the police exists for many reasons besides criminals like him."

Chernoff, who was far from impervious to the mocking tone of the cards, received this comment with a good deal more appeasement than his faint nod of acknowledgement suggested.

"The perfect crime. I am thinking of the theory of one of my professors. Laliberté is his name, but that's besides the point. According to this theory, the perfect crime is not one the perpetrator simply gets away with, leaving no traces. Not at all. Such crimes are often committed. If we say that a personality susceptible of criminal action is torn between his need for power and his need for humiliation, the perfect crime, the one which satisfies completely his criminal longing, his contradictory longing, yes? is the one that the criminal has the power over his own humiliation. That is to say, the one that he controls when he will be captured, and how he will confess."

Chernoff could not help being distracted by his paternal affection for PF and by PF's slight accent, which made Chernoff think of the fluttering arpeggios of accordions. At the same time he was aware of his friend's bare shoulder breaking through the curtain of her unbrushed, aluminum hair, he did not know why.

"By the way," he said, "how's the snort with our lady of the joe-maker?"

PF's seriousness did not relax. "After so much time, I still don't know why she is sitting there."

"You think she has a reason?"

"Oh yes, I do."

Chernoff was almost wounded by this response, having come to believe that PF's interest in the coffee-maker lady was unrelated to police business, based only on a shared and human enthusiasm.

"She talks very much," said PF, "very fast, but not about herself. She has never even said her name."

"You haven't asked?"

"No. It is Olivia Cottinjon."

"How do you know that if you haven't asked?"

"It is written in a book she reads."

Chernoff's gaze slid down his friend's shoulder, along her upper arm, over to her somnolent breast. "Not necessarily *her* name. What's the book?"

"The Sand Reckoner."

"What's that, Barbara Cartland?" He might have taken a handful of sand and let it trickle down his friend's back. The sand might have clung to the bosses of her spine for him to blow gently away. There was no sand in the darkened kitchen.

"Archimedes wrote it," said PF, with only the suggestion of a smile. "About 200 BC."

"Oops," said Chernoff. He might have used the trickling sand to waken his friend's stout, sleeping nipple. He changed position to disguise a shiver of delight, sat up, invigorated by the thought that the evocation of his friend's body continued to be more immediately arousing to him than its actual presence.

"The eureka guy," he said, adjusting his pants discreetly. "So. Getting back to the card, what do you have to say about the hints?"

"The first one is not complicated."

"No. We'll be taking the obvious precautions although . . ." He did not seem to have much confidence in obvious precautions. "We'll have a bunch of extra men on the 28th, I don't know from where, the state force likely. That's Hrbek's job. The second hint."

"Where is Melrose overpass?"

"Not in San Buenaventura. Melrose crosses over 101, the freeway, north of here about half an hour. Santa Barbara technically, I believe. Hrbek's feeling is the guy was afraid he had given us too much with the first hint, so he added the second as a distraction, a false trail."

"Yes, yes," said PF, his conviction enthusiastic enough as to not seem particularly convinced. "He could have just started over, but that's a lot of cutting and gluing." He was silent, bobbed his head meditatively. "I will think about it."

They were both silent.

Chernoff's friend, her unbrushed aluminum hair falling over his open thighs, ran her tongue over the creases of Chernoff's midriff. She stuck, one by one, onto his wet skin, the prickly letters of the word "crunch."

"Tell me," said Chernoff loudly, scrubbing his face briskly with his dry hands, "how much longer will you be with us, Canada?"

"Eh? Oh, two weeks about."

"Is that all? You're going to miss the 28th. You can stay here forever as far as I'm concerned."

"After I'm going to Santa Monica. For paramedic training."

"Really."

"I am thinking, Captain."

"Sorry," said Chernoff, smiling at PF's raptness.

Again they were silent.

"I am thinking about the second hint. As I said, I believe this person's criminal longing is to control how he will be captured. It is not to commit another crime. For me, it is the first hint that is false." He closed his eyes. "The second hint, the second." He opened them again, observed Chernoff with a striking fixity. "The second hint is about the crime this person has already committed. On the 28th, yes, but a month ago, two months, whatever. At Melrose overpass."

Chernoff grunted with a scepticism surprised enough as to seem partly convinced. "Why don't you get in touch with the Santa Barbara police, Canada? We'll see how good you are."

He felt a pang of solitude as the door closed behind PF. The fluttering accordions disappeared instantly, taking his friend and her aluminum hair with them, leaving his office swollen, pulsing with silence and familiarity. He was in a strange mood, the shrewd and vibrant agitation that had seized him at the arrival of the cards had disintegrated into a bemused, restless detachment that he found disappointing. He looked at his watch. Four o'clock. He could not stay there, the very familiarity and silence seemed to observe him facetiously, to cheer in secret for the would-be killer, the sender of the cards.

For Chernoff knew who the sender was. Or rather he knew that he would know. He had only to resist himself, to live through the passing of time, to not try too hard, to not over think. And he would know. He had only, simply stated, to be alone.

"Prick," said Hrbek, placing his soft, strawberry hands on PF's shoulders and giving him a good push backwards.

PF beamed timidly, pleased with himself certainly, but unsure whether the colour in Hrbek's cheeks was an indication of esteem or of displeasure.

"It would have been my next idea," said Hrbek bluffly. "Chernoff would have never figured it out."

PF beamed more confidently. "Where is Captain Chernoff? So I can tell him."

"Gone for one of his walks. Don't expect to see him before tomorrow."

Chernoff had been walking for an hour when he felt the first drop glance off his cheek. He did not look up. The drops continued briefly, light, almost musical, speckling the beach-coloured sidewalk.

And then the deluge began.

He did not look up. He did not dance, did not sing. He was not, strictly speaking, happy again. And yet he received the rain with a good deal more appeasement than his cumbersome gait seemed to suggest. He was living through the passing of time.

And in time, drenched, he entered Dimitri's Gyro Grill, where the sweetness of rain and garlic clung to the particles of meat fat suspended in the air. He went into the men's room, dried his hair summarily with paper towels, crumpled the towels into a ball and looped the ball towards the waste basket, missed, did not pick the ball up, stepped, instead, out into the restaurant, over to a window booth and said:

"Do you mind if I join you, Olivia?"

"You know my name," said Olivia Cottinjon, "Captain Chernoff."

Chernoff might have made some reference to their common acquaintance from Canada and his knack with names, but he was, for the moment, unable to speak. He was wet through, his heart was knocking in his chest, he was in the presence of the woman he had been observing every day now for close to three weeks and had followed on a sufficient number of occasions to know she ate almost invariably at Dimitri's Gyro Grill. He was fascinated by the details of her face: by the current of freckles that began at her hairline, moved slowly down her temples, trickled under her nose and over her lips, flowed with increasing speed along her throat and funnelled into the V of her bulky sweater; by her eyes, so heavily scribed with eyeliner they appeared to be wounded and healing badly. Above all, he had heard his name spoken by her voice, and having done so, he knew that he was, at this moment as in so few moments in his life, unequivocally Captain Chernoff.

The waiter's arrival startled him.

"Christ," he grumbled, irritated more by his own nervousness than by the waiter's stealth.

"Sorry," said the waiter.

"Bring me, just a plateful of baklava."

"A plateful like two, or a plateful like six?"

"Like six. And the largest cup of joe you serve."

Having ordered, he had little choice but to sit.

"Nice name, Olivia," he said blandly, adjusting his chair. "Not a particularly common one."

"It was my mother's name," said Olivia Cottinjon. "She died before I was born."

Chernoff raised his sluggish eyebrows. "She what?"

"Not long before. Twenty-two minutes."

The waiter brought the baklava. Chernoff offered the plate to Olivia, watched her surprisingly graceful fingers close over the pastry and disappear out of his range of vision. He was thinking of ambulances, commotions, emergency Caesareans, Olivia Cottinjon, bloody, squawking, dangling by the ankles over her mother's corpse. His testicles tingled with curiosity.

"Did you make that sweater yourself?"

Olivia nodded, unable to speak, her mouth full of baklava. Chernoff waited.

"So, Olivia Cottinjon. What interests you about the police station?" He bit into his own piece of baklava.

"Oh, the comings and goings. The stories. I like talking to the officers. They're good company."

"That," said Chernoff, pausing to chew, brushing off his pant leg as he did so, "is complete and utter," running his tongue over his teeth, "bullshit. You're bored stiff." The dry pastry thickened his voice. "You don't read. People who read, people who are engaged in reading, besides turning pages every now and then, have a severity, an irritability about them, as though they didn't approve of their own book. You just sit there with your ridiculous coffee-maker, as blank as blank, your mind in neutral. You twist and squirm all day long. If it wasn't for Canada, you'd have given up long ago."

"My coffee-maker is not ridiculous."

"Your coffee-maker is ridiculous. Take it off the table."

"I will not."

"Take it off."

"Take it off yourself."

Chernoff stood, seized the coffee-maker and placed it on the floor with an exaggerated delicateness meant to applaud his restraint in not breaking it into a thousand pieces. He reseated himself.

"Furthermore. You arrive every morning exactly at eight o'clock and you leave exactly at five. What, are you on salary? You then get yourself and your ridiculous coffee-maker over to this restaurant just as fast as your little legs can go. Furthermore. I never wear flip-flops, much less walk on crushed glass with them. Furthermore. You may be forgiven for concluding from the fact that I carry a putter up to my office occasionally that I play golf. In fact I do not. I do not play golf. Furthermore. Don't you dare call me Captain Crunch!"

The growths appeared white and lifeless in the blood-rich, angry furrows of the skin under his eyes.

"I'm not like Canada. I'm not good at games. Stop playing yours."

Pastry flakes clung to his mouth giving the impression that his lips were moulting.

"Now then, I want you to tell me, in plain, simple English, exactly what it is you are up to. Not now, mind you, not here. This is my card, my address is on it." He looked at his watch, although the intensity of his emotion prevented him from either deciphering the numbers or performing simple mental calculations. "You have twelve hours."

Captain Chernoff stood, did not indicate what might occur at the expiration of the 12-hour period, did not pluck at his wet shirt although it was glued to his chest and revealed his stimulated nipples, was not aware that the money he placed on the table would have paid for several platefuls of baklava besides the one he had barely touched, did stride out of Dimitri's Gyro Grill.

Into the radiance of the Pacific, evening sun.

It had very little in common with Olivia Cottinjon's coffee-maker. It was nothing more than a decorative, 20-cup, thermal pot. Its base was pinned between Chernoff's pyjamaed, midnight knees, its crown served as a support for his hands, which in turn served as a support for his unsleeping head.

He did not know at what moment it had occurred to him that Olivia Cottinjon was the sender of the cards. No doubt at the very moment the accusation had hurled itself from his throat, thick with pastry.

Nor did he remember in which words the accusation had been formulated. He remembered, in fact, very little of what he had said. Very little, but he knew he should not have said it. He would not soon see the joe-maker lady again, on the park bench or anywhere else.

He remembered the freckles trickling over her lips, the diluted eyeliner dribbling down her fleshy cheeks. Her eyes healing badly. Above all, he remembered the pang that had pierced the small of his spine at the moment he had seized her coffee-maker, that had scorched the fibres of his nerves and bent them all, without exception, towards his sex.

He closed his eyes, brushed his lips over the hard, plastic pot, but his imagination was not convinced. His imagination required the presence of Olivia Cottinjon.

He stood in his doorway, the palm of his left hand directed towards the living room, his eyes darting anxiously from his left foot to his right, his pants plumped with the pyjamas he was wearing underneath.

Olivia Cottinjon remained in the hall. Cagey, caged.

"Are you in a good mood?" she said.

"Yes."

"No, I can hear in your voice that you're not in a good mood."

"My voice? All I said was yes."

"There, you're starting to yell already."

Chernoff concentrated on moderating his breathing. "I apologize. About the restaurant. I let myself get carried away. I . . ." He shook his head, as though at a loss to comprehend his own behaviour. "I don't even remember what I said."

"You don't remember saying, 'You have twelve hours!'"

"I remember that, yes."

"Ah."

Olivia Cottinjon remained in the hall. "I'm not going to sleep with you, if that's what you're after."

Chernoff's embarrassment was so pervasive he felt sure it was reddening his pudgy skin under his pyjamas under his pants. He rolled his eyes, made a brave attempt at a sigh of exasperation. "I just thought . . ." He concluded with a second sigh, not having any idea what he just thought.

Olivia Cottinjon entered his apartment.

"Let me take your coat."

The removal of the coat caused Olivia's sweater to pucker at the neckline, so that Chernoff could see briefly the current of freckles that ran out of the erratic hairs on the back of her neck, flowed around the island of her seventh cervical vertebra and dropped into the abyss of her back. Her coat in his hands was so heavy it might well have been chiselled from a quartziferous formation with a naturally greenish-blue hue.

Olivia, with deerlike guardedness, prepared to bolt at any second, perched herself on the edge of Chernoff's luxuriant and rarely occupied sofa.

Chernoff in turn sank into an armchair, crossed his legs, smoothed his hair mechanically. "Whenever you're ready," he murmured.

Olivia delivered her story then, speaking very rapidly and with a tension in her voice that suggested it had been well-rehearsed, but never performed. She had been minding her own business in Dimitri's Gyro Grill one day when a man had introduced himself, had talked with her briefly, and then asked her if she would be willing to help him out. He had showed her an Asymptote Market Research business card.

"Do you have that card?" broke in Chernoff.

"Somewhere," said Olivia, patting the pockets of her slacks. "Maybe in my coat." The man also had a letter of authorization, seemingly genuine. He said that AMR had been hired by the city of San Buenaventura to do time-efficiency studies of various civic institutions, the town hall, the fire department. What he wanted Olivia to do, assuming she agreed, was to observe the police station, to keep track of the movements of the various officers, to look for patterns, habitual occurrences. Every day. For a week. He gave her an envelope containing a surprisingly generous amount of money. There would be another envelope at the end of the week. He would be in contact with her to discuss the results.

She had asked him if he made a habit of hiring people in restaurants. He had said it was extremely difficult to find people who were bright enough and at the same time willing, basically, to odd-job. He had learned to rely on his instincts.

She had agreed. What the hell. A week. She liked the word "asymptote."

At the end of the week, she found the second envelope in her mailbox. It contained far more money than expected and a note telling her to continue. She had been uneasy, but had done so nevertheless.

She had gone to Dimitri's every day hoping the man would be there, but he never was. And yet the money kept coming. Therefore they knew she was at her post. Therefore she was being observed herself. She did not know what was going on, had not dared do anything but carry on, had not dared even confide in Canada. She had been hoping someone from the police, the big man maybe who didn't like her, would become suspicious and intervene.

"So you were right, Captain Chernoff, I am on salary. Very brilliant of you. I should, I suppose, thank you. Very impressive."

Chernoff could not resist letting himself be soothed by this comment. He absorbed Olivia's story without either accepting or rejecting its veracity. He would let it ripen, rise in his mind.

"And what have you found out," he said quietly, "through your observations?"

"Nothing at all. You're right about that too. I am bored stiff. Thank God for the Canadian. I hope the police are busy at night, because nothing much happens during the day."

"Nasty, nasty."

"It's true. I can't understand why anyone would pay so much to know so little. But as for the rest of what you said, the other stuff about the golf and the Captain Crunch, I don't have the remotest, not the remotest idea what you were talking about. Utter madness. Of course you don't *remember* that."

"I remember, Olivia, I remember." He continued for many moments to smooth his hair mechanically. "I'm on edge," he confided at last. "I've been receiving threatening messages." Olivia looked over at him sharply. "No, no, not threatening to me personally. Threatening to kill, at random, no specific victim."

"Here? In San Buenaventura?"

"Oh yes. Things do happen, even if it doesn't look like it."

Olivia rocked back and forth tensely. "And you thought it was me."

"No, no. I don't know what I thought. My emotions got the better of me. The rain, the rain. I'm really . . . very sorry." He paused. "Do you want something to eat? Coffee?"

"I'm too tired. I haven't slept. What time is it?"

"Twenty past five. You can sleep here if you like."

"No, no."

Chernoff stood sternly, disappeared, returned with a blanket and pillow.

"Give me that," said Olivia, taking the blanket. She wrapped herself in it, discreetly removed her formless slacks and lay down on the sofa, clearly disinterested in human affairs of any sort.

"I'll need," said Chernoff, "the best description you can give me of the Asymptote Market Research man."

She did not answer.

"Do you mind if I look for the business card in your coat?"

Silence.

"I'll head out to the station then and leave you alone. Don't worry about locking the door when you go." He would have much preferred to stay, to tiptoe vigilantly around the apartment.

"Your coffee-maker," he said softly, "is not ridiculous."

She did not answer.

"Not long ago," said Police Sergeant PF, "Quebec was very Catholic. The French part, that is. Even when my father went to school, he was taught by nuns."

"That so," said Hrbek. "Have you been to the Franciscan mission here in San Buenaventura?"

"Not yet."

"I think you'd find it interesting. And you say that nuns are criminals?"

"No, no! You are laughing at me. I say that nuns and criminals have, both, a need to give themselves up, to surrender themselves, but to a high force, a great authority. They have no faith in men and women. They want something bigger, noisier."

"The great authority for the nun being God obviously. And for the criminal?"

"For the criminal the great authority has no name. He is never there, never anywhere. He couldn't care less."

"Nice thought."

"Because, you see, the nun seeks humility. The criminal seeks humiliation."

This idea, all the more bleak in PF's avid, young voice, caused Hrbek to shrink into himself. "So look," he said sombrely, "this is what we now know: 28 April, sometime after dark, a woman falls from the Melrose overpass onto the highway below, nobody sees her, she lands on the grassy median, her body isn't discovered for many hours. The Santa Barbara police go through the motions, but as you and I both know, if it doesn't solve itself in the first twenty-four hours, it doesn't solve itself. So it's filed away as a possible suicide. Now then, we have an individual sending us anonymous cards. He admits essentially to having caused, deliberately or not, the death of this woman. Also, having lived the big thrill and gotten away with it, the individual is expressing an interest in going after the big thrill again. But you're saying what he really wants is to give himself up."

"Yes. That is why he sends the cards and why he told us about the 28th."

"I can buy that. But now, Canada, what do we do?"

"Ignore him. Not care less. He will surrender himself."

"Yes, but how many victims later? We're not paid to cater to the twisted. We're paid to protect the untwisted. Supposing we put a man in a flashy uniform on every corner. Wouldn't our individual, according to your line of thinking, find a way to get himself caught in the act? Commit the perfect crime as you put it."

"Maybe, yes. If he has still some faith in people. But maybe also he will say wow, all these cops after me. That is not too humiliating. That makes it fun pushing women off overpasses."

"Christ, Canada."

"But it is certainly you who are right and I who am wrong. Unless we're both wrong."

"Maybe I can help," said Captain Chernoff. He had been listening, unobserved, to the conversation, intrigued, not by the flutter of jealousy he felt at hearing Canada talk so openly with Hrbek, nor by the mild impression he had of his two colleagues being busy behind his back, but by the fact that he was not offended. No, he felt almost liberated. But from what?

"Chernoff!" said Hrbek. "I didn't see you come in."

"You didn't see me come in because I've been here since five-thirty this morning. I got your memo, Canada. You were right about the 28th. I should, I suppose, thank you. Very impressive." He pronounced these words with an odd distinctness. "I had a conversation yesterday evening. With Olivia Cottinjon, the joe-maker lady."

"Ah, I was wondering why she didn't show up for work today," said Hrbek.

"No?" said PF. "I didn't notice."

This remark stung Chernoff. He had forgotten how lightly young people manoeuvre inside friendships. "For work, you say, Lieutenant. You're closer to the truth than you think." He then related Olivia Cottinjon's story, making no mention of Greek restaurants, apartments, or 12-hour ultimatums.

"So what does the asymptote guy look like?" asked Hrbek.

"She didn't give me a detailed description," said Chernoff, blushing slightly. "She was too tired," blushing slightly more.

"Something else for you to check out, Canada," said Hrbek. "Asymptote Market Research."

"It's a crock, guaranteed," said Chernoff.

"Yes, I think so," said PF.

"Are you ever wrong?" snapped Chernoff.

"Easy, Crunchy," said Hrbek.

"Don't call me Crunchy!"

Chernoff glared for several moments at Hrbek's tie, which rode the unbroken wave of the lieutenant's rolling chest like a pointed, toy surf-board. He struggled with the genteel obligation of modulating, if not apologizing for, his sudden outburst, was unable to meet this obligation, strode off in his cumbersome way to his office, unlocked the door, entered quickly, and relocked the door behind him.

His morning's work lay on his desk: words and letters, cut out from a New England magazine containing lavish, although now decimated, photographs of mist-bound, Searsport fishing boats. The words had been placed side-by-side, unglued, to form an invitation:

"Princess Ptoot, may I have a brief encounter to discuss   you together traveling."

This was as far as he had got. He found it extremely difficult to come up with a coherent sentence, such that the number of letters in each word would be equal to the corresponding number in the value of pi, but he was determined to do so. He was aware that "discuss" had one letter too many, and he was afraid "traveling" might have two l's. He was sure that Olivia would be outraged at being referred to as "Princess Ptoot," which was what he wanted. He had, in any case, no intention of delivering the invitation.

"One thing's been bothering me," said Hrbek. "Why golf? Why the Almendros club?"

Police sergeant PF was not listening.

"Crunchy doesn't play golf. He has a wooden boat he likes to take out."

PF, having rolled down his window, was gazing out over the peopled beach towards the ominous, seductive ocean waves, back-lit by the late afternoon sun. To be a Californian, he was thinking. Surely the sound of the surf must, over the years, penetrate your eyes, your hands, your pancreas even, your brain, until you see farther, touch with more finesse, digest more efficiently, and think less clearly. He adjusted his teardrop sunglasses unnecessarily, turned towards the lieutenant.

"I feel like I'm living on television."

Hrbek snorted. "You've got to be good-looking to be on TV, Canada."

"I'm good-looking!"

"Better than Chernoff, I'll give you that."

They were driving back from Santa Barbara, having been briefed, briefly, the session having lasted no more than minutes, on the police investigation into the death of Joyce Q. They had been supplied with a copy of the report, appallingly flimsy, padded with redundant photographs.

Joyce Q. had, at 37, been a much-admired music therapist. Her admirers, however, were all under 13 years of age and, to varying degrees, autistic. She had had few colleagues. Her friendships seemed to have been fairly numerous but short-lived, transitory, dissatisfying. And if her daytime conduct had been unassuming and selfless, her nocturnal deportment had, at times, been extravagant. She had not, perhaps, been entirely without autistic attributes herself, had been known, in crowded nightclubs, for no apparent reason, to scream with manic perseverance, to spin and pant until she lost consciousness. On the last night of her life, however, Joyce Q. had not seemed to create any such disturbance. She had consumed only alcohol and not to excess. There were no signs of physical outrage. She was made-up heavily, dressed entirely in black, wearing a silk blouse, very sheer but strategically ruffled, a very short leather skirt. Presumably she had been to a club within walking distance of the Melrose over-pass, but this could not be established with certainty.

Presumably her admirers mourned her disappearance. This could not be established with certainty either.

Captain Chernoff stood outside the door to his apartment.

He entered.

No.

No, but the sofa had been smoothed, the blanket folded. He inspected the kitchen, discovered a glass on the counter, sitting in a film of water. He sniffed the glass without touching it, examined its rim for lip smudges, went into the bathroom where the free end of the toilet paper was trailing on the floor. He had not left it like that.

He strode through the apartment where Princess Ptoot had done nothing more than sleep, drink water, and relieve herself, but which, nevertheless, resonated with her presence.

So much so, thought Chernoff to himself headily, I feel like I'm the intruder.

He was almost disappointed that she had not taken anything. It seemed to him that there was an exceptional amount of light in the apartment, almost as though the apartment were airborne and had broken through cloud cover. He could feel the faint but steady trembling of the fuselage, the occasional shudder of the wings.

I wonder, he wondered, if she'd be interested in flying to Maine with me. I just wonder.

He took up the receiver, dialled.

"Olivia! How did you sleep?"

"Captain Chernoff," said Olivia, stiffly.

Chernoff was particularly silent for a moment, having again heard his name spoken by her voice. "I was just wondering," he said, wishing he had chosen his words beforehand, "if . . . uh."

"Certainly, Captain. Would you like me to come to the station?"

"Yes," said Chernoff, although his mouth was suddenly dry and his chest clenched into a tight nub. He had forgotten the description of the asymptote man he had requested, had forgotten the anonymous cards. Forgotten. Utterly. He had been on the point, the very point of inviting, of calling her. Princess. Ptoot.

"I'm sorry I'm going to have to call you back," he said, although he could not be sure that Olivia had heard because he could not be sure of having heard himself. He was panting, spinning, he thought he might even be screaming, but if so with such an unpractised, gasping tentativeness that he could not establish this with certainty either.

"Have a seat, Olivia," said Police Sergeant PF nervously. "Captain Chernoff has asked me to do this so I will get some experience. I hope you don't mind being interrogated by a guy in training. I've never do it before. Done it before. This is Lieutenant Hrbek." Olivia and Hrbek acknowledged each other. "In any case it is not a real interrogation. You can leave your coffee-maker on the table, sure. It's good for your dignity. Now then, if this was a real interrogation I would start by saying, 'State your name,' and you would say, 'Olivia Cottinjon.' And then I would say, 'Occupation,' and you would say?"

"Retired teacher."

"Retired? But you're too young to be retired."

"I taught mathematics for twenty-three years. That was enough. I retired at forty-four."

"You're not forty-four!"

"Correct. I'm forty-six."

"Forty-six!"

"Almost forty-seven."

"Forty-*seven*." PF shook his head incredulously, as though the attaining of such an age were of an equivalent probability to tanning on Uranus. "Forty-seven."

"Six," said Olivia.

"Six. Right. So then I would say, 'Do you know why you are here?' And you would say?"

"To supply the police with a description of a man who claims to represent Asymptote Market Research."

"Is that the only reason? Asymptote Market Research is a crock, by the way. I checked it out."

"What do you mean by 'a crock'?"

"A crock is something that doesn't exist."

"A crock exists. It's a big pot."

"Ah. I didn't know. In that case, Asymptote Market Research is a crock with nothing in it. So I would ask, 'Is that the only reason?' And you would answer?"

"Yes, it is."

"Good. So I guess that's it." PF grinned anxiously into the silence. He could tell by the air of anticipation in the room that there was something more he should ask. He looked at Hrbek. "Ah," he said, remembering. "Do you have any questions, Lieutenant Hrbek?"

"Maybe one, yes," said the lieutenant dryly. "Could you tell us, Olivia, what the asymptote man looked like?"

Lieutenant Hrbek stood in the glassed-in front corridor, gazing out, down towards the empty bench in the park, his knees flexed, his pelvis rolled under slightly to maintain his lower spine in a position of therapeutic straightness.

"Don't tell me you miss her," said Chernoff, rounding the corner of the central stairway.

"Miss her? No. Not exactly."

Chernoff stopped, appraised the tenor of Hrbek's unexpected response, negotiated silently with himself.

"Why don't you come into my office, Lieutenant?" he said. "I've something to confess."

They entered the captain's office. Chernoff closed the door.

"Olivia Cottinjon," he muttered, sighing breathily through the tufts in his nose. "You wouldn't have taken an interest in Olivia, Hrbek?"

"An interest?"

"Because if you have, say so."

"What?"

"No, okay." Chernoff gathered himself. "I don't know how exactly, I wasn't really aware of it myself, but somewhere along the line I got it into my head that there was a connection between the anonymous cards and our lady of the joe-maker."

"On what basis?"

"On no basis. That's the point. Feeling."

"You're not saying you suspect Olivia of sending the cards?"

"Nohh! No, no."

"The asymptote man."

"Definitely. Unfortunately, I'm not definitely convinced of his existence."

"Fair enough. But we do have a reasonable description. We circulate it, we see what happens. We do what we can."

"We have a description of a man with a head. You've seen the drawing. It could be you. Scaled down a bit. Why don't you find a reason to take a little run through her house? It's a neglected duplex on Carlsbad Avenue, see if you can't find some loose cash, the business card, something. Maybe there are more hints in the messages than we've hit on, the golf angle, I don't know, something."

"Chernoff. Don't think so much. Listen to the woman, respond to what she says. I do, and I conclude that the asymptote man — assuming he exists, if he doesn't it doesn't matter — knows she is not on the bench. Therefore she should be given a measure of protection. I know where her house is, I already have a man watching it. I conclude further that if the asymptote man, still assuming he is real, is having the station watched, and if, as your feeling leads you to suspect, he is also the sender of the cards, you should not go traipsing off by yourself the way you do."

Chernoff scowled under his clumsy eyebrows. "You don't tell Canada to not think so much."

"Canada is a kid. He's leaving in a couple of days. Besides, what he says depresses me. That gives me the impression that it's true."

"Oh. And what Cottinjon says, does that depress you?"

"Not especially."

"Well then." The captain, despite himself, glanced at his waste basket where a clump of papers covered the decimated New England boating magazine. "Christ," he said, "I'm getting bored with all this."

Only in California, marvelled Police Sergeant PF to himself. On this, his last day in San Buenaventura, formations of stratocumulus surf scudded over the clear blue ocean. The sky teemed with squid, magenta rays, black crabs and spinning starfish, striped eels, pink octopi. Bare-legged, sun-basted fishermen thronged the beach, casting their lines a way way up. PF wrote his new English words in his notebook, "parafoil," "drogue," "carabiner," "laundry," and beside them, "Playa Rincón Kite Festival." He imagined Hrbek, inflated to giant proportions, swimming through the sky, observed a policeman in shorts accept the offer to attempt to fly one of the enormous, tentacular kites, saw him take the line, stagger, be lifted bodily off his feet and dragged over the sand a short distance before being hoisted onto the laughter of his rescuers.

"*Salut*," said PF. "*Adiós* San Buenaventura."

Lieutenant Hrbek would never forget the moment when he was seized with the certainty that he understood the nature of existence not more clearly, but less so. He was at the Almendros Golf Club, braced against the timber and adobe wall of the trophy room, an invisible wave having broken over him, leaving him gasping in his own insignificance.

He thought of the authority who was never there, never anywhere, who could not care less, knowing that if Canada had been there with him, he, Canada, would have clapped him on the back excitedly, would have eagerly examined the awkward, brass golfer perched on the wooden trophy adorned with columns of rectangular plaques the size of business cards, would have read, over and over, hungrily, the letters engraved in the three tarnished plaques in particular: "Winner, Club Championship, Alex Cottinjon."

But precisely, Canada was not there. He was gone, his training stint over. Hrbek was entirely alone with his discovery, which he might as easily have made five weeks earlier as not at all. And it was precisely the finding of the brass plaques that left him overwhelmed with the impression of being a mere flunky of happenstance. Had he not found them, he would have remained himself, the master of his fate.

He could as easily go running to Chernoff with his discovery, as not mention it to anyone. Who would know? What, ultimately, did it matter?

A small piece of Hrbek never left the trophy room. A small piece that had gone limp, that could not care less.

"I knew it!" hissed Chernoff. "I knew there was a connection. I just fucking knew it." The intense sparkle in his eyes was enhanced with a vengeful glint. "But tell me, Hrbek, what induced you to go up to the golf course?"

Hrbek's voice was distant, calm. "I don't really know. You said it yourself. The golf angle."

"What a cop, uh. What a cop!"

"A fluke, Chernoff. A fluke. If I hadn't looked right at it, I would never have noticed."

"But you did look right at it, Hrbek. That's the point. You and no one else. That's why you're good!" His face had taken on a rosy luminescence so that the growths under his eyes were barely visible. The thickness of his lower lip was attenuated by an eager grin. "This guy's our man, Hrbek. I can taste it. I can just taste it."

"State your name."

"Alex Cottinjon."

Captain Chernoff observed the man sitting on the opposite side of the melamine table. The resemblance to Olivia was not perhaps immediately apparent, but could be retraced easily enough from the knowledge that he was indeed her older brother. The same after-thought of a nose. Similar lips, drained, in need of moistening. The face was more plump, however, flushed, as though the surface skin had been peeled off in a single, refreshing instant. Freckles there were, but greenish, unhealthy looking, contained within a stagnant pool in the area that had once been covered with hair, and that now was bald.

The eyes, however, bore no relationship to Olivia's. They were content, for the most part, to skulk behind the dissipated, fatty lids. But when they did reveal themselves, they were strangely, invitingly blue, boy blue, intimidating, beautiful.

"Occupation."

"Professional . . . loafer."

"Occupation."

"Unprofessional loafer."

Chernoff did not insist further. He knew perfectly well that Cottinjon was without employment. He knew a great deal about Alex Cottinjon, having quickly discovered that he was the sort of person about whom people were only too willing to talk, for whose unsuccess, despite every natural gift, people were only too willing to exposit personal theories, as though Mr. Cottinjon were a statistical hedge, a talisman against the undoing of their own assumed success.

"Do you know why you're here?"

"Does anyone?"

Chernoff reached under the table for the bottle and glass, placed them on the table.

"Jameson's," he said. "Your favourite whiskey I believe."

"Any whiskey is my favourite whiskey," said Cottinjon, not looking at the bottle.

"The bartender at the Almendros Golf Club tells me they used to have it sent down from Canada for you. Quite a lot of it." Chernoff was sure of himself, confident of his strategy. "So we had some sent down too."

Cottinjon had, at one time, been the map librarian for the Department of Lands and Surveys, a solid job, but one which, although it allowed him plenty of time to get caught hiding out and eavesdropping in the women's washroom, did not allow him enough time to work on his golf game. He was young then, fairly young, still able to nourish hopes of playing professionally on the California circuit, by so much the best player at the Almendros Golf and Country Club that the board of directors, distinguished fans all, voted an amount of money to the "trophies and prizes" budget sufficient to import annually several cases of Jameson's whiskey for his personal use.

"Are you still a member at Almendros?"

"An honourary one. I don't play there."

"When was the last time you did?"

"Must be . . . quite some time ago. Seven, eight years maybe."

"That the last time you drank Jameson's?"

"Could be, now that you mention it."

"Your glory years. Right? How many times were you club champion? Three?"

Cottinjon quit his job. Not that he ever had any great difficulty getting himself hired, having, among other things, done an obligatory stint as a financial consultant, sold deluxe roofing systems, been an assistant director of the Santa Barbara marina, there being always someone willing to acquire, at a quietly reduced salary, the services of a star golfer to adorn their mid-week, deal-doing foursomes.

His nerves however, undermined by his favourite whiskey, were never quite able to stay him during clutch bunker shots and crucial putts. His game never quite came together. His sense of repartee on the other hand, enhanced by his favourite whiskey, did. So that if at first Cottinjon's services were engaged out of respect, they were later engaged out of fellowship. Ultimately, when he had become a bantering, over-par alcoholic, his services were engaged, when they were engaged, out of straight-up affection. With a chaser of disdain.

So Chernoff was confident. He would wear Cottinjon down, make him face the hollowness, the disappointments of his life, not allow him to drink, and only then, when he began to unravel, would he ask, nonchalantly, if, say, he ever had occasion to cross the Melrose overpass. Indirection was the key. It was indirection that created rapport, that incited the person being interrogated to wonder why such-and-such a question were being asked and to explore therefore, if only out of self-interest, the mind of the interrogator.

And it was rapport that would incite Cottinjon to confess.

"Your mother died when you were young."

"Yes."

"How was that? Was it tough?"

"Truthfully, I don't remember. I was two."

Opinion was divided as to the nature of Cottinjon's love life. Many accorded him a venereal aptitude concordant with his talent for golf. Breathtaking for some. Lacking finish for others.

"Was it your dad who got you interested in golf? Did he play?"

"It's difficult to play golf with only one arm."

"I'm sorry, I didn't know."

"So yes, it was my dad. I'd do anything as long as he couldn't."

Chernoff nodded wisely. "Your mother died giving birth to your sister. Olivia."

Cottinjon ran his index finger along his eyebrow. "Yuh," he said shortly.

Olivia. The other game-player of the family. Olivia's role was less clear to Chernoff. He presumed her intention had been to protect her brother by deflecting suspicion towards an imaginary asymptote man. If so, she had come very close to succeeding. Very close. Only the unusualness of the name had defeated her.

"Did you hold that against your sister in any way do you think? That she was, not deliberately of course, the cause of your mother's death?"

Cottinjon was slow to answer. He looked up at Chernoff, observed him for several moments. And Chernoff, whether because of the riveting, repellent blueness of Cottinjon's eyes, or because of the suggestion they contained of his sister's wounded eyes, felt his testicles tingle with curiosity.

"Excuse me," said Cottinjon. He reached across the table, gripped the neck of the bottle in his right palm, hooked the glass with his index finger, and sat back again. He unscrewed the metal cap, poured out an ounce and a half, slid the glass over to Chernoff.

"May I ask you a question, Captain?"

Chernoff acquiesced with a minuscule nod of the head. He resisted the temptation to slash the glass away with the back of his hand.

"Do you play? Golf, I mean."

"No."

"Golf is a difficult game. I still hit two, three hundred balls every day. I used to do that and then go out and play thirty-six holes. I am what's known as a ball-striker, Captain. I hit the ball. Where I want to. Every time. The short game has always eluded me. What I enjoy most in golf is watching the ball diminish into the sky. I wish it would diminish forever. The moment the ball starts to come down, my chest tightens, I look away. I know where it's going to land. There is a part of me, with every shot, that is trying to get the ball out of the game. And therefore myself I suppose."

"I heard this story about you," said Hrbek admiringly. "You were coming up to the tee at some par-four somewhere. You asked the gallery how long the hole was and somebody called out, 'For you it's just a drive and a wedge!' So you hit the wedge off the tee, used your driver from the fairway and put the ball right on the green. That story true?"

"Golf is a cruel game," said Cottinjon. "Because the more you work at it, the more shots you learn to execute, the more your memory is stuffed with the holes you've played, with yardages, over-hanging trees, invisible breaks in traitorous greens, with decades of shots, thousands upon thousands of them, all there, each and every one, so that all it takes is a word, an odour, a cloud formation in a particular afternoon sky, and you can remember the very feel of the sand grinding under your feet in the bunker on the seventeenth at Carmel Valley in the Monterey County Invitational eighteen years ago, eighteen years, Captain, but you are right there, the golf ball is right there off your right heel, partially buried, and it will pop out again eighteen years later, bounce twice, and again roll just past the hole so that you will know next time to be looser in the knees, to open the club head a fraction more in order to better execute the shot to which you have already sacrificed how many hours of sweet sleep and how many more tonight now that you've remembered missing it again. But what was I going to say? Right. A cruel game. Because, Captain, the more the game of golf invades you, binds your life into innumerable variations of one single event, aims its spotlight at your very soul, the less it lets you so much as glimpse its own light, its own soul. Which is to say, there comes a time when the game of golf simply will not let you forgive yourself. How I long, Captain, how I long for your capacity for incompetence. For your capacity to play like a plumber. I cannot."

Chernoff gathered all the sarcasm he could muster. "My turn now?"

"Sorry," said Cottinjon. "Let me just ask you one other question. Nothing to do with golf."

"One," said Chernoff.

"What," said Cottinjon, "were *you* doing on the night of April the 28th?"

"So he confessed," said Hrbek. "The way he told it, he went to a club that night, drank too much, and left with, in his words, the 'wrong person.' Was Joyce Q. the wrong person? We'll never know what she would have to say about that. They were walking to her car, over the Melrose overpass. She went berserk, out of control, screaming. Why?

He swore he hadn't done anything. He tried to calm her down, they struggled, but he was totally hammered and landed on his ass. Did he crack his head? Did he pass out from the booze? He doesn't know. He just knows that he lost consciousness because when he came to, he looked over the edge, and there she was."

"Pretty convincing," said PF, "given the police report."

"Oh, Cottinjon's certainly convinced. He wants to be responsible. Hasn't had a drink since, hasn't played a round of golf. Now that he's got the confession out of his system, he just wants to get into jail as fast as he can so he can get out and do good things for autistic children."

"Like his Jesus is Joyce."

"Something like that."

"And Olivia?"

"I called Olivia just before I called you, pointed out to her that obstructing justice is an indictable offence. Chernoff doesn't want to have anything to do with her. What the hell, he says. We've got her brother. The asymptote man was a fabrication. The idea was for us to go chasing after him, not find him, give up and close the case. Her brother would have been safe then."

"So this is the guy who sent the cards to Captain Crunch and cut out all those little letters. Did you ask him if he was good at kindergarten?"

"Nope. I did say to his sister that it was the best thing that could have happened to a has-been golfer and a drunk. 'Don't you dare insult my brother!' Like he was God's gift."

"Not the best thing that could happen to Joyce Q."

"No. So how's Santa Monica?"

"The palm trees look like giant golf balls on tees. Pom-pom trees."

"Easy on the English, Canada. When you heading back to Montreal?"

"Couple of weeks."

"Well, bone voy-ahge. Prick."

———

Captain Chernoff was lying, perfectly naked, on his back, on the rigid mattress of his friend's bed. The moon had attained an altitude such that it shone directly into a standing mirror, filling the bedroom with an aquatic eeriness.

"May I," he said, "have a brief encounter to confer about our going together traveling? Kittery? Kennebunk?"

The friend herself was perched on top of him, her snub-nosed nipples aimed directly at the brown, oval targets of Chernoff's own. Their nakedness was the sort of nakedness appropriate to a midnight coition.

The friend smiled appreciatively. "Searsport, I think, would be just a piece of pi."

They drifted for a time in silence. The friend roused herself. "So," she said with gentle mockery, "your instincts were right about the golfer."

Chernoff was struck by how his friend's hair, in the moonlight, appeared white, airy.

"The streets," she said, "are safe again for the honest people of San Buenaventura."

Again they shared their intimate communion for a time. Again the friend roused herself. "I want you to show me how to play snort."

Chernoff opened his eyes. "Snort? Now?" He had the impression that if he crushed his friend's hair between his palms, it would disintegrate into ash. "It takes a piece of paper and a couple of coloured pencils."

"Want me to get that?"

"Not particularly."

The friend disengaged herself carefully, returned with the required material, refitted herself onto Chernoff. "Okay, what do I do?"

"You just doodle all over the paper, make a bunch of loops."

The friend placed the paper on Chernoff's chest, doodled, held the paper up. "This good?"

"The loops are too small."

The friend crumpled the paper between her palms, redisengaged herself, returned with a fresh sheet, re-refitted herself.

"You do it," she said, holding the paper like a bib against her breasts. Chernoff doodled, although neither the nature of the surface, nor the trembling of his hand, were conducive to clean work.

"Now what?" said the friend.

"We colour in the loops, taking turns."

They coloured.

"Mmn," said the friend, "I can tell you enjoy playing snort. Who wins?"

Chernoff had difficulty finding his voice. "I forget."

"Either," said the friend, increasingly under the empire of her senses, "I am more, receptive, than usual, or else you . . . I think," she had to concentrate on the act of speaking, as though, "you like," she were learning a new language, "being right."

Police Superintendent Paul-François Bastarache was intrigued to find in his mail a letter from San Buenaventura, California. The letter had reached him despite being addressed simply to Sergeant PF, 11th Precinct, Montreal. As host of the popular television program *Citizen's Arrest*, PF received a large volume of mail, a fair amount of which was delivered despite being improperly addressed.

The letter was from Olivia Cottinjon. As he read through it, PF paused frequently to consult his past. It had been almost 30 years since he had done a 12-week training stint in San Buenaventura, and his memories were not easily summoned.

Not that he had forgotten Olivia. She would be over 75 by now, a fact that accounted perhaps for the distracted style in which the letter was written. PF remembered her sitting on the Parisian park bench beside the burbling coffee-maker which kept her dignity up.

He remembered the sun, the snort.

But he had never laid eyes on her brother. He did recall that he had been a golfer, a pro or semi-pro, and that he had confessed to pushing a woman off the Melrose overpass to her death. He had an idea that the woman had been mentally handicapped. Having been involved with the organization of security for the Playa Rincón kite festival, PF had not had time to give the case a great deal of thought. Chernoff had asked his opinion once or twice, and Hrbek had driven with him to Santa Barbara to consult with the police there. Ultimately though, he had left San Buenaventura before the case had been resolved, so that his impressions of it remained disparate. Parts of Olivia's letter baffled him completely.

It did strike him as ironic, however, that Olivia had clearly never known that the Melrose overpass was not in San Buenaventura, but Santa Barbara, and that the Santa Barbara police had barely pursued the case. Had she and her brother simply done nothing at all, they would never have been under the slightest suspicion.

PF entertained briefly the idea of getting in touch with the San Buenaventura police. But there was always the oppressive possibility that Chernoff might no longer be alive. Or Hrbek. If so, PF did not want to know. He read the letter several times, ran his fingertips over the handwriting, tried to imagine the swollen, discoloured fingers of Olivia Cottinjon as they gripped with difficulty the ball-point pen. He remembered her raincoat, her kinked and floating hair. He made a soft "vrrmm" in his throat.

And then he crushed the letter between his palms, and dropped it into the waste-paper basket.

My mother died before I was born. Not long before. Twenty-two minutes. My father's brain was so eaten with grief he couldn't even come up with a name to give me. Except my mother's name, Olivia.

I never knew my father with both arms. He strapped the right one to his body so he wouldn't forget my mother, stuffed his empty coat sleeve into his pocket, taught mathematics left-handed at Las Palmas de Oro High School. Writing was easy one-armed. He said. Even with the wrong hand. What was hard was getting the chalk off his fingers.

Why are you writing with your left hand? He yelled at me. Write with your right! He was off-balance trying to hit me with his right arm tied to his side. I could jump away easily. Bitch, he called me.

Why are you working so hard at your mathematics? I don't want you to. Oh no, you're not going to be a teacher. I forbid it. I'm not going to pay. Get away from me. Do something else.

I taught math left-handed for twenty-three years. Not at Las Palmas de Oro.

Bitch.

My brother's hair was made of candied wheat, his eyes were crystalline, semi-precious. At their best when he was lying.

He was always in my room, my brother was, in his undershorts, giving me presents, drawing me with colored pencils, to look like himself. Telling me about the girls who wanted him to do this with them, or to wear that, or to move like this other. I'm myself with you. He said. Just you.

When he was with me, my brother's eyes were always at their best.

There must have been a time when my brother didn't play golf, but I don't remember it. Before my mother died maybe. Every week my brother and I did the World Bedroom Golf Championships in my room. No day clothes allowed. Bare feet only. Using the putter like a cue was legal, if you shanked one under the bed.

Just when I was about to drain a putt on the last hole to beat Boris Kutchakokov, the Crushin' Russian, Boris would suck in his breath, and his undershorts would drop off.

One day, my father turned into a pumpkin. Bloated, orange. Bright's disease. He told me in the hospital that I might as well untie his right arm, seeing as there was no longer any danger of his forgetting my mother before he died. The tendons were so weak his elbow popped out. He screamed blue murder.

After my father died, my brother started to dislike me.

I kept an exercise book of all his little women. Whatever I could get.

Sometimes just a date and a word. Sometimes a name, an address, a bra size, whole pages of empty conversation. Sometimes a snapshot.

It's natural to know lots of women. He said. Inconsequential. What is perverse is an obsessive devotion to only one.

I drove him. Everywhere. He lost his license once from driving drunk and discovered he liked being taxied. I drove him to his clubs, his skin dives, as he called them. He thought I just went home again, but I waited. I always did. Waited to see who he would dig up.

He left with her. I followed. I always did. For once he wasn't Mr. Clutch-ngrab. Not all over her.

Halfway across the Melrose overpass the fight starts. She's yelling, punching him. Serious stuff. Hey, I think, if anyone's going to knock him out it's going to be me. I move in fast, and bash him.

Bitch.

Think she thanks me? No. Keeps screaming to high heaven. I've just saved her the infamy of having to beat the shit out of the 50-year-old booze-bunny of her own choosing, and she just carries on carrying on, hollering, hysterical. The cars are pounding by underneath us. My brother is uncon-scious, hurt maybe, and she's screaming as though he doesn't exist. Or me.

So I nudged her. See who doesn't exist now.

All I did was nudge her. Not my fault if time wouldn't let her fall back upwards. It won't let any of us.

I hustled home. After a while my brother calls me. Beside himself, whim-pering. Spills the story.

Sit tight, I said. Nobody must've seen you, therefore nothing happened. Sit tight.

I tried to follow my own advice, but I was just waiting for some cop to sidle up and say, "Don't I know you? Aren't you the Nudger?"

That's when I sent the first card to Captain Crunch. Get him running after anybody but me.

But then what? I couldn't just do nothing. I thought if I have to sit and wait and wait, I might as well do it in front of the police station, where I can see what I'm waiting for.

It was a ride. Terrifying. I thought he had me, the captain. In the restau-

rant. Had me. If he hadn't stomped out when he did, I would have told him everything. "You have twelve hours!" Reprieve. Even at his place I would have given myself up if he got mad again. Ever see him mad? But he'd gone all muttery and head-scratchy.

My brother doesn't acknowledge my existence anymore, now that he's a good person. He launched a breakfast cereal, here in California, with his picture and life story on the box. The profits go to an institute he founded for the mentally mental. Untold millions. He'd be devastated to know he wasn't a womanslaughterer after all.

I am writing this letter for three reasons, apart from the obvious.

One. Because I can't imagine it will ever get to you.

Two. Because, like my father before me, I have turned into a pumpkin.

And three. To tell you not to feel bad, no one has ever proved that four colors are enough to color a map. Although they are.

TWO BASS BIRDS

"Who's goo-brain?" he said, referring to me, looking at Luc.

The he was eating a mille-feuille, squeezing it so the cream oozed out, licking the cream.

"His name is John," said Luc. "He's good."

We were fast friends, Luc and I, and had been for all of three hours, during which entire time we had been living together inside the tilt and twitch, the eye-banging egg-land of video games. I was still rehatching, readjusting to the suppleness of the actual world, its luring perspectives pulling me in all directions.

"We don't need freshettes," said the he. His cheeks were trimmed with pastry flakes and smears of cream. I saw myself wrench the mille-feuille out of his mouth, its soapy filling flecked with bloodless bits of his lips.

"He's not a freshette!" said Luc who, being French, did not presumably know what a freshette was. He certainly knew nothing about me. Other than that I was something new. "Hey," he had said, "want some laughs? I gotta meet this guy at Cantor's Bakery. *Viens. Viens-t'en!*"

"What does he know?" said the he.

"He knows nothing," said Luc.

"Then he can just go ay-way."

"I told him he can come!" said Luc, petulant, aglow with nascent fraternity.

"So, goo-brain," said the he after a time, still looking at Luc, "you're keen to come along."

"Yeah," I said. "Yeah I am. I can always go for a few mutinous laughs."

"Mmn," he said. "Mutinous."

He wedged the decreamed body of the mille-feuille behind his teeth, compacted it, swallowed bigly, and wiped his mouth with his knuckles.

"Well," he said. "Let's go then."

I watched the wires inside the metro tunnel spin and glide as we rattled along, but all I could hear was the he dozing beside me, his breath creaking with every inhalation, the back of his throat still tacky with sugar.

Luc preened in front of the glass doors, posing jumpily. He pulled his stunning locks back from his forehead to examine his rudder-shaped nose which was bent hard to starboard, causing him to breathe through his mouth and lick his lips frequently. Eventually though, his vanity required more attention than even his own reflection could provide, and he flopped into a seat, jouncing his knees feverishly up and down. "Sad day for the mosquitoes," he said.

I looked at him interrogatively, followed his liquid gaze to a cartoony ad for house insurance: two white, bare bodies standing in the greenery, the more feminoid of the two biting into an apple, a frowning, cloud god looking on. "If *they*'d had home insurance, maybe we'd all still be living in paradise."

"Sad day for the mosquitoes in the garden of Heden," said Luc, clapping his hand onto my shoulder. "When they fell out, Adam and Heve."

He gave me a leering, wet-lipped smile, pleased I was party to his satiricalness.

"When they escaped you mean," said the he, softly, distinctly, the smooth triangles of his eyelids firmly closed.

We slipped quick down a street lined with trees so overgrown they absorbed what little light was provided by the stunted, blank-faced street lamps. And then we dodged into a back alley, the nocturnal din falling suddenly to a murmur, as though a piece of night had broken off and dropped in a clump around us.

"What time is it?" whispered the he.

Luc twisted and turned, trying to find a stray piece of light to shine on his watch.

"One-fourteen."

I could feel the vigour of the giant dandelions bursting through cracks in the asphalt. I could hear Montreal cooing, the doting trees groaning in their sleep. Luc's head sawed back and forth in time to the music he was singing in his head. I caught the he looking at me, measuring me, caught myself thinking of clever things I could say to him.

"Well," he said. "Let's go then."

We skulked up the alley and dropped into a tiny backyard crawling with sleepless tomato plants. Up the backstairs we tiptoed, very rascalous, and slid into the shed.

"Luc," said the he, "the key."

"In the woodpile, under the first log near from the door. It's what he told me."

The he found the key, unlocked the door gingerly. And then he motioned to me to go in first.

My heart still races at the thought. My index finger still remembers the pressure of the trigger-shaped lever that lifted the latch. The kitchen smelled of summer grease and mildew. I can still see it, bathed in inframarine blue, the garish light of the refrigerator that Luc could not resist opening, the refrigerator itself crammed with forgotten jars and packages and emitting a bubbling miasma of fermenting cheese that so creased Luc's bent nose even the he had to smother a laugh.

"Don't close the door," he whispered to Luc.

"Come on, man. It stinks!"

"Shhh."

"Shit, man," said Luc, closing the door slowly.

"Open it."

"Shit," said Luc.

"Luc," said the he.

And Luc reopened the door, started taking out ancient jars of pickles and maraschino cherries, open cans of breathing sardines, half-sucked candies wrapped in paper napkins, holding it all as though it might explode in his fingers. "Ah *que ça pue.*"

"John," said the he. Pride scorched the inside of my lungs at the sound of my given name in his voice. "You look in the bathroom while Luc here does the kitchen."

"Sure. What'll I be looking for?"

"Lucky lucre, John."

I looked at him blankly.

"Money," he said.

"Oh. How much?"

"However much she's got hidden."

"She?"

"The old bone-bag who lives here, goo-brain."

The he could see through my eyes, he could, right to my suburban-boy's bravado. I tottered down the corridor, feeling my way, my cheeks burning.

The bathroom was papered with flowers as big as human heads. There were little bars of soap shaped like pieces of fruit. I found no money. I found books. One was an ancient *Reader's Digest* about Pablo Neruda and Montgolfiers. The other was a woman's medical book, so old the pages were brown and crumbly. This I looked at for some time, afloat in its stifling, feminine intimacy: tincture of digitalis to be rubbed over pregnant abdomens, a paste of soda, heavy cream and oatmeal to be inserted into inflamed rectal passages, lettuce leaves to be applied to cracked nipples.

When suddenly I heard a squawking and screech worthy of a parrot on fire, I tore into the bedroom to find the he holding down the bone-bag, her turkey-legs flailing, Luc pumping her about the coin.

"Où-ce que c'est, l'argent! Chioune!"

"Fuck it," said the he. "Hold her."

Luc pinned down the thrashing woman while the he dug out his X-acto knife.

"Hold her chin up," he said, "so I can get at the white meat," whereupon I drew their attention to my presence by collapsing on the floor.

Vaguely I felt the he coming at me, felt the heat of his fury wrap itself around me, lift me off the floor and send me hurtling back down the corridor, through the kitchen, the shed, down the stairs, and crashing through the tomato plants. It dropped me hard in the alley. The X-acto knife was under my eye now.

"We," murmured the he, "will never meet again, will we?"

He vanished then. I felt no pain at all, although my ear was filling up with blood.

Luc pulled me to my feet, shaking me sick.

"Run!" he hissed. "Run, hassole!"

And so I did.

I had a room on top of a depanneur. I stayed there for two days. I couldn't eat. I didn't dare sleep, for fear the jerking, wrinkled nudity of the bone-bag would take hold of me. The fever of my humiliation wrapped itself more and more tightly around my head, until all I could hear was its relentless, pulsing hum.

They were strong, Luc and the he. I remembered sliding slick into the kitchen, I remembered Luc's pleated nose in front of the steaming fridge. It had been a gas. It had.

I was starving and I had no money. I went down to the depanneur to mooch a box of Pop-Tarts. The Korean woman was there, smelling like limp onions. She hated me, she'd already caught me trying to sneak out with shit. She wouldn't give me the Pop-Tarts. I screamed at her, flung the Pop-Tarts into the back of the store and stomped up to my room.

I can't stand it here, I thought. I'm going back. Tonight. *I'm* going to knife the bone-bag.

Me, a murderer. Hoo. I slid through the broken tomato plants with pantherine elegance, my eyes gone soft, the taste of meat in my mouth.

The door with the trigger-shaped lever was wide open. So too was the refrigerator, its contents still piled high on the kitchen table.

The bedroom light was on, the bone-bag asleep in her bed. Her spindly white hair curled away from her neck, revealing the sweet shadow of her sternocleidomastoid muscle which, in my innocence, I believed was her jugular vein. Pure patience I was. My head was crackling with an exhilaration of blood. Pure patience, poised. I knew the thrill was coming. It would seize my hand in a flash of soothing cruelty.

And then.

And then the bone-bag raised her eyelids with doll-like slowness, looked at me balefully and said:

"*Ah, c'est toi. Merci, merci. I' t'ont pas fait mal?*"

"Mairsee?" said I. "Poorqwah?"

"For chasing them away from me. Did they hurt you?"

The affection in her addled voice subdued my blazing nerves. Has she not so much as moved? I thought. In two days?

"No, no," I said.

I was dizzy, my pulse was whistling in my failing body.

"Sit, sit," she said. "Your eye is like black butter. What did they do to you?" She sat up to make room for me on the end of the bed. "Ohh, they really scare me. They won't come back. Eh? Do you think? Not with you there. Say, if I was making some tea for us? Eh? I don't think you like tea. Do you? Hungry? I have maybe something you like."

She jumped out of the bed. The ridges in the pink-striped bedsheet made an abstract drawing of her body, the drawing gave off an odour of moist potato.

"*Mon doux! Mon doux!*" she called from the kitchen. "They have left everything on the table! *Ah là là là là.* The ice cream is soup."

It was all I could do not to lie down on the drawing.

"My friend once used to put her money, all, in the fridge. She always was saying: theivers will look never in the fridge. Hah! Oh-oh, the water's boil."

I ran my fingers lightly down the furrows in the bedsheet, the drawing rolled over on its back.

She carried in a teapot on a tray, with thick turquoise dishes and a gaping, yellow box of cereal. We ate heaping bowls of the sweet, styrofoam pellets floating in a pond of milkless tea. I say we ate. We ingurgitated, gobbled. She more than me. I felt bloated, nauseous. And she was spent, her transient energy sapped by the bilious cereal. She cupped her hand to her mouth, leaned into me so the knob of her shoulder pressed into my upper arm and I wanted to push her away. She leaned still harder, reddening, straining.

And farted. We both did in fact. Two bass birds fluttered into the air almost at the same moment, graceful, and so intertwined that it was impossible to tell which bird was emanating from which nest. They rose together and disintegrated into a faint spray of silence that caused us to look at each other in sparkling connivance.

"I think," she said, "I have never done that before. With a man."

Me, a murderer.

Marie-Claude Demougins. An elegant name.

Up against me hard she rubbed.

"What's it your name?"

Her breath was wet with tea, her grinning knees eased out curiously from her colourless nightgown, like the heads of baby tortoises. The swarming cities of bacteria growing on her released their dense fumes, acrid, arousing.

"John."

"*Djunn. Y en a beaucoup, des Djunn.*"

"Wee, boe-kooo."

"*C'est beau pareil.* You know your eye? What's it the best thing to put there? Mud. *Oui oui,* some good mud. Listen, you lie down. I have my idea. Lie down there."

She made me lie on the drawing and then she disappeared. The drawing held my shoulders softly, ran its finger between my buttocks.

What's your name, sport? Djunn. *Djunn?* Yeah. I'm with the bone-bag. *Say? Boanbagh?*

All Montreal orbited as I lay glued to the bone-bag's wrinkled drawing, defending, supposedly, her cold piece of debris.

Good enough, Djunny Boanbagh, what's yer pyzen? A peck of cracker-snow jack? Cream of dristan, man. Sorry, I'm out of coin. The bone-bag does all my finances. *A hundredweight of cuervo mould? Turn your brain into a red dwarf.* Hey, I said I got no fluff. The bone-bag pulls my strings. *You're cool with the boanbagh, eh Djunny? No preggers, no safes, no raw-raw diseases. The life, eh. Tell you though I've got this Yanomama maiden can whistle Amazon songs through her, her nether lips shall we say. C-note gets you a geek.* No way man, I'm with the bone-bag. *Strange music she makes. A tenspot, a feuille de Laurier. Crackling nipples she has, Djunny, as rich and brown as mushrooms. You can smell them under her nightgown, goo-brain.*

"Djunn!" said the bone-bag then. "What's it the matter?"

She had a potted plant in one hand, a fistful of wet earth in the other.

"Oh," she said. "I can see your heart that's beat. There in your neck. Bup bup bup. Lie back down, Djunn. *Là là, ça va aller. Couche-toi, mon Djunn.*"

She made me lie down again, clucking me calm, and plopped the mud onto my eye. A drop trickled over my cheek and deposited its load of silt on my lips. She tugged at the upper gathers of her nightgown to wipe me. The warm cotton stuck to my mouth, making my stomach lurch.

"*Là, ça va aller mieux.*"

The stain of dirt was pinned to the bone-bag's nightgown like a wounded insect bleeding water. With just my one eye open, I had the impression the insect was limping up the bodice. I could still feel the colourless nightgown in my mouth. I saw myself tearing at it with my teeth, snuffling at the bone-bag's skin. I sat up smart again, holding the mud to my eye.

"*T'es pas bien comme ça. J'enlève tes souliers.*"

She took my shoes off.

"Your stocks too?"

"Socks!" I shouted, excited by the accent of her fingers on my blue, English ankles. The bone-bag stared at me. Her eyes were gelatinous and flat, like licked china. She stared and stared. Like a piece of radium, I thought, staring at Marie Curie.

"You want to go now?" she said.

We should both go, I wanted to say. To Venezuela. There's a waterfall there so high the water rises in a mist even before it reaches the bottom.

It's possible? she would have said.

Oh yes, I would have said. You can stand under the falls at the bottom and look up into this massive cloud. You barely get wet. Want to come?

Oui, Djunn. Ah oui, je veux.

"No, no," I said.

Murderers are not necessarily monsters, no.

She sat beside me on the bed, slouching inside the transparent cylinder of her existence, distracted by the images flitting over the inside of its walls.

And I was so sleepy, so hungry and young.

"I can pay you," she said.

"Pay me?"

"Oh yes, I can. I had a cat. Borborygme. *Stupide eh, comme nom.* You know what's it? Borborygme? Anyway. It had kittzen, kit-tens, just three. I kill the kittzen, you know I must, and then I . . . I beery them? I bury them. *Voilà*. I put them each one in a chocolate box, you know for a . . . *cercueil?* a coffin, a Black Magic chocolate coffin, and I bury them in the tomatoes. Just three kittzen, kit-tens. But four boxes."

"Why four?"

She looked at me, a gleam in her flat eye.

"One box for my money! Good idea eh!"

"I guess."

"So you can have it, my money."

"I don't want your money!"

"Wait to you see how much!"

"I don't care how much!"

"But I don't give you. I pay you."

"For what?"

"For . . ."

"What?"

She was staring at me again, squinting, as though I were passing under a bridge far below her.

And then it was as though one of the members of the bridge yielded, she gasped, took my hand and pinned it like a broach to her falling sternum, smiling the idiotic smile of a preteen with a crush, her teeth shy in her marshy gums, little teeth, shaped like the toes of elephants, her eyes melting, dribbling down her cheeks.

"J'ai peur, Djunn," she said. "They really really scare me. Really. *J'ai tellement peur. J'en peux plus. Plus!"*

So I tried. It was what she wanted. I held the pillow taut over her face. But the strength bled fast from my wrists, my neck trembled with stringy hysteria. I hurled the pillow across the room.

"I can't do it," I said.

"That's alright," said the bone-bag, without the trace of an accent.

An electrocution of fear discharged itself into my spine. How could she speak with no accent? How could she? Because it was not her voice, was it, no, but a delusion of my gooey brain. The bone-bag no longer had a voice, did she.

No. Murderers are not monsters. Victims are monsters.

I wanted to scream every insult so loud her dead brain would cringe and squeal. I wanted to smash the dead daylights out of her.

The contents of the refrigerator were still piled high on the kitchen table. I wanted to set fire to them all.

The Black Magic chocolate box was indeed full to bursting with money. I stuffed a handful into my pocket and reburied the box for future reference with the three little kittzen.

And then I ran.

No sweat, Djunn. Luc and the he nixed the nixie good. They're the culprix. You're just the foul player, sport.

I watched the wires inside the metro tunnel spin and glide as I rattled along, but all I could hear was the bone-bag dozing beside me, slumping in her transparent cylinder. I hated her. She'd sucked me and my fizz into her mawkish maw, hadn't she?

Actually, you noticed, did you, that the boanbagh just lay there neat as a pin for Djunny-djunn-djunn. For lucky Luc and the he, she did the pea-hen-squawk. The primal-flail extravagant. Notice that, sport, did you?

The murdered are the monsters. Monstrous bullies of us little livers.

Hand it to you, sport, you got the hands. Goodnight, Djunny, you got the feel for it. Luc and the he are dead-lousy snuffers beside you. They make their wicktims want to liiive!

She's still sitting beside me, my Mary-Cload Demuggins. Here, in the office of the sporting goods store I now own. Where the price lists of my ski-wax suppliers brush the acrylic trophy given to me by the Chamber of Commerce as Young Businessman of the Year. Where the fabric samples are pinned down by the Black Magic chocolate box, full to bursting now with purchase orders and receipts.

My bully, my nixie indeed.

I hated the bone-bag for slipping her sob-story around my neck.

But not for long. Even as I rode down the metro, I felt her brighten beside me, dye her nightgown purple, spit on her fingers and smooth her eyebrows. Station after station slid emptily by as her breath, still wet with tea, blew the invisible cylinder of her existence around us both.

And when at last I pushed open the metro doors, the weak sky was dawning spongily. I walked among the scuttling secretaries and muddled night-timers, still young enough to believe that the present did not penetrate far into the future, and that, ultimately, I should be corrected for my bad actions.

I had decided, bravely, that I would go home and sleep. And then I would go to the police.

I rounded my corner, stepping firm, when the blow came from behind. I saw nothing, but the hands were on me, pulling me to my feet, stapling my arm between my shoulder blades, pushing my chin hard up, goosing my gooseflesh and my pockets triumphantly.

The Korean woman in the depanneur was beside herself with glee at the sight of me. She tongued and tittled and held up the policeman's hand for all to see, the hand with the bone-bag's money in it.

Some poor jerk had robbed the depanneur that night. That very night. The Korean woman wanted it to be me so badly I felt almost privileged.

"I advise you," said the policeman, "to keep it shut good and tight and get in the car."

Which I did. I was found. I was a murderer. And no one would know. A murderer dressed up as a petty thiever.

I looked up into the massive cloud of the Korean woman's hatred. Barely getting wet. Celebrating.

I turned to my Mary-Cload beside me in our cylinder and said, "I don't know how you pulled that one off, but I know you did. Mairsee, eh. Mairsee."

Two Bass Birds

Djunny Boanbagh's my name, sport. I'm with Marie-Claude Demougins. She's my bully, my Egeria. And will be, till death do us bring together. At least till then.

SMALL WONDER

I knew I was preggers. I didn't even have to miss my exclamation point. I could smell it. I could smell my insides softening, turning to pap for the fucklet. Yuck.

I stroked the two, blind, friendly fish of my breasts, looked at myself in the mirror, saw what I would look like when the fucklet had got done turning me into a vertical turtle, with my jellied eyes, my beaky nose, my dry feet splayed, my middle a pink, loafy carapace.

July it was. Sweltering. I was sitting in front of the open fridge, sweat trickling down my throat, between my friendly fish. The fridge was vaporous, pestilating bluemeat, bubby cheese. The uggs especially were gutting on my nerves something fierce. I cracked them all on the floor. Not one had a red thing in it. Lucky.

In flew a shitfly, slow-mover, hanging thickset under his work-wings. Buzzing made my brain swell till it touched my skull. Slashed away at him, slammed the fridge door. Ha! It wasn't the bluemeat the shitfly wanted to sniffle. It was me. Busy all around my kinobby-kinees looking for an upward passage. Hot cud burst into my mouth, right up my nose. Kept me from screaming.

I ran out of there, sure the shitfly was on me. Or in me. Divested double pepper, fumes from my zooterus making me weep. Small wonder the shitfly. Locked bathroom door, turned on shower full blast. Ahhhh.

Centuries. Soaped myself down and up and down and down and up. Water ran off my hair in falls. Twiggled the red noses of my fish-heads, funnin just.

Couldn't get clean. Not clean clean. On the inside I mean.

Eased my sloapy middle fingling into my nanus. Ahhhh.

My erectum glid all around my fingling so liscious I didn't know what was cleaning what. Centuries. Eons. Gleased out my fingling at long length, my nanus sighed, popped shut. Gleased in all my eight finglings and my two thumbs. Not all at once! Wish.

Squatted down on stall floor to do vulvet. Repulsion. Weep made me. Wanted to reach in, yank out zooterus, fucklet, vovaries, whole bit. Hystericalectomy. Same time, didn't go for inserting nice clean finglings. Vulvet puffy, nidorous. Uck.

Soap bar thin white blade. Introduced it my regina. Tentative. Tiny bit. Hmmn. Bit more.

Close eyes, clean.

Pain, soft in bedwoomb. Make me shiver. Fucklet not happy? Poo-hoo.

Clean bit harder, mmn. Cry. Harder, bit harder.

Big pain. Sudden. Big!

Bedwoomb alive, breathing inside me. Shit. Soap stubs in fin-glings, broken bits, zooterus panting, crackling something fierce.

Filled tub. Half bottle foam bath. Fell in, held myself open, heaved forward-like to get water up, soap out. Over and over, splash-kaplash! No go. Zooterus breathing heavy, heaving, I stifling, like someone scooped my brain out, plopped in candies.

Pain punctured, *tttssssssss*, draining out of me.

Ahh.

Shit! Suds going pink-like. Blood-pink-like! Fucklet want out.

Exit tub pronto. Bloodslugs noodling down inside of my leg-meats, foam lechers, leeching, leaking black dribbles. No end to them. Dizzy me. Nanus doing a do-do. Swunk down on toilet, all holes exuding goo, brain-candies tumbling, tumbling.

Woke up on floor. Soon as I fell awake, I was dreaming again.

Rooted around in my mess, looking for it. Had to be sure it had got born. There it was, lumpish clot, icky, eye-sized.

"Hello," I said to the mcembryo. You're supposed to talk to your children, you know. "Hello. You hurt Mommy big time, but Mommy not mad, not anymore, now that her neuterus is hers again."

The mcembryo scowled, not happy with me. Cold likely, thirsty.

Snicked it with the nail scissors. Seemed more chipper, not so scowly. My imagination maybe. Snicked it again, many times. Looked more natural to me, less like a mcembryo. More culinary.

Question: if I zapped it in the mickey-wave, two minutes? two and a half? and ingested the thing, would it be like a vaccination? Keep me from getting another?

Laugh.

So I got dressed, stuffed a handful of lite-days into my undies, put the mcembryonics into a sandwich bag, the sandwich bag into my pocket.

Outside, the heat wrapped me up like a white bandage.

"Oof," I said, "do you have to be so tight? I can barely breathe."

"Do you good," said the heat.

We got on the bus together, me, the heat, and the mcembryonics. We didn't fight, didn't argue. We watched the sweat-stainers get on and off, staggering under their load of sun.

After a while I said, "I fucked up, eh."

"No, no," said the heat, "not at all. Unsuccess stories are the ones we like best, by far. We like the angel in full moult, the vampire wearing braces."

"Right," piped in the mcembryonics, "for us a success is just a failure that didn't work out."

"You're kind, the two of you," I said. "Maybe I *am* invisible under my white bandage. I feel like it."

"Sure you're invisible," said the heat. "We all are. If they could see *me* sitting here, they'd get off in a hurry."

"Or me," said the mcembryonics. "Seeing as I'd have had bug-eyes, work-wings, and been some uglysome."

We drove way out, past the stadium. It smelled of concrete and flags.

"Our stop," I said.

The botanical gardens were gasping in the torrential sun. The heat put the big arm around me, making me walk semi-sideways. The heat's the tactile type, extravert.

"I'm not crazy about flowers," said the mcembryonics. "Find them rather rude. I prefer the grass."

"Grass it'll be then."

We came to the entranceway at the Chinese gardens. I dug a hole in the grass at the base of the gate. The mcembryonics got in.

"People will be buying postcards of you every day and sending them all over the blue plummet," I said.

"The ba*loo*," corrected the heat, "pa*lan*et!"

"What letter do you want," I said, "to mark the spot?"

"*S*," said the mcembryonics.

I scratched an *S* in the gate with a sharp stone.

"*S*," I said, "as in sleep?"

"*S*," said the heat, "as in sit up and eat your earth."

"*S* as in sssssssssss," said the mcembryonics.

After that, the heat and I got on the bus together. We didn't speak for listening to each other.

We drove in past the stadium. The lights were on, the black flags asleep.

The heat started kissing me little kisses on my neck.

"What are you up to?" I said.

"You smell good," said the heat. "You smell corporeal, clean. Like a newborn smells."

"Like a what?" I said, moving away a little.

"You smell," said the heat, sniffing the skin between my friendly fish, "like the newborn you are. Learning to breathe, right? Ready to rip."

"You're kind you are," I said, not looking anywhere but out the window.

THE THIRD PATIENT

Jane Bing climbed into her hospital bed with almost ethereal slowness, as though a steaming bowl of paint were perched delicately on her head, which, as always, was throbbing.

"Hi," said the woman in the window bed beside her, "my name's Farinaz."

"Jane."

"What are you in for?"

"Bff."

"I'm here because I can't walk. I don't know why not. Nobody seems to. Least of all Lu. Do you have Lu?"

"Christopher Lu is my neurologist, yes."

"The strange thing is, I walk in my sleep, or I have. I tie myself in now at night. I just can't walk when I'm awake. Ever since my miscarriage."

Jane Bing stopped attempting to wrap the hospital smock around her thighs, pulled the covers over herself, held herself briefly in prim tranquility, and then, addressing her knees, said rapidly:

"I'm here because Dr. Lu suspects — *I* suspect, Lu is noncommital — that my heart and my brain have changed places. At any rate the organ in my chest just sits there like a grey lump while the one in my skull bangs away day and night, night and day. Have you had successful pregnancies?"

"Oh, sure. Three."

"You've a partner I hope."

"Darby."

"Darby? You've three kids, a partner named Darby, you're what, twenty . . ." she looked over at Farinaz, ". . . six? seven? And you wonder why you can't walk? What are you watching?"

"The Olympic games. It's either that or the Olympic games."

"Mmn." Jane nodded then towards the curtain drawn around the bed nearest the door and lowered her voice. "Who's the third patient?"

"That's Lydia," said Farinaz, barely audibly. She made a grim face, tightening the muscles under her Persian jaw, rolling her bittersweet, black eyes, as though to say, "She's *really* weird."

"Jane," said the intern, the palm of his hand directed towards the seat of the wheelchair. Jane was not sure whether it was the shrill white-ness of his outfit that hurt her eyes, or the precise, styrene quality of his decorous torso. The knob of his smiling, human head had a dull, yellowy sheen that seemed to call for a fresh coat of varnish.

She drew back the covers weakly, made only the blandest effort to hide her flagrant, chevaline legs.

The intern scooped her up, plunked her into the wheelchair, steered her down to the consulting room.

"So," said Dr. Lu, "how are you feeling?" His neutral expression varied so little Jane could work away quietly at deciphering his moods.

"I was doubled over with colic this morning, an improvement from being tripled over. Excavation work is continuing on the subway system inside my brain."

The doctor's featureless silence was at least as fluid as her own noisy irony.

"Have you received your Devianol?"

"That rot gut?"

"Have you received it?"

"No."

The doctor noted this down. "Understandable on the first day. The situation will quickly become normalized." He paused. "This is a hospital. You have a task ahead of you here. It is to get better. You must eat, you must sleep. You must be disciplined."

Jane raised her eyebrows at this frontal attack. "I'm sorry to be such a red mark on the long list of your successful cases."

Dr. Lu remained impassive.

"I will try, I promise," she said, a deliberate note of schoolchild penitence in her voice.

Again, silence.

"Your roommates," he said. "You have met Mrs. Agharabi?"

"Farinaz? Yes, I like her very much."

"A warm and open person. Mrs. Kwaznievski is different. Do not let her disturb you. She is elderly. Utterly harmless. A gentle soul."

The crepuscular hospital night was soothing, ominous, filled with hummings, tricklings, muted voices, brief cries. Jane's headache became a faithful presence, intimate and yet disinterested, a tubular halo inside her skull that burst into pain, disintegrated, remade itself, ignited, fell apart. The particles of her headache drifted down the inside of her face, infiltrated her veins, gathered in her fingertips, her armpits, her anus, and upper lip.

In the neighbouring bed slept Lydia Kwaznievski, rigid, her white hair purplish in the dimmed, fluorescent light. Each of her exhalations was a sustained moan, so melodically sad as to be almost humourous. Only when the moan stuttered and fell silent did Jane's heart accelerate with dread.

The night inched forward. Jane shuddered, realized that she had been dreaming, therefore sleeping. Lydia Kwaznievski too was awake, gazing emptily at the ceiling. Jane decided she would introduce herself, was on the point of speaking, when Lydia sat bolt upright in her bed. Her beaming, periscopic face swivelled around until it was aimed directly at Jane. The face seemed to record a brief series of observations, and then re-centred itself.

Lydia Kwaznievski lay back in the identical position as before. Her eyes snapped shut.

———

The intern scowled at Jane's untouched cereal.

"I never eat breakfast," said Jane. "Especially when it looks pre-eaten."

"I am a sensitive man, Jane. If you don't eat, I will feel badly."

"I bet you will. So you're Mexican are you?"

"Canadian, through my mother. Mexican through a friend of my father. Manolo's my name. I was born in Sarnia. I just work in a hospital to keep up my image."

"Ah. And Lydia? She doesn't get any food?"

"Lydia prefers to eat air."

Lydia Kwaznievski did not appear to hear this or any other part of the conversation. Her covers were drawn up smoothly to her armpits. Her entire attention was absorbed by an unmoving spot on the ceiling. It must have been a familiar spot, because she was smiling the sort of smile reserved for friends.

Manolo went on his way. Farinaz leaned towards Jane.

"You don't look super great," she said. "You sure you're alright?"

"My head's throbbing. I barely slept." She lowered her voice. "It's *her*. I'm scared of her."

"I'm scared of her too," said Farinaz, although she hardly appeared to be so. "She's doing her angel imitation right now but don't let that fool you. She can do that for hours, for days."

Farinaz's visitor took his leave, nodding elegantly towards Jane as he backed away. He was a somnolently vigorous individual whose dangly beard appeared to be stuck on with tape.

"He's really a brilliant physicist," said Farinaz with confidential admiration after he had disappeared. "He has calculated the speed of heaven, using the mathematics of special relativity, which is his thing, but introducing a time-dilation factor based on certain verses of the Qur'an. Abstruse, amazing stuff."

Jane receded into her headache, resisted the variegated exuberance of her neighbour whose paraplegia was all the more arresting in that it seemed to enhance rather than dampen her vitality. She felt the familiar solace of rejecting what she knew was good for her. She could feel the question coming, she did not know how she would answer.

"So what are you interested in, Jane?"

There it was. She paused, tried to steady her breathing. "Hot paint," she said, regretting it immediately.

"*Hot* paint. I haven't heard of that."

"You haven't heard of it because it doesn't exist. Yet. Officially. I invented it. I spent four years developing it."

"Really. What is it exactly?"

"It's what it says. Paint that gets hot. You can heat your house with it."

"But that's an incredible idea. You've got it patented I hope."

"I have twenty-seven patents."

Farinaz regarded Jane with open admiration. "That's really impressive."

She leaned over to give Jane a congratulatory pat, but could only just reach the edge of the mattress, so she patted that.

Jane pressed the heels of her palms into her pounding temples, closed her eyes, tried in vain to silence her clanging brain. "No," she said, "it is not really impressive. It is not interesting. Not anything. Four years of nothing. I shouldn't have mentioned it. Really what I'm interested in, I think, is me. Yes, I think that's right. Me. Me, myself and I, I, I."

"Are you alright in there?" Manolo could hear Jane being sick in the bathroom. He was carrying Farinaz in his arms. She was dressed for her water therapy, her black bathing suit muting her own decorous torso.

Jane opened the door.

"I'll be okay," she murmured, hugging her ribs.

"I'll be back soon," said Farinaz. "Get some rest."

Jane lay on her stomach, her cheek buried in her pillow, and observed with one eye the turned-back sheets of Farinaz's bed beside her. She could see a miniature version of the dangly-bearded visitor busily calculating the speed of her headache.

She rolled over suddenly. Lydia Kwaznievski was sitting up stiffly, looking straight at her, her eyes wide with alarm, her mouth grinning.

"You must eat," said Dr. Lu.

"The Devianol makes me hurl!"

"Devianol does not have that effect."

"For me it does."

Dr. Lu did not respond.

"I'm onto your game. You just sit there, never smile, never frown, no expression at all no matter what I say because you know I will just project onto you whatever I want to see and what I want to see is everything that is not me."

Dr. Lu did not respond to this either.

"Can we talk about my roommates? Farinaz humiliates me with her strength."

"Farinaz is not strong. She is ill."

"And Lydia Kwaznievski. Who is she? Where does she come from? What happened to her? If only I had something to go on. She scares the shit out of me."

"I can't discuss my patients, you know that. I've already told you you have no reason to fear Lydia Kwaznievski."

"Jane," said Manolo, "what are you up to?"

"Just walking," she said. "I can't sleep. I can walk for hours at night. And the hospital is so quiet. So alert at the same time. How come you're still here?"

"I'm an addict."

"What can you tell me about Lydia Kwaznievski?"

"I can tell you that she's something of a legend here."

"A legend."

"A legend, yes. Like you, she likes to explore at night."

"Like me? Don't say that."

"According to the legend, whenever Lydia Kwaznievski visits a ward, somebody gets better."

Jane grunted doubtfully. "People are always getting better."

"Sure they are. But I know this to be true: she was found in maternity one morning, in the special care nursery. Maternity, yes. I was the one who found her. She had broken a glass pane in the door to get in. Apparently no one heard. There were premature triplets in the unit at the time. Their incubator had been disturbed. The triplets were all very frail but one especially was tiny, tiny, a matter of ounces, written off, hopeless. He is alive and kicking today. The mother worships Lydia."

Jane shrugged. "She should save her worship for her child."

"I want to be moved, Doctor. How can you expect normal people to get better when you put them in with crackerjacks like her?"

"Normal people?" said Dr. Lu tensely. "I would not wish normalcy on anyone. Not even you. Also: hospital beds are at a premium, you're lucky to have the one you've got."

A man came to visit Lydia Kwaznievski. Reasonably assured, pushing plump, richly haired, above all, young. He barely glanced at Jane, either out of respect for her privacy, or else with a lack of human curiosity bordering on rudeness.

He leaned over Lydia Kwaznievski, the fringe of his scarf falling onto her face, and gathered her up into an openly tender embrace which Lydia did not resist, and did not return. He lay her back down and drew the curtain.

Jane and Farinaz looked at each other with ribald pertness.

Farinaz returned then to the 100-metre backstroke while Jane, the pounding in her head serving to whet the fricative rustlings emanating from behind the curtain, closed her eyes and listened.

She heard a series of sharp, dry clicks, was puzzled, recognized the sound and yet could not identify it. A pause, more clicks. Nail clippers! Instantly she felt a curious tingling crowning the tips of her own toes. She was sure she heard the visitor utter the word, "fluff."

"What," whispered Farinaz, "are you smiling about?"

"Oh, nothing." She sniffed rabbitly, nodded in the direction of the third bed as though to say, "What's that smell coming from over there?"

Farinaz too sniffed, shrugged.

But Jane knew it was perfume.

In time, the visitor drew back the curtain, prepared to leave.

"How's Roger?" said Lydia Kwaznievski suddenly.

Jane had not, till then, heard Lydia speak, had, in fact, presumed she could not.

"Roger? Roger's fine," said the visitor.

"And Tim?"

"Good! Good."

"And Lydia Kwaznievski? How is she?"

The visitor smiled broadly, undeterred. "I haven't seen Lydia lately."

"If you do see her . . ."

"Sure, I'll say hello. Goodbye."

Early afternoon, the worst hour, lethargic, breathless. And solitary, Farinaz having gone to the day room to sit.

Every part of Jane's body wanted to squirm, to thrash and squeal under the flux of her sinuous, reverberating headache, and yet she applied all her concentration to remaining perfectly still and silent, to taking the full brunt of each blanching node and peak. Her palate was clammy with nausea. She was drifting through her own brash perversity, taunting herself with the snide promise that it would all soon be over, yes, the next throb would be the last, wouldn't it, not that one but the one after, the very last, no, the one after that.

The covers were thrown off. She started, the sharpness of the movement making her skull glow.

Lydia Kwaznievski stood beside the bed, weird, contradictory, her mouth smirking thinly, her eyes round with warning.

"Lydia," she said, her voice low, urgent.

"Get away from me," said Jane.

"Lydia!"

"Get away I say." Jane grabbed the covers and yanked them over her head.

"It's time to go, Lydia."

"Stop it," said Jane, wanting to weep. "Please."

"Get up, Lydia. Get up. It's time to *go*." She pushed Jane vigorously in the back, her touch soaking into Jane's spine like icy ink, turning her nerves into feathery crystals, making her wild.

"Don't you touch me!" hissed Jane, flailing viciously through the covers at Lydia Kwaznievski, who pushed and punched all the harder.

"Get up, Lydia. Get up this minute!"

"The fight's on!" cheered Manolo, attracted by the uproar.

A nurse, following closely on Manolo's heels, wheeled in Farinaz who immediately screeched, "They're crazy, both of them. I want them out of here!"

"Can it," said the nurse, whereupon Farinaz discharged a screaming flare from her mouth, her ears and nose, her black, metallic hair.

Manolo, wincing in the din, hoisted Lydia Kwaznievski onto his hip and put her back into her bed. He drew the covers up under her arms, clucking a mysterious formula that quickly restored her angelic calm.

"I think we can go now," he said quickly to the nurse. "Afternoon, ladies."

They made good their escape. Farinaz pouted, Jane sniffed.

Night. Gently, gently, Jane's pain seeped out through the taut skin of her forehead, forming sticky droplets that the snuffling air licked away immediately.

No, she thought, smiling, this is a dream. The air doesn't snuffle. It doesn't lick.

She opened her eyes, shook her head to clear her senses. A nurse stood over her, rotund, shadowy.

The pain oozed out from under Jane's jaw and the small of her skull. The nurse wiped it away with her fingers, licked her fingers, drew them across her uniform. It exuded from the inside of her knees, of all the strange places. The nurse turned back the sheets, spread Jane's chevaline legs and scraped off the clear syrup with the edge of her stubby thumb. So soothing was her palliative touch that Jane might almost have laughed.

"Where," she asked, "do you think it will come out next?"

The nurse shrugged, sat down on the edge of the mattress.

Wherever the glistening beads appeared, the nurse wiped them off until her own fingers were shiny, until Jane's nerves, so long thwarted by her bullying headache, prickled and stretched, like drying seaweed. She could feel her pulse fluttering in her lower lip, the ridges of her teeth against her tongue. "Kiss," she muttered, woozy, delicious. "Kiss, kiss."

The nurse lay down on the bed beside her.

"Lydia," said the nurse.

Jane's brain burst into wakefulness. She leapt off the bed, clutching herself, squealing with horror.

"Get her out of my bed! Get her out!"

Lydia Kwaznievski looked up at her with her canine, wounded eyes.

"Not too tight," said Christopher Lu under his breath to Manolo as they tied the straps onto the metal rungs of Lydia Kwazmievski's bed.

"Alright, Jane," he said, raising his voice, "we're done here."

"Why me?" said Jane. "What does she want from me?"

"She's strapped in now," said the doctor. "She won't bother you."

Farinaz growled, tossed, hid under her blanket.

Lydia was sleeping uneasily under her straps. Each of her exhalations was a languid call, not loud, not especially intense, tailing away, stuttering, alone.

Jane thought of a puzzled mare-moose, shot in the spine, unable to drag her useless hindquarters any farther. A tragic sound certainly, and primitive, but also welcome, loving.

Farinaz punched her pillow and sat up.

"Are you going to be able to sleep?" she asked.

Jane shook her head.

They listened together, in the imposed and privileged intimacy of the half-lit hospital, to Lydia Kwaznievski's breathing, daunted, fascinated.

Lydia shuddered, opened her eyes. "I'm hungry," she said simply.

Farinaz and Jane looked at each other.

"I'm hungry," said Lydia Kwaznievski. "I'm hungry. I'm hungry."

"Why us?" muttered Farinaz.

"I'm hungry."

Jane got out of bed and padded over to her locker.

"I'm hungry."

She took down from her cache two vanilla pudding cups, and a plastic spoon, went over to Lydia Kwaznievski's bed and untied her straps. Lydia instantly sat bolt upright, her mouth avid, her tongue lolling.

"I' h'ng'ee."

Jane slid in a bland, starchy spoonful. Lydia gulped it down, reopened her mouth. Jane slid in another spoonful.

Farinaz rolled over then and went to sleep, while Jane fed Lydia her entire cache of vanilla puddings. She scraped the corner of Lydia's mouth with the edge of her stubby thumb, drew her thumb across her smock.

Lydia Kwaznievski lay back in the identical position as before. Her eyes snapped shut.

Jane remained sitting for a long moment. There was a tingling about her headache, a buoyancy that was almost pleasant, that might almost have heralded its breaking up altogether. It was the time of night for which she was best suited, abeyant, subversive. The hour for princesses with open sores, gnomes with bewitching voices. She stepped out into the hall, filled with a nocturnal curiosity, a longing that was disquieting certainly, and primitive, but also welcome, loving. She began to walk.

She was very hungry.

Hungry, yes. At last. Hungry, starving. Not that I wanted to eat, no. I wanted to be hungry. I walked all night, all through the maternity ward, ogling the little ones, the pewlers and mukers. I walked, thinking about the pristine breakfast cereal I would refuse in the morning, so I could stay hungry. I walked, getting hungrier and hungrier, building up my strength. I needed to be strong. Eddy Constantine was coming.

"Ahh," said Farinaz as Jane came out of the washroom tying a towel around her head, "look who's decided to wash her hair. Company coming?"

"No," said Jane. "Eddy Constantine is coming."

Eddy Constantine had lovely teeth, rectangular, beady spectacles, short-pile hair.

He sat down beside Jane's bed, saying, "Hi" to Farinaz. He

nodded in the direction of Lydia Kwaznievski who was doing her angel imitation.

"What," he murmured, "is that?"

"Be strong," Jane said to herself, and to Eddy:

"That? That's a crackerjack."

"You're too fragile, Jane, to be around people like that. I'll get you moved."

"I don't want to move."

"You need decorations, something that's alive. I'll bring a plant next time."

"I don't want there to be a next time." A runnel of perspiration skated unskilfully down Jane's ear.

Eddy dug in. "You realize," he said to Farinaz, "that this is a very brilliant woman you have beside you here."

"I know," said Farinaz. "She's told me a little about the paint she invented that heats up. Abstruse, amazing stuff."

"Mmn. The walls of her basement are covered with four years of experiments. The fire marshall went ape-shit. Incredible tenacity. Some people just have the most startling insight into the way the world works."

Eddy had a lovely voice, round, floating *i*'s, deep-pile *r*'s. There was nothing between Eddy's voice and Jane but a smock, a meagre white blanket, and the thinnest of air. Still, her hunger held.

"Me?" said Farinaz. "Oh, I seem to have lost the use of my legs. Ever since my miscarriage."

"Really." Eddy's gaze moved over Farinaz's Persian knees.

"I have sensation," she said, pinching the tops of her thighs by way of illustration, "but it's all I can do to make my muscles behave. It's coming. I'm learning to walk again, a little."

Eddy continued to direct his gaze over Farinaz's decorous torso in a way that would have been luridly frank had he not managed to convey the impression that his mind was entirely elsewhere.

"My dad," he said, "had this way of getting me to learn stuff. Like, he just threw me into the lake, whuff, splash, like that, and yelled, 'Swim! I dare ya.' So I started swimming. After I got the rock untied from my ankle."

Farinaz laughed brightly, while Jane closed her eyes, struggling with her pounding head and rising nausea. Her hunger could withstand Eddy's flattery, but not his humiliating playfulness.

Lydia Kwazbievski sat bolt upright in her bed then. Her beaming, periscopic face swivelled around until it was aimed directly at Eddy.

"Hullo, dear," said Eddy, waving gooily.

The face aimed itself at Jane.

"Lydia!" said Lydia Kwaznievski.

"Lydia?" said Eddy.

"What," said Jane.

"Lydia!"

"What do you want, Jane?" said Jane Bing.

"Lydia!"

"Jane! Tell me what you want." She was almost shouting.

"Li–dee–ya!" hollered Lydia Kwaznievski.

"They're crazy," squealed Farinaz. "Both of them."

"Jaayne!" yelled Jane Bing.

"Stop it! Everyone!" commanded Manolo, entering.

"Love a duck," said Eddy, exiting.

The intern lay Lydia back in her bed, clucked his soothing formula for some time into her ear.

"I want another room," grumbled Farinaz.

"What," said the intern once Lydia was calm, "got into you, Jane? You could see she was overexcited."

Jane did not respond. She was trembling, perspiring. Her scalp was growing under her hair.

"Why did you egg her on? She mustn't get like that. It's dangerous for her."

Jane dared not speak. It was not her scalp but the surface of her headache that was growing, growing, becoming thinner, more tenuous. It was on the point of disintegrating, surely.

"Are you listening to me?"

She could feel her pulse fluttering in her lower lip, the ridges of her teeth against her tongue. "Bing," murmured Jane Bing.

"Dangerous as in life-threatening."

"Bing. Bing."

Bing! You weren't there, Bing.

I go back for a visit and what do I find? Farinaz stumbling about with braces on her legs, greener than ever around the gills, still talking pep.

And no Bing at all. None. Bed unoccupied. Almost as if I'd made you up for my own benefit. Could I have?

I didn't dare ask anybody where you were. I split quick.

Walk, Bing. Walk with me.

Ah, the great poisonous outdoors! The uproar, the tumultitude. The millions-nillions. My head's fine, I'm hungry all the time now. Can't get enough to eat. I don't either, and I'll keep it that way.

Call me Lydia if you like now, Bing. It's my name.

Technically, you know, no mass can be subtracted from the universe. Contrary to technique, however, people do die and when they do, they leave behind a hole that no mass can fill, no energy illuminate. This hole is what we call their portrait.

A self-portrait is, therefore, an egocide.

Bing, Bing, old artifitrix. You did me in. You painted me to me. I don't know how or why, I just carry your hole around in my pocket. I always will.

I'm off to forge in the smithereens of my soul, sweet squat all.

I don't have to think anymore.

And I don't.

I don't think. Therefore I am.

THE MAN ON THE STAMP

Seventy-eight. A ripe, an overripe old age. No surprise that a 78-year-old should feel like weeping. "That's alright, old fellah. You go right ahead. Can't expect to have the same tear glands for 78 years, can you, and not have them leak a little."

July. The parasitic humidity of Montreal worming its way under your skin, nibbling at your nerves, but doing you no real harm. I was in my favourite store, McCluskey's Coin and Stamp, on Lagauchetière, observing the wan dust in the panels of sunlight that slid between the bars covering the storefront window, when my eye was caught by a miniature man wearing glasses not unlike my own.

Eyesight is a gift certainly, but one given with the proviso that it must be used. We must look, whether or not there is anything to see. Our eyes, consequently, spend much of their time flitting nervously about, hoping to detect a clue that might lead to a hint that might suggest something of some interest. Hence the attraction of the eyeglasses.

The miniature, bespectacled man in question was on a blue, Russian, two-kopek postage stamp, 1990, in which year — if you remember — the Soviet Union was perestroikaing and glasnosting, rebuilding and publicizing it, in literal terms, falling apart and trying to hide, in accurate ones. Gorbachev's bloodstained forehead was everywhere, except Moscow. God was at the cottage. And me, what was I doing?

Not a particularly well-executed portrait, mind you, not a particularly attractive stamp.

"You can't buy that," said McCluskey, whose real name is Ben

Friedman. He placed the tip of a pale, arthritic index on a thin pile of sheets placed beside the stamp. "Until you've read this."

"I'll buy anything I like," I said, taking up the sheets nevertheless. A magazine article, photocopied. I read the article. From first word to last. Half an hour. After which I threw the sheets across the room.

"Give me the goddamn stamp, Ben," I snapped.

"Didn't like it, huh." He gave me his pale, arthritic smile. "I did."

"Just give me the stamp."

"Your eyes are . . . trouble with your eyes?"

"Never mind my eyes. Who wrote that?"

"Joseph Brodsky. Died some time ago. Won the Nobel Prize."

"Did he. Give me the stamp please, Ben."

"Sure. But you're . . . why are you . . . ?"

Why. Why tears? Why indeed. After all, the miniature man, like Mr. Brodsky and unlike me, was perfectly defunct, seeing as his bespectacles were gracing, or disgracing, a postage stamp. Perfectly defunct, harmless, not worth getting upset over surely.

Philby. Kim Philby. Soviet secret agent. You will have heard of him, particularly if your tear glands are starting to leak a little from time to time.

I picked him up on Lagauchetière, I remember. He got in and barked out an address at me, as if he would have preferred to go somewhere else.

Elderly he was, his combed white hair shone like wet feathers. He manoeuvred his head so that he could see around the glasses which stood up straight on his nose and blocked the view of his bovine, distorted eyes. His hands were spotted, fluent, they slid telescopically out of the sleeves of his suit jacket, which might well have been made from the skin of a shimmering, deep-water fish.

Later, when I knew him better, it struck me that Mr. Litvac insisted on dressing with a ministerial elegance that aged him considerably, but not so considerably as time itself, making him appear young, relatively.

"Why are you not in school, young man?"

"I am. I'm an autodidact. I learn in my car. My taxi's my carrel."

Mr. Litvac didn't know what a carrel was because he hadn't been to university either. He had made a great deal of money in the construction industry, his orange, trestle barricades still lined the choking, jack-hammered streets of Montreal every summer, although he himself had retired and was devoted to buying his way back into his own good graces through philanthropic activities.

"I got wind of a group called *J'écoute/I'm listening*, a telephone service for people needing encouragement and an understanding ear. They had financial problems and were about to lose their premises. So I took them over, and set them up in my condominium."

I found this admirable, was genuinely interested, I asked a number of questions, and then a quirky thing happened.

"Stop," he said. "Pull over here."

That wasn't the quirky thing. That happens every day.

A quirk is the opposite of a surprise. The proposition of a surprise, like that of a dream, is unexpected, apparently illogical, and therefore menacing. Once the logic of its proposition is revealed, however, a surprise is reassuring. A pink, plastic toy that falls out of a box of breakfast cereal is a surprise.

Mr. Litvac examined me with a strange, iatric intensity, as though debating whether to request a urine sample. "Would you be interested," he said with tactical deliberateness, "in a coffee?"

The proposition of a quirk is extra-logical, often pleasant, seemingly harmless. But a quirk has no resolution, its implications persist, become disquieting, ominous. A bit of breakfast cereal that falls out of a box of pink, plastic toys is a quirk.

"I have a family vehicle," said Mr. Litvac, ploughing the sugar particles into a pile with the edge of his hand. "Which is incongruous seeing as I don't have a driver's licence now, and I've have never had a family. I would like to put my vehicle at the disposal of the handicapped, the housebound, so they can get out, go to the movies, get their errands done. For this I need a driver."

I was doing well with the taxi. Reading Motoo Kimura. My friend's name was Irène. She was taking the pill to regulate her menstrual cycle, but we abstained during the ides anyway. I always used a condom. If we ever had a kid, we were going to call it Houdini.

"Come and see me," said Mr. Litvac. "If you like."

And I did. Surprisingly.

Ben Friedman was right. Read Mr. Brodsky, do. "Collector's Item" I believe it was called. Know it was called. Unforgettable. Moving. Mr. Brodsky came across the man on the stamp also, a blow-up of him, in a newspaper. Do read his tirade of disgust.

Disgust. My sludgy, overripe imagination is not anything like as perceptive as Mr. Brodsky's, but even I, having lived through too much of it, am capable of recognizing the twentieth as the abhorrent century.

But why? Why anger? Why tears? My life has been very different from Mr. Brodsky's. Mr. Brodsky was a Russian living in exile in the United States, whereas I, albeit born in Kharkov, am a Canadian, living in exile in Canada. I have no right, none whatsoever, to his majestic nausea.

I have even rooted for the miniature man. For Kim Philby. I have felt, as you very likely have too, the murmured thrill of that arcane talk, filled with rain, with footsteps and foreign accents, with words like "cover" and "mole" and "operative." Espionage.

And, if I close my eyes, I can see Mr. Philby dressed in his favourite tweed, favourite because although of the finest domestic wool (British I mean), it is too tight across the shoulders and the sleeves bag at the elbows. The dazed knot of his tie is half-hidden under the limp collar of his shirt, he is lying on his back, wearing the glasses that are not unlike my own, needlessly, seeing as his eyes, also like mine, are perfectly closed. His chest is sporting a red cushion sporting an array of medals, the Order of Lenin notably. And around him, a solemn brace of the Blood Red Army's finest stands to attention, bearing his rosewood casket lightly on their heavy shoulders, their military caps like khaki haloes.

Not represented on the red cushion of course is the O.B.E. he was

awarded in 1946, nor the medal presented him by Generalissimo Franco after
he was wounded in Spain. Oh yes, Philby was there, I was not. A corre-
spondent for the Times *he was, pro-nationalist, anti-communist. The only*
time he was on the winning side. Although he wasn't. He was just deepening
his cover. Oops, that arcane talk.

I turned the mezuzah counter-clockwise, as Mr. Litvac had told me
to do. The door lock cracked open with an imperiousness that elim-
inated all thought of not entering.

There was a waiting room full of magazines and green chairs.
Nothing waits with such pallid stoicism as a room. I crossed it
quickly, afraid it might think it was waiting for me, found myself in a
sort of sound booth, painted white, with egg cartons on the ceiling,
squares of cork on the walls, and four partitioned areas for telephones.
One of the operators pushed herself out when she saw me.

"Hi," she said enthusiastically, hooking her hair behind her ears.
"It's not as easy as you might think. We know so much about ourselves now. But the foundation of hope is precisely ignorance, isn't
it, in the strictest sense of the word. We can no longer exult in the
fear of not returning from any undiscovered country. We know there
is no such place. The challenge of the sentinel, and we here consider
ourselves sentinels, is to relieve, to add relief *to*, the unending, bad,
blandlands of self-familiarity."

"Ah, actually, I'm here to see Mr. Litvac. Not for the phones."

"Oh." She was the-Béliveau-twins, although I didn't know that
yet. "Through there," she said, disappointed I didn't know myself
well enough to be useful.

I make no claim to know what I'm talking about. I know about Philby what
a lot of people know. He was one of the Cambridge spies, with Blunt,
Burgess, and Maclean, upper-class young Brits, attracted to the world's
workers by their disdain for the middle class and by their taste for immorality.

Like their fathers, they had their club, the Apostles they called it. Only their club was Marxist.

"Come in! Come in!"

The broadloom in Mr. Litvac's condominium tracked my every footstep, although the oil paintings barely glanced in my direction, and then moved on. A shaft of sunlight was seated at the piano, while Mr. Litvac himself was seated at a table whose glass surface was illuminated from underneath, making his white shirt appear to have been made from flower petal.

"I'm working on my stamp collection," he said.

"Stamp collection? Didn't a meteorite strike the Earth sometime during the Mesozoic and destroy all the stamp collections?"

"Philately, young man, has never been more popular or worthwhile. Gone are the Lillys and Burruses with their gazillions. Today anyone can own a rarity. And may I say that stamps outperform mutual funds, by far. Ever heard of Kim Philby?"

"Sure, Swedish actress. She worked with Bergman."

Mr. Litvac took up a stamp with tweezers, and extended it towards me. I stooped, like an adult bird being fed by its fledgling, towards the stamp.

"What," I said, "is Mr. Dressup doing on a 1990 Russian stamp?" I knew it was Russian because the letters were in Cyrillic, except for the CCCP.

"Who?" Mr. Litvac inspected the stamp and nodded, I felt sure, in agreement. "That, young man, is Kim Philby."

"No, no," I said, quirked. "Mr. Dressup's real name wasn't Kim Philby."

Mr. Litvac laughed out loud then. Although I was sure I was right.

"I have an errand for you," he said.

I told him I couldn't start until the first of the month because I'd paid up my taxi fees. He wrote me a cheque.

"Take it, take it. And don't look at me like that. You haven't much time, young man, whereas I have nothing but."

Now, recruiting spies is a thankless job because should you recruit one who really does fine work, you are in the unfortunate position of being able to reveal your protégé's identity. It is generally thought, therefore, that whoever recruited Philby at Cambridge was quietly retired by a deeply appreciative KGB, and rewarded with a golden parachute. That did not open.

Philby did so well at working for the U.S.S.R. while he was working for the U.K., that before he was 40 he was in Washington, chief liaison between the CIA and its British counterpart, MI-6.

Unfortunately for Philby, in 1951, or thereabouts, the aforementioned Maclean and Burgess, feeling the pinch, defected to the Soviet Union. Burgess, moreover, had been working in Washington and living with Philby-dilby. Nothing too intimate, mind you, Philby was wived and well-mistressed. The occasional goose in the loo, perhaps. A spy's salute.

As a result, Philby was subjected to a lengthy interrogation (this was when I rooted for him) and eventually cleared of all suspicion by Harold Macmillan, soon to be prime minister. His MI-6 days were over though. He was in Beirut after that, journalist, still dishing to the Soviets, encouraging them to cultivate the Middle East countries, build Arab confidence with a view to skimming oil revenues, an initiative that worked so well the said countries took their new-found self-importance and formed the OPEC cartel leaving the Soviets out in the poorhouse.

Kim, consequently, was removed to Moscow where he lived the rest of his life on his government vodka pension. With his last and Russian wife.

So I began delivering bouquets of flowers, magazines, recycled computers to the ageing boomie vanguard and the older still. It wasn't as easy as you might think. These offerings were frequently received with mistrust, not to say terror:

"C'est qui, qui m'envoie ça?" The Siamese cat regarded me with placid contempt.

"Je suis désolé," I said, *"il ne veut pas que je vous dise son nom."*

Curled up she was, in the dais provided by the arms of her pet owner. *"Mais je n'accepte pas de fleurs de parfaits inconnus! Dis-lui, à ton boss, d'envoyer du cash."*

Which supported Mr. Litvac's central premise that it was important for elderly women when they received flowers, and more important when they didn't.

I was still a youngster when my parents left Russia, crossed northern Europe to Cherbourg and secured passage to Canada. Of that time I have, perhaps, a single memory: my father strolling the deck during loading, the cables and derricks squealing, a cargo hook swinging by, snicking off his hat. Lucky. His skull might as easily have been crushed, leaving me fatherless forever. It is true that my life has been dogged with luck. Still, perhaps I am wrong. My father has no memory of the incident. Very likely I dreamt it. Let us say then, to be safe, that I have no memories of Russia, or of coming to Canada.

Mr. Litvac was a prodigy, already, at seven, an incredible pianist. Every morning he practised for three hours, after which his father, who was the owner of the imported food shop below their apartment, came upstairs with a tray of poppy-seed cakes and made frothy, Viennese coffee for himself, his wife, and his grown-up son.

And no memories of the Russian language either, although I babbled it as a rebionok, *and my parents spoke a proud dialect of Russian which they called English.*

At 12, Mr. Litvac was told that with just a little more work, he could earn a scholarship to Vincent d'Indy, a music school even I have heard of. He practised harder, the poppy-seed cakes were larger, the coffee more robust.

I have never been a member of the communist party, or an exponent of Marxism-Leninism.

At 14, he was working all day long, he would certainly have got the scholarship except that his friend, Cyra Weinberg, who was a year younger and whose name you may know if you are familiar with Canadian pianists, asked him if he would help her prepare her Murray Hall debut, so he learned all her music too, better than his own. After the concert, she was invited to study in Europe. She could never have done it without Mr. Litvac, she said. Or his father's coffee.

I have been a romantic.

   I have not forgotten the forgotten war, the Spanish Civil, the international brigades, the Mac-Paps, concert pianists fingering explosives, fish-handed Catalans dressing cracked heads. Bethune was there. Philby was there. I was not. I was 16.

   I knew nothing, of course, but I knew I was a fan. Not of anarchism, because, I think, if you can see an anarchist it is only because you are afraid of him. Of communism. How it reached into me, with its vast ambition, its unshakeable fraternity, its chanting celebration of the underdog.

By the age of 16, Mr. Litvac was practising round the clock. One day, his parents entered the music room and gave Mr. Litvac a long and affectionate embrace. His father then offered him a tray of florentines and a glass of brandy. Mr. Litvac understood then that he didn't have to play the piano anymore.

A fan I was.

And his stamp collection, which he had started as a refuge from the necessity of being more gifted than he was, became an escape from his lack of mediocrity.

So sure, if you like, an old man's overreaction. But the sight of the miniature man on the stamp and what Mr. Brodsky didn't say, upset me, made me angry. And I'll tell you why. I'll tell you why.

Close your eyes again. See him? In the drab kitchen of his wife's Moscow apartment where he has been lodged now for 15 years, leaning against the metal table, the clatter and buzz of the refrigerator as relentless in his ears as the Russian language he can still only half speak. Watch him drop to his knees, crawl over to the cupboard under the sink, pull out the garbage, dump it, flatten the paper bag with his red and swollen fist, and write, with the childlike deliberateness of the totally hammered, "I hereby state that should my Russian wife murder me, she was fully justified in doing so."

No, it is not that.

That, for Philby, was fairly brave.

As a complication of his philatelism, Mr. Litvac suffered from deltiology. He had thousands of postcards, mostly old. We pored over them together, tried to make out the handwriting. People depended so much on handwriting in those days, which is why they wrote illegibly.

"You're not asking for a response," said Mr. Litvac, "when you send a postcard. You're just saying, 'Hello, I am here, in this place.' What else is there to say?"

"Right. Postcards are sort of like human birdsong."

Don't think that Philby bothers me because he was a spy. Spying is — numberless authors and moviemakers notwithstanding, or perhaps not notwithstanding — spying is a childish occupation. And I like children.

A spy is someone who loves to gossip about family, but who is an orphan.

One day I drove Mr. Litvac to the dentist's office. After a long time he came out, tight-lipped and very grey.

The next day I found him in front of the mirror, examining the remnants of his dentition.

"Scale model of Stonehenge?" I said, to make him laugh.

Mr. Litvac turned to me, holding back his lips with his fingers to reveal a gleaming, ceramic wall of perfectly calibrated, bevelled teeth.

"I hdth ntst . . ." He released his lips. "I had the dentist put new jackets on all my teeth."

"Jackets? On all of them?"

He returned to his mirror. "Never another," he said, tapping his front incisor, "cavity. Lifetime guarantee."

"Lifetime? Mr. Litvac . . ."

"Oh, I know what you're thinking, young man. And you're right of course. He *should* have put pants on the lower ones."

Treachery? Please. Treachery is to an intelligence operative of any sort what technique is to a pianist.

"What do you think of this baby?" said Mr. Litvac.

"Ah, it's a red, U.S. 24-cent stamp," I said, "with a blue airplane flying upside-down."

"The plane should be right side up. It's a printing mistake."

"Oh. And the stamp's still a stamp? It's not like, worthless?"

"Not worthless, no. It's called an inverted Jenny, issued in 1918, there are a hundred in existence. Want to help me put it up for auction on eBay?"

"Sure!"

Mr. Litvac had his own rooftop microwave antenna. You only had to breathe on his mouse and you were screaming through the net.

"I don't want anyone to know it's me, though. Stamp collectors like anonymity."

"You're a self-philanthropic group."

"Make me up. Somebody who's not a collector and not too bright. Yourself, if you like."

So this is what, with Mr. Litvac's guidance, I posted:

OK *this is a stamp we acquired it in a will hinged in great condition to explain we are not a dealer we operate a janitereal service we have limated knowledge as to the orgine of the stamp but understand this stamp is medium rare and worthy of a collecter that would welcome this rarity into his/her collection only a short sale please no reserve happy bidding.*

Thousands of hits, e-mails unlimited. Such as:

Ah, janittereal has two t's. Or:

Frawd is an indytable offence!! Or:

I cannot possibly bid seriously without seeing the reverse of the stamp. Are you willing to have it escrowed? Can it be delivered to an escrow attorney with clear title?

Mr. Litvac took the controls:

Number written on back 86 looks like maybe 98. Sorry forgot to ask what does escrowed mean?

"Mmn," I said, "you're pretty good at this."

"Bff," he said. "Everyone's a chameleon."

Betrayal. Ah. Let us look at the question of betrayal.

We do not like to be easily betrayed. Because it hurts, yes, but also because it eats through the protective coating we bake onto our curiosity. "Perhaps I too," we think softly, "because it's just got to be a rush, perhaps, if it can be so easily done, I too . . ."

Therefore we would like those who exercise their capacity to betray to be exceptional. To be something we are not. Finding them perplexingly ordinary (we did let them betray us after all, and we're not stupid), we make their very ordinariness exceptional. "As they say," we say, "a double agent is the sort of person not even a waiter notices." We smile, say to ourselves: that calls for a refill, and glance up at the barman who, strangely, does not seem ever to look our way.

In order to betray, you must belong. And to whom or to what did Kimmy belong?

To communism? Ha! You are not a carpenter just because you can afford one and you like the smell of sawdust on his coveralls.

To the Soviet Union? The stamp, the stamp. Listen to it wheedle in your ears: "Colonel of the Red Army Philby, Kim, was ours. We watched him, watered him. We gave him wife, we give him stamp. Ours."

Such sniping insistence. Clearly, Kimmy did not belong to the Soviet Union.

Forget England.

To the bottle? Yes, but he was faithful to that.

Did he belong to betrayal itself?

Ah, but in that case, there's really no reason to waste any anger on him.

Did he belong to one or other of the women he slept with, four of whom he was variously married to at the same time as he was sleeping with various of the others? To the one who didn't murder him perhaps? Yes. Perhaps.

My favourite postcard was a relatively recent one, 1950s, a spectacular photo of a monastery chiselled right out of the Himalayas. It had been sent from Kathmandu to a destination in Iowa. On the back was written:

It's the same here. Love Turps.

So maybe I won't tell you why. Maybe we'll just put it down to an old fart's inability to oxygenate his brain due to the close air of McCluskey's Coin and

Stamp, and leave it at that. Shun the Philby-the-scum camp and the Philby-the-spy-for-all-time camp and steer a middle course to no conclusion. Why not? A conclusion is only what you come to when you stop thinking.

Besides, Philby's occult machinations did not deflect the course of events the 60th part of the 60th part of a degree.

As double agents go, Ronald McDonald outperforms Philby, by far.

The-Béliveau-twins was never seen together because her one didn't work at the same time as her other. No one could tell her apart or dared use her names. Many sentinels lasted a week, some only a shift. But the-Béliveau-twins was always present, bimorphous, the soul of *J'écoute/I'm listening*, a corpulent duo with a radiant voice, like a flightless angels squatting in a bent-over palm tree.

She filled me with misgiving. I was terrified her adiposity might stifle her heart at any moment. I had confused dreams in which I screamed and threatened to drown myself in her foaming, rapid flesh while she talked me out of it with a patience that was slow and indifferent.

"Read Motoo Kimura," I said to her one day, because I say this sort of thing when I'm under human influence. "He argues that the development of life on this planet has been so statistically miraculous that there can be no possibility of its having developed elsewhere. That life is a quirk."

"Which we've always suspected and which is why," said the-Béliveau-twins, whose telephone light was flashing, "we've always turned space into heaven, and filled it with strangers and gods."

"Yes," I said quickly, as she fitted her earphones over her head, "we want so much for life to be a surprise."

She nodded so vigorously I could tell she hadn't heard.

A personal note, if I may.

When I was 20, a childhood friend who had moved to Europe sent me a present of a set of old French postcards, 1890s. Cyra her name was.

The cards were sepia-and-cream photographs of a town called Baume-les-Dames. The messages were on the front, as they always were then, inconsequential, and yet I read them over and over, I could see the fingers holding the pens, I could hear the scratching of the nibs, as though the words were being written inside my own head, calling me, claiming me.

I decided I would go to Baume-les-Dames. I would drink Pernod until I had no more money. None.

And then I would shoot myself.

As I say, I was 20.

Years later, I happened to run into Cyra, it doesn't matter where or how. What matters is that something, the intervening years I suppose, kept me from identifying myself. She continued on her way, and I found myself following. I felt, at first, very uncomfortable, but I was still hoping to run up suddenly and say her name. And then, I was simply following her, watching the cadence of her walk, the cadenza of her hair. It struck me, not that she was entirely beautiful, I'd known that for a long time, but that I had never really seen her beauty in its entirety because I had never seen it entirely oblivious to me. Is this clear?

Anyway, such, I imagine, is the privilege of the spy.

Mr. Litvac's favourite postcard had been sent by a Corporal Mainwaring to his mother in England. It was postmarked Namur, which is in Belgium, August 1918. It had been written hurriedly, because soldiers in 1918 didn't have much time:

God keep you from your loving son Ralph.

So what shall we do with the miniature man?

Well as it happens, I possess a stamp of a certain value. Six figures in point of fact. But only just.

I have unearthed a buyer, call him Mr. Escrow, whom I have enticed to Montreal by convincing him that present greed and philatelic ingenuousness *are leading me to sell the stamp for a ridiculous, albeit cash, amount. $39,412 to be precise. Plus the use of my Mercedes S-500 station wagon until the stamp is authenticated.*

A ridiculous amount indeed for the 1990, two-kopek Philby commemorative.

I am hoping the sight of the man on the stamp will fill my buyer with indignant outrage.

Better yet. You are perhaps aware that the owner of the world's most expensive stamp, the 1856 one-cent magenta of British Guiana, is a convicted murderer. Maybe the good luck which has dogged my life will hold, and our man Escrow will be of a similar nature.

The last evening I spent with Mr. Litvac started with a party. Mr. Litvac had found a buyer for his inverted Jenny. He was to meet the buyer that evening to complete the sale, and then he was going to go live in Europe.

He played the piano for us.

Gérard was there, a transient sentinel, always anxious about his partner learning of his working at *J'écoute/I'm listening*.

"It's a open relationship. I have lovers, all I want. But I'm coming here, it's like, so un*faith*ful."

The-Béliveau-twins was there, together, except the one working the phones.

Irène put in an appearance, but escaped early. "Maybe our relationship is more open than I thought," I thought.

Mr. Litvac announced that he had established a trust fund for *J'écoute/I'm listening*, which would be moving to new quarters, and we all ate Viennese pastries and drank frothy coffee.

After which I drove Mr. Litvac for the last time.

"Where to?"

"The Chaim Batista Theatre on Dundonald. That's where I'm meeting this guy. I'm lending him my car as part of the deal. Going to drive me to the airport in it.

"Remember the man," he said, "on the Russian stamp?"

"Looked like Mr. Dressup. With your glasses on. Sure. Phil Kimby you said his name was."

"I bought that stamp the day I met you, so I'd like you to have it." Mr. Litvac stuffed an envelope into my pocket as I drove. "Might be worth something someday."

"Thanks."

I parked on Dundonald, down from the theatre. "This good?" I said.

"Very best."

"So where you off to in Europe?"

"France. I'm going to a place I've wanted to visit for sixty years. Baume-les-Dames. Ever heard of it?"

"Sure," I said, "it's on the Boamlay River." To make him laugh.

"I like you, young man," he said, "a great deal. I like, if I may put it this way, your triviality."

We shook hands, I got out, started walking, and that was that.

Close your eyes. Look, over there. Use your binoculars. See the raccoons? Climbing over those huge, white chunks of rubble that used to be Lenin's impressive head. Aren't they delightful? See them disappear down the hollows that were his pupils. They'll curl up there, where it's cool, and go to sleep. Sweep over to the left. Oop, too far. There. See her? On the balcony outside the drab kitchen of her Moscow apartment. What's she holding? The binoculars aren't strong enough likely. It's a letter from the Committee for State Security, of emphatic praise for her late husband, and it contains the stamp.

The immense, psyche-withering monuments the Soviets loved to erect to their ephemeral heroes have all fallen.

But the stamp will be collected. Not by me, mind you. It will, like so much that is trivial, endure.

So the letter contains the stamp. And the stamp was issued to honour not one of the 50 million Russian citizens sacrificed to the communist adventure during the course of the abhorrent century, but rather to commemorate the ine-

*briated, wrinkled Brit, whom, although she had clearance to do so, she did
not murder.*

She, it is said, loved him. I wouldn't know.

Loved the miniature man. Loved him profoundly.

You should just be able to make out her tears.

The quirky thing wasn't that the envelope didn't contain the Russian stamp, but the inverted Jenny.

That didn't even surprise me.

I pictured to myself the distinguished man whose white hair shone like wet feathers. I had known him for half a summer and part of a winter.

And it struck me that I could easily conceive of the universe rolling through time without me in it.

But not.

Without Mr. Litvac.

That was the quirky thing.

YOU, KWAZNIEVSKI, YOU PISS ME OFF

Bing! Bing! Are you there? Walk, will you! The fuckles are out in force. Piyum piyum piyum. Walk, I said! Sleep good?

Like a nail. Are we going to Saint Sylvestry's?

No!

Lydia, why not? I'm hungry. It's cold out.

It's not cold.

It is so cold. It's cold as a titch's wit.

You've nuzzled into the warm, Bing. You should have stuck with me instead of going to sleep. What a night I had!

Sure, Lydia. Like you walked again for nine hours, phosphorizing.

Shit no. Way better. Way better. Listen: last night. Nine twenty say. I'm working the Chaim Batista Theatre. On Dundonald. Opening car doors for the fuckledrops.

They're filling your pockets with bat's asses.

No, no, I'm making some fluff. Now, there's a car kitty-corner, down a way. I'm not like, positive these are theatre fuckles, but I ease on all the same over and joyk the handle. I jerk the handle, like this, tock, and whungg! the driver falls out on me. The fuckle's dead, Bing. Dead!

Sure, Lydia, his eyeballs are bouncing on his cheeks.

His eyeballs are fine, Bing, except for being extinguished, like the rest of him. I'm terrified, I'm holding him with my body, my like, pelvis, this way, I'm not sure if I can lurch him back into the car.

No way, Lydia.

I heeeeave, inch him up, he topples over and I slam the door. There's an object on the ground, a bag thing. I'm not opening that door again to put any

97

object back in. I pick up the bag thing and go.

You're making this up.

I'm not making this up. And I'm not finished. The bag thing, Bing.

Don't tell me. It's full of money.

Alright, I won't then.

Lydia! How much?

Three, nine, comma, four, one, two.

How much?

Thirty-nine gees, Bing. Four hundred and dust. There's postcards. One with mountains that says, "it's the same here, love Turps."

Holy, Lydia. Holy dying. That's whack enough for living quarters, heated, with food.

Can't spend it! The police'd be all over me.

True. Only too. So?

Phosphorize, Bing.

Detective Inspector PF sat alone at his newly assembled, resinous, modular desk, and pressed his fingertips into his sleepless eyes. It was almost midnight, there was no reason for his being there. None.

There was, however, less reason still for his being anywhere else.

He heard, in the foyer adjacent, the relentless, finch's voice of Lydia Kwaz012-nievski and his face, behind his hands, flushed with antipathy.

Lydia Kwaznievski was well known to Detective Inspector PF. She was a vagabond, an incompetent one in his view, jailed upon occasion so she would not freeze to death, six feet tall, taller therefore than Detective Inspector PF himself. Her forehead in profile angled outwards, swelling her skull so that it appeared to house a brain that was still growing, an intelligence that was domineering, oppressive.

He pressed his eyes hard, making luminescent stitches sew painfully through the geometric clouds that shimmered behind his lids, but even this did not prevent his hearing Kwaznievski's chirring voice say to the night sergeant that she had an envelope she wanted to deposit with the police. An envelope she had found. A second voice, which PF recognized by its officious, chunky grammar as belonging to Constable Laliberté, said that he had been with her at the moment of and had witnessed the envelope, her picking it up of, that was.

What is this noise? thought Detective Inspector PF, standing, moving to the distal end of the room, where the finch's voice soon spotted him and flew him down.

"Then you have to give me," said the voice, "a receipt for the envelope's contents."

Detective Inspector PF was further exasperated by the inaudibility of the night officer's reply.

"How should I know how much?" said Lydia. "I just found it. Constable Laliberté is a witness. You have to count it and give me a receipt."

A silence followed.

Why silence? thought PF. Is he counting money? Why is it taking so long?

"Because," said the finch's voice, "if I leave it here, and you announce it publicly, and it's not claimed within a year and a day, it will be mine. You don't know that?"

Is that true? wondered Detective Inspector PF. He recrossed the room surreptitiously, as though exposing himself to enemy gunfire, flattened his back against the wall, and inched towards the open door.

"Laliberté!" he called, gruffing his voice deliberately to disguise it. "Would you come in here, Constable?"

Constable Laliberté inserted his head into the room. "Sir?"

"What does *she* want?" hissed Detective Inspector PF.

"She found an envelope, sir," whispered the constable.

"*Claims* to have found an envelope. You saw her?"

"Yes, I did, sir. I saw her find, claim to find the envelope."

"What," glared PF, "is in the envelope?"

"Money."

"How much money?"

The constable pointed an index finger ceilingward, disappeared briefly, returned.

"Thirty-six thousand seven hundred and nineteen dollars."

"*How* much?"

Constable Laliberté, with the same index finger, wrote the numbers invisibly in front of his chest. He inserted a comma after the six.

The intense light in Detective Inspector PF's eyes may have been consternation, anger, it may have been the setting Ipanemian sun he had always and only dreamt of seeing, or it may simply have been the reflection of the numbers smouldering backwards in the air in front of him.

"Book her," he said. "Vagrancy, whatever. Put her in jail."

"Fine by me!" chirped the finch's voice from the foyer. "Colder out than a titch's wit." The voice's short bill pecked into Detective Inspector PF's ears: "You're working late," it said, "Inspector."

So I get off the metro, Bing. First thing, I check the Caisse Desjardins garbage bin for vanilla envelopes.

Manila, Lydia.

Okay, manila enmelopes. Tons, as always. I take two. Stash money in one, all but two thousand and some. Trash bag thing with balance. Hoof it to Tournesol and Saint Josephat Square. Drop empty enmelope in gutter. Hide monied enmelope under coat. Berate fuckledrops full blast till Constable Laliberté drives by and gives me the yellow card. "Lalibby," say I, "whuzza in the gutta?" Pick up enmelope. Wipe on coat, executing deft exchange with other, monied enmelope. Y'follow? Tear open corner. "Lalibby," I say, "look! There's fluff inside. Bags. I'm taking this to the cop shop! Drive me?" Hard on midnight by now, Bing. PF's working late.

Okay. But why, Lydia, the two thousand and some that you threw away?

Simple. Some fuckledrop comes claiming his coin. Lost thirty-nine gees in a bag thing on Dundonald. What's in the cop shop? Thirty-six and some gees in a manila enmelope found in Saint Josephat Square. With a witless.

With a witness, Lydia.

We're talking Laliberté, Bing. So no go for the fuckledrop. All mine in a year and a day. Year and a half-day.

Good. Adventure over. Can we go to Saint Sylvestry's now?

No. Too much yellow food at Saint Sylvestry's. Too many fuckles, too many drooling eyes. Keep walking, Bing.

Detective Inspector PF sat on his heels in the dark hallway where the narrow cells were located, and observed through the shadowy bars that appeared to hang loosely and undulate, the obscure form of Lydia Kwaznievski as she slept.

You, Kwaznievski, he thought, you piss me off.

He knew she was highly trained, an engineer of sorts. He was not at all impressed, therefore, with her mouthy, mountain woman incarnation. He had had to do, in the earlier part of his career, with individuals far more liable to drown in the on-rushing, normative current of daily life, but who managed, nevertheless, to keep a little air in their lungs. Kwaznievski, in his view, had let herself go limp. She lacked stamina, courage. She lacked imagination.

The idea that chance should pour kindnesses into the pockets of such an individual offended his sense of propriety.

Jealous? he thought. Yes, I am frankly. I could do with 36 grand.

Detective Inspector PF was not an easy man to please. He suffered from persistent, attritive grief. His wife had died. Of technical difficulties. So stricken had he been by the loss that he had not changed a single observable detail of his conduct, had kept working, kept tinkering with his career, kept plodding unblinkingly through the same semi-suburban townhouse, the same groceries and hardware stores, while his stockpot of sorrow simmered away continuously, unwatched, reducing itself eventually to an overcooked, dense syrup. He became merely irritable, rebarbative, difficult to predict.

He sat on his heels and watched the breathing mound of Lydia Kwaznievski.

"Of technical difficulties, yes," he said out loud, induced by some nocturnal force to join the swirl of incessant conversation that seemed to emanate from Kwaznievski even as she slept. "She, my wife, was living, at the end, in a state of chemical mushiness. So wasted the biggest lump under her covers was her diaper. She said things like . . ."

He adopted an airy falsetto.

"'. . . the show will go on. It will. My show will go on. In living colour. It's just the transmission of it that will be interrupted, due to technical difficulties beyond, beyond anyone's control.'"

He returned to his natural voice.

"Technical difficulties of an aggressive, cancerous nature."

Very tired but unable to sleep, Detective Inspector PF let himself slide into a similar state of mushiness where he could see himself on a young and sun-bleached airplane bound for Rio, at the same time as he could see the airplane itself drifting off to sleep, his own body sailing out of it somewhere over an endless expanse of wrinkled ocean that was not unlike elephant hide.

A vigorous shudder unravelled itself through his body. "Kwaznievski," he said, looking enviously at her sleeping form, fingering the manila envelope for which he had given the night officer a signed chit, "where did you really find this? *Did* you really find it?"

Bing, Bing, it's a dolphin of a day. I was made for this life. I was. I have the knack that puts me onto the neighbourhoods where the garbage is out, wraps my chewy gloves around the tubs of shortening with the generous dregs, plunges my numb index into the warmish mash of dead weggitables the snots didn't like. I stuff myself, Bing, I do. But even so I have to push myself away from the garbage can, leaving half my dinner untouched. The knack I tell you. Big-time men, holding their coats closed, open doors for me. Fur-bearing women slip bills into my pockets, with suppurating tenderness, while my head is turned. Pigeons throw bread. I couldn't be better off, Bing, I am in my worm. I climb into its nose, screw down the portals, flip switches, and my worm starts worming.

You walk, you mean.

I walk.

Good. Didn't you say the fuckle was dead, Lydia?

Which fuckle, the car fuckle?

The car fuckle, yes.

Yes.

So you're scared. Shitless.

Shitless? No. In fact I'm rather full of it, I could do about now with . . .

You could do with a newspaper, Lydia.

Right, to wipe myself.

To inform yourself as to the identity of the croakee whose money was in the bag thing wherein the contents of which you absconded with.

Detective Inspector PF set out. He had not followed anyone, had not, in fact, done fieldwork of any kind, in several years. The January air stormed up his nose, so that the cumbersome device which the sleepless night had clamped into the muscles of his neck, dislodged itself and dropped into the snow.

Sleep, he thought, picking up the pace to narrow the distance between himself and Kwaznievski, who needs it?

The rule, as he remembered it, was to make your footfalls match those of the individual you were tailing. This did not seem necessary in the morning uproar and sloppy footing that characterized the current exercise. Nevertheless, PF endeavoured conscientiously to observe the rule.

This had the additional advantage of requiring him to concentrate on the heels of Kwaznievski's military boots, thereby sparing him the irritation of observing, except peripherally, the gesticulated punctuations that accompanied her perpetual conversation with the air.

The sun was white, the sky cold and brittle, the steam-breathing pedestrians slid through his field of vision like vertical fish swimming sideways while Detective Inspector PF navigated the snowy sidewalk, step for step with the military boots.

Kwaznievski stopped.

PF did likewise. He adjusted his hat to hide his face and looked negligently through the restaurant window beside which he found himself. A man with a shaved head was sitting in front of a plate of eggs, dribbling ketchup over them, and weeping. The man lifted out a ripe, bleeding forkful, tendered it towards his mouth, but could not, due to the violence of his sobs, slide it in. A young girl approached, concentrating on the soup spoon she held in front of her in whose bowl were seated three gleaming maraschino cherries. She plunked the cherries proudly, generously onto the man's eggs. The man's eyes widened. He straightened, stood quickly, hurled the maraschino cherries furiously across the room and stormed out of the restaurant, not four feet from PF himself, who realized then that he had forgotten Kwaznievski.

Angry with himself, PF hurried up the sidewalk, and soon enough re-established eye contact with the military boots.

Shit, Bing, there's nothing.

Nothing? Give me that newspaper!

Not a word. Squat-all. No missing cars, no missing cadavers. Too soon, you think?

Maybe.

Phosphorize, Bing. Two possibilities. One: the car is still parked on Dundonald, the croakee has not yet been missed. Two: the car is not still parked on Dundonald, somebody drove it away. Unless it was towed away without the body being discovered. Possible?

Think not.

And if driven, who drove? Maybe the croakee was not totally croaked. Maybe there was somebody else in the car.

Maybe.

Okay, I've got the body . . . Bing! Look back there!

What?

Isn't that PF?

As I living die. It is.
What's he doing way up here? This isn't his beat.
Beats me.

The military boots faded and lurched over the uneven snow while Detective Inspector PF followed in concentrated, cool pursuit.

He imagined to himself all the places the hurled cherries might have landed, against the wall, in hair, on the spluttering grill, and the respective sounds they might have made.

The sun continued to shine whitely, the short-lived urban snow was still young enough to appear eternal. Detective Inspector PF, exceptionally, was happy.

He's footing it, Bing, with deternimation.
Indeed he is.

And he continued to be so right up to the moment he discovered that military boots were a not uncommon choice of winter footwear, and that the ones he was so doggedly in step with did not belong to Lydia Kwaznievski.

He discovered this . . .

He's coming right at us, Bing!
He should be wearing his flashing hat.

. . . when his face entered into sudden contact with the black duffle of her greatcoat, and when her penetrating, fringillid voice piped:

"Inspector! Are you alright? You're not nearly as, as dense as you appear on television."

2

"YOU there! Who are you looking at? Eh! Eh! Look a little closer! Come on! Eh! SHIT!"

Am I bleeding, Bing? Another fuckledrop who doesn't know it yet. First PF *piles into me, now this fuckle dings me with his elbow. What's with them? Why do they want to get away from me so quick? Must be my stink, the muskrat I ate what, the day before the day before . . . So I'm not bleeding? Shit. Where were we?*

Where we are.

More than likely.

Detective Inspector PF felt ridiculous, inept, he upbraided himself mercilessly, recognizing as he did that whatever his suspicions, he had absolutely no business following Kwaznievski without the proper authorization. He stumbled hurriedly over the same sidewalks but in the opposite direction this time, not daring to look through the restaurant window as he passed, knowing he would see himself dribbling ketchup over his eggs, and weeping.

He was tired, tired. He had the impression, the certitude, that a steel barrier, spotless and perfectly smooth, was rising in front of the police station at the same time as he was approaching, so that by the time he arrived, the barrier would be just high enough for him to be unable to climb over. If he retreated, the barrier would lower. If he rushed it, it would rise to meet him.

You were getting the body, Lydia, back into the car.

Right. Right! So I've got the body here like, it's leaning into my abdomen, threatening to push right through me and drop between my feet, I heave, eeeeewah, and there, just there, gravity snaps, thoing! *the body leaps back into the car, there, I feel them, I do, shit, the eyes are on me. There were other eyes in the car, Bing. There were. What if the bag thing belongs to the eyes and the eyes belong to the croaker? What if the car is still parked on Dundonald, with the eyes still inside? What if the eyes are waiting for me? What if they're on me now?*

And in truth, the closer he came to the station, the more intense, the more redoubtable the idea of the barrier became, until he simply could not proceed, could not breathe.

Detective Inspector PF stopped, lost in the familiar streets of Montreal. Wherever he looked, the sun ricocheted off the young snow into his eyes, whiting him out.

Walk, Bing, walk. I wish PF were still following me.

He wasn't following you! A pro cop doesn't bang right into someone they're following.

I wish he were here then. What say we head back in the direction of the cop shop?

Lead on, Lyd.

Detective Inspector PF started to walk. Just walk.

I've been doing my headwork, Lydia.

Have you! Let's hear it then. Go, Bing.

Okay the epochs of the Tertiary are: the Paleocene, the Eocene, the Oligocene, the Plasticene, the Hyliobscene.

No, Bing. There you're in the Neozoic. And the ganoid fishes subordinate to the teleosts?

The Cretaceous.

And the cycads and evergreen trees?

With the flying reptiles.

Go, Bing. The Pennsylvanian.

The Patuxent, the Ar . . .

Bing! Bottle it! Who's that?

As I living die. It's PF *all over again.*

Look at him. He's doing his Mr. Inconspicuous imitation, coplike. He sees without being seen.

Y'think? I'd say he's walking. Just walking. Could be he needs to pick up some carpet shampoo.

It's him, it is. The best view of a man, Bing, is like this, from behind. Shhh, he's stopped. Look. An even better view is from behind a man who stops to wait. A stooped back straightens when a man waits. A straight back stoops. The most, the only, sincere part of a man is his back.

I can think of other parts.

The best view of all is from behind a waiting man just, just at the moment he is about to turn around. Just now.

PF *is about to turn around?*

Shhh, Bing. Do I stink?

As the host of the popular television program *Citizen's Arrest*, Detective Inspector PF was not unaccustomed to being recognized. He had observed moreover, that the more he was greeted with animated congeniality by random strangers, the more his genuine acquaintances, out of respect no doubt for his privacy, offered him the mere suggestion of a smile as they passed, when they did not ignore him altogether. Therefore, on hearing a treble voice behind him say, "Hello Inspector," PF categorized the voice instantly as belonging to an unknown individual and made no attempt at identification.

He simply turned to face the voice, and was surprised by the same pleasure of adventitious recognition he so frequently inspired in others: "Oh! Hello . . ." which pleasure, even before he reached the end of the third syllable, curdled, ". . . again."

He averted his eyes. And yet he could not deny to himself that the same embarrassment that was turning his cheeks paint red, was also drawing him out of the white invisibility through which he had been dragging himself. He looked up at Lydia.

"It's money bags," he said, with the mere suggestion of a smile.

3

"Everything is what it is, Inspector," said Lydia with animated bravura, "but also not everything that it isn't. Example: we are walking. What is our destination?"

"Our destination? Could be anywhere. You tell me."

"I don't think we're going anywhere."

"Alright. Nowhere then."

"No. Wherever we're going, it'll be there when we get there."

"So we *are* going somewhere."

"No. Dayton, Ohio, is somewhere, but we're not going there. We are anti-points, Inspector. A point has position but occupies no space. We, on the other hand, occupy space but have no position. Like whole black pages. Our destination is everywhere, minus the sum of all the places we're not going to. Which is?"

"Where we are?"

"You see? Every step we leave to arrive again to leave again to arrive. Every step."

"Good for you, Lydia," muttered Detective Inspector PF, looking out into the traffic, hoping to spot a green LeSabre, like his own.

Bing! He called me Lydia.

"What!" PF's head snapped back. "Listen. Either you talk to me, or you don't talk at all."

They stepped sturdily on then, she stuffing Bing as far into her brain as possible, he thinking how much easier it is to be with people, like Kwaznievski, for whom you have little regard. A short refrain was turning over in his head in time with his footsteps, I leave, I heave, I yarrive, I weave . . .

"Do you remember," he said, "the ice storm? No electricity for several days. How many years ago was that? Was it that many? Anyway, the station was equipped with an auxiliary generator, still is, so we had heat, partial lighting. Crammed with people. From all walks of life, you know, a true sense of community. Very little criminal activity at times like that, very little vandalism even. There was a young kid. I say kid. He was almost twenty. Only a couple of years younger than me really, at the time . . ."

Detective Inspector PF listened to his voice at the same time as he listened to the short, silent refrain. The sun was paler, cooler, it drew the warmth from him, leaving him chilly under his coat. He was aware that he had begun this story obliquely, as a moral tale intended for Kwaz07nievski's improvement, the kid in question having since become the successful owner of a sporting goods store. But his voice seemed to take little interest in this aspect of the story.

"Everyone had to be registered of course, and as it happened, it was me who registered this, this young man shall we say. He'd showered, shaved, been disinfected. He was completely off heroin by then, but he was still undernourished, chronically ill, he still walked with a forward lean. No doubt he felt me watching him as he filled in the card because he glanced up. He looked like death. His face was flat, a mask, without feeling, not in the least bothered by the scabs that the shower had opened and that were leaking bright new blood. Like death. Death, I assure you, has no difficulty looking almost twenty.

"But not his eyes. His eyes still had their adolescent vitality, not very clear thinking maybe, but defiant, and yet inviting at the same time.

"Of course there was no privacy anywhere, the washrooms were constantly packed, you didn't know where to look, you couldn't speak without being overheard, so there was no possibility of getting to know anyone. But . . . you're sure you're in the mood for this?"

"Oh absolutely, Inspector. Go on, go on."

"Well, we ran out of sleeping bags. So I had to share a blanket with Raoul Leblanc, he's not in the force anymore, moved to New Zealand, something to do with forest management, very clever guy, and as it happens we're assigned to a piece of floor right next to John, that's the young man's name. So here I am, in this incredible, artificial intimacy, sharing my bed with two other men, in the middle of this equally artificial non-intimacy, and I sleep, believe it or not, the sleep of a child.

"Morning comes. Raoul whispers to me that his night was one long parade of erotic dreams and he's sorry if he had an erection to beat the band. I say, 'That's okay, I slept very well, I didn't feel a thing,' and he goes, 'What! How could you not feel anything! Tonight, you'll feel something all right. Butter yourself up!' He storms off, I roll over and there's John beside me. His scabs are starting to bleed again. Because he's straining so hard to keep from laughing."

Detective Inspector PF's voice paused here for a long moment because, having lead PF this far, and having reached the part of the story it found most telling, it did not want to continue without being repossessed by PF himself.

"I have never," his voice and PF said together, "felt such a, such a strong sense, of proximity with another person."

Bing! Bing! Are you there? Ah, Bing. Come on.

What.

Hey, it's not my fault. Hang on while I urinate. My kidneys can't metabolize all this coffee. Not my fault, Bing. I can't talk to you. He won't let me.

Sure, Lydia.

He won't let me talk at all. He's on and on and on. Never stops. And he hasn't said a word. About, I mean, the events of last night.

He's buttering you up. Keep an ear peeled.

Shit, Bing, look at me pee. I'm losing all my good vitamins and my electrolytes. My tongue's going to go black and drop out.

So what's he on about?

I'm not really sure, I can't listen fast enough. He started off with some kid with scabs that bled so much it gave him a feeling of proximity. Lately he's been quoting from his wife's ghost. She got late early.

———

Detective Inspector PF gazed out the restaurant window, his chin fitted into the heel of his palm, causing his head to bob as he spoke. "She said that we had grown so much alike, we had become twins. That we would be twins separated at death." He snorted softly. "Maudlin I know, but she was very ill, heavily sedated. And I was moved, you get caught up in these things. I said, 'If you're going, I'm coming too.' I meant it, I think. She was furious. 'Death doesn't deserve any bonuses!'

"No indeed. Death does not. Her favourite expression, or saying, whatever you want to call it, was that we should all carry a label: 'Shake well before opening.' She thought we should all challenge each other, shake each other up. She hated complacency.

"She improved suddenly, briefly, around March, so I drove her down to Vermont. We stopped at Venise. The lake looked hard, cold, the beach was deserted, there were patches of snow still, but the sun was so strong, you couldn't help but hear the hordes, the motorboats, the piped-in music. 'The surest way to forget who I am,' she said, 'is by never loving anyone else. Sometime, bring her here.'"

Bing! I'm back. Save me, please. Mrs. Ex-PF just will not stop. She keeps flying around the table, flapping her peppermint wings and clubbing me with her broom. She's not going to let a little thing like death keep her from sinking her syringe into his future, is she, Bing? Please, Bing. The place is crawling with fuckledrops. With proximity. Bing. Answer me, Bing! Shit.

Get off the can, Lydia.

"One thing she said," said Detective Inspector PF, his elbows planted on the table, his wide head drooping between the uprights of his forearms, his square fingers combing his undulant hair towards the back of his neck, "has meant a great deal to me as a policeman. She said we'd been happy together." He looked up. "A privilege that carries with it obligations towards the less happy."

"Yes," said Lydia brightly, "that's very good, Inspector. I shall endeavour to continue living up to my obligations towards the less unhappy."

The restaurant, as apprehended by Detective Inspector PF, fell silent, grew distant, looked elsewhere.

"I'm not sure I like your tone," he said.

No, he was not sure. He would, in fact, have liked Lydia to repeat herself. Lulled by her mute attentiveness into a mood of warm concurrence, he had not been prepared for the irony of her response and had not fully grasped her meaning.

He would also have liked to point out, with pinched, martial dignity, that if he was devoting so much of his time to her that day, it was in the hope that she might learn something from what he had to offer.

He sustained Lydia's difficult gaze for several seconds, cleared his throat unnecessarily, stood, adjusted his winter coat to lie correctly on his shoulders, and made his way to the cash.

The waitress crinkled her hydroponic eyes, spread her bills into a fan, picked PF's, flattened it meticulously on the top of the glass dessert cabinet, and began studiously to perform the addition.

PF swore under his breath, was sorely tempted simply to leave $20, did not dare watch the waitress for fear of protracting the apparent length of the arithmetic operation underway, did not dare look back towards Lydia Kwaznievski, observed instead the inaudible television.

A cooking show. Extravagantly cheerful. Cake, cream. The chef's assistant unscrewing the stubborn lid of a jar of maraschino cherries.

Detective Inspector PF smiled inwardly. Everything, he liked to say, is coincidental, is it not? Everything happens at the same time. Coincidences are the fibres of time. This second appearance in his day of maraschino cherries charmed him, gave him the impression of life as bound, spinning, exploratory.

The lid flew off, the cherries leapt out of the jar. Hilarity. Buffoonery.

Detective Inspector PF was not aware he was smiling broadly.

A member of the television audience, a white-bearded gentleman with a mariner's cap, shuffled in from the side of the picture, concentrating on the soup spoon he held in front of him in whose bowl were seated three gleaming cherries.

Detective Inspector PF's smile vanished. He gasped, was filled with an eager, an almost joyous, trepidation.

"Lydia!" he called to Kwaznievski, whose greatcoat was wafting through the restaurant door, "I've just seen the most, the most incredible what? the most incredible coincidence. Wait, wait up. I just happened to be looking at the television . . ."

Colder it was, darker. Montreal was as though sinking through an icy, gelatinous semi-liquid, twilit, murky. Detective Inspector PF shivered, stopped to do up the buttons of his coat, and discovered he did not know how to begin describing the temporal spark that still glowed between the girl and the gentleman, the soup spoons, the maraschino cherries, was no longer convinced, in any case, that he had not misremembered, misinterpreted, misconstrued.

Bing! I'm out! At last. Are you there?

It's cold, Lydia. Can we go to Saint Sylvestry's?

I just ditched the PF's, Mr. and Missed, and you want to go to Saint Sylvestry's? Too many fuckledrops, Bing, too much drooling soup, too many yellow eyes.

It's cold out.

Cold? The cold, Bing, is a childlike thing, a gourdy, plumply-faced girl, needing affection, approval. Well I approve, I do.

Good.

Her fingers are stubby. Like breakfast links filled with yoghurt. Her name is Tina. I see you, Tina, I do. Wave to Tina, Bing. With her oily organs and her excellent pinkskin.

Lydia. The cold is cold.
Walk, Bing.
What about the Piffer?
PF's ditched me. He's got work to do. Obligations to the less happy.

Detective Inspector PF gazed at the pedestrian signal, waited for the white johnny-walker to light up so he could cross the street.

He was as though drunk with his own weariness. He had talked, he thought, far too much. Far too much. He should never, for example, have mentioned Venise, there are stories like that that can never really be retold again once you've told them once, once, the way serial killers, say, can kill over and over but you can execute them only once, only once, and God knows he might have found a better pair of ears to tell it to.

He could see himself feeling his way along the black, stainless barrier surrounding the police station, searching for an opening, a seam even, finding at last a crack through which, closing one eye, he could just glimpse the pale incandescence of the next barrier.

Boff, he thought, one pair of ears hardly hears any better than another. He watched the smoke billow around the heads of the passers passing him by and wondered if he had put on the proper breathing apparatus. He could not seem to inhale the semi-liquid. He thought that the air was likely fresher close to the ground and that, consequently, he should sit down.

"No, no, I'm fine, I'm fine," he said to the knock-kneed business-women who bent beside him, holding their sleek hair away from their faces with their black gloves. "No really, fine. Thanks, thanks. A little tired maybe. Bit of a sit, as they say, in Liverpool, is it? I'm fine, I am. Didn't get all the sleep I maybe might've. Thanks to Kwaznievski and her fifty-eight thousand dollars."

"Thirty-eight thousand," said Lydia Kwaznievski.

"I beg your pardon?"

"Never mind, Inspector, just get up. The girl in the restaurant came trumpeting after me. You didn't pay apparently."

"I didn't?" said Detective Inspector PF standing smartly up. "Well, where is she? How much was it? Here, give her twenty dollars."

"That's alright, I paid her."

"You paid her? How did you. . . ? Let me pay you back then."

"Turn around, Inspector." Lydia knocked the snow off PF's backside. "Your coat is wet through."

"Lydia," he said turning to face her, "I can't believe how much better I feel. Which is odd because I wasn't aware of feeling anything but fine. Is there something you'd like to do? To eat? Somewhere I can drop you off?"

"Shhh," said Lydia soothingly, confidingly. "You don't have your car, Inspector."

"Oh I don't mind walking."

Montreal touched bottom with an impalpable, mysterious shudder, causing the faintest of ripples to rise languidly through the gelatinous air, which brightened momentarily before becoming darker still. The nocturnal winter insects had been roused, thick-voiced, playful.

"I have to go to work," she said.

"Work? You work? Oh. Well how far do you have to go?"

"It's an hour from here on foot. A little more maybe."

"That's fine."

"You're not going to suggest we take a taxi?"

"Sure, if you like. I thought you wanted to walk."

"Alright then, Inspector," she said, "we'll walk. But on one condition."

"Sure."

"That you don't talk. Unless you talk to me."

4

"This is where you work?" said Detective Inspector PF.

They entered Saint Dunstan's Church. The dark, woody silence of the nave was barely illuminated by a man at the far end talking in flickering undertones. His listeners stretched towards his voice like lilies towards a patch of sunlight.

A woman sat at a table. There was a Bible on the table and beside it a white card on which had been written, artfully: $12.49.

"Hello," whispered PF, smiling beneficently at the woman. "Sold any?"

The woman consulted a paper. "Eighty-five today."

"Oh! Well. That's quite a few. Can I buy one?"

"If you like."

The woman put his money into her black cash box, made a note on her paper, handed him a Bible and a starched, white rose with a plastic stem.

"You must be quite religious," said Detective Inspector PF lightly to Lydia.

"Me!? I have my own linen flower business. They give me work-space in the church in exchange for flowers to decorate the altar, hand out with the Bibles and so on. Come on, I'll show you."

She led PF outside through the deep and crisp and even blue snow to a low side door which she unlocked with what might have been a Jacobean, gaol-keeper's key.

"Woo," said PF, following her into the solid darkness.

"It's not far," murmured Lydia, "put your hand . . . yes, like that," feeling the touch of PF's hand on her shoulder run down her back and merge with the brush of his coat spreading up her spine. She aimed her bundled breasts on a course dead ahead, advanced through the dense blackness, rattled another key into its slot, turned a cold knob. A blast of light wheeled around, drew her in roughly by the arms, and struck PF hard on his dry forehead.

"It's alright, Inspector," said Lydia. "You can come in."

The room was small and very white. The pipes and wires lining the ceiling were white. It contained a white table, boxes of stalks, clear bags bursting with petals, a telephone, cubicles containing baskets and flowerpots filled with pieces of moulded foam.

"This is it," said Lydia. "This is where I work." And then, "Let's go up."

She opened the door of a narrow cupboard that served to conceal a vertical ladder with metal rungs and started seamanly up. PF followed more lubberly, pressing himself against the rungs, where the flow of gravity seemed less strong. The wall into which the ladder was bolted smelled so strongly of stone that he had the impression of climbing up into the earth.

"Shhh," whispered Lydia, "take your boots off. We're over the sanctuary." She was lying on her stomach, looking over the edge of an ornate, wrought-iron grille several feet in diameter. Her cheeks, in the reddish light rising from below, appeared swollen and sore. PF rubbed his tense, exhausted thighs, stepped across the wooden floor with apneic wariness, and settled himself gingerly beside her, surprised by the warmth.

A white, young face looked up at them through intelligent, closed eyelids, unimpressed by the exaggerated wood grain and glowing hardware of the casket in which its body was lying, unperturbed by its own death.

Beside the casket stood a woman scratching the back of her neck with a microphone, talking to a man holding a television camera. Viewed from above, they appeared to be wearing shoulder pads, their feet seemed to fit directly into their knees.

"What are they saying?"

Lydia shrugged. The voices rose, evaporated, with limpid clarity, but the sedimentary words stayed below.

After a while, the man and woman packed their equipment away and left the church. Lydia reached into a pocket of her coat, took out a linen petal and dropped it through the tracery of the grille. It slid across the rising air currents, and drifted into the aisle. She dug out another petal.

"You try," she said. "Try to get it in the coffin."

PF poked the petal through the grille. It tumbled straight down and landed on the quilted padding of the casket's open lid.

"Al*most!*"

A second petal struck the edge of the opening and dropped to the floor.

"*So* close!" squealed Lydia.

PF rolled over onto his back. "Such enormous rafters," he said meditatively. "Imagine the building of this church, the sky-high scaffolding, the giant tie beams heaved up one by one with ropes as thick as your arm. You can almost see the workmen, can't you?"

"Their shirts," said Lydia, "soaked with sweat."

"See that one? See him spit?" PF raked his throat and expectorated richly into the rafters. "Look at him set his sledgehammer down at the very edge of the scaffolding, place his grinning boot beside it, nudge it over the edge. The sledgehammer drops faster even than a warning voice can reach the ground. *Thup!* He looks over the edge. Oops, sorry, horse."

Lydia shivered. She saw PF's sputum stuck to a rafter like a glistening, red pupa.

"So what'll you give me if I get one in?" said PF, rolling back onto his stomach.

She stared at the pupa, trying to remember the word for what was inside it. She could see the June elms, could see PF grab hold of the sledgehammer of another worker whose back was turned, sling it onto his shoulder, deliver a blow, his back dark with sweat.

"Eh? What do I get?"

Chrysalis? No it was not chrysalis. She wanted to disperse, like pollen, to cling to PF without his knowing, to make him sneeze, to make his eyes water.

To disperse. She did not move as PF's hands tugged at the flaps of her coat pockets, plunged inside to retrieve more petals.

"Slim pickings," said PF, pushing the petals into a small pile. "We haven't discussed bonuses. Supposing I get two in. Supposing I get more than five."

He dropped the petals one by one, his hands meticulous and alert, through the grille.

But none fell into the casket.

"Bad luck," he muttered, defeated, seemingly, by the fibres of time. "Any place else I might find some, if I looked?"

"No," said Lydia.

"No?"

"No."

"No?"

"No."

They were silent for a time, after which Detective Inspector PF worked himself to his feet, lumbered over the wooden floor, brushing off his shoulders needlessly, and descended the vertical ladder. Lydia listened to the muted, diminishing echo of his boots against the metal rungs.

The pupa opened wetly.

"Imago," said Lydia out loud. The imago attempted unskilfully to deploy its liquid wings, and nose-dived onto her shoulder.

"Oops," it said, "sorry, horse."

The church doors opened. Steps thudded down the aisle. Detective Inspector PF was loaded down with clear bags of petals. He tore the bags open with his teeth, emptied them onto the sanctuary floor, sprinkled handfuls inside the casket, and placed the last one, delicately, almost primly, on the forehead of the young, white face.

He looked up towards the grille, snapped his heels together, saluted and disappeared.

Lydia sneezed, inexplicably. A draught of sleep made her shudder. She sneezed again and brought her knees to her chest, not without appeasement. Her lip did not tremble, her nose did not crinkle, her expression did not change. Her tear ducts simply opened. The imago sniffed her wet cheeks, and flew woozily off.

A fast learner, she thought, falling asleep.

5

Detective Inspector PF woke up as always at 20 minutes past six, fully-clothed and lying where he had collapsed, on the sofa in the living room of his semi-suburban townhouse. He was refreshed, starving, he allowed himself to drift briefly through the tropical darkness of the January morning before standing with brisk impetuosity and discovering that his hamstrings had turned into wood, his kneecaps into chalk.

I must have walked for five hours yesterday, he thought. Fifteen, 20 miles. How many kilometres is that?

He was pleased with himself. Destiny, not neon-lit destiny, but the simple weather of events, had at last involved him in a system of some intensity. He limped into the stainless steel kitchen of his chilly house which, because he was seldom there, he did not heat above 19 degrees, and performed the breakfast routine he had elaborated and honed to perfection.

He was generous in his praise for the incompetent vagabond. He had not so enjoyed the company of another human being, had not talked so much, in donkey's days. It was as if she had scraped the leftovers out of his stockpot of grief, and thrown the pot in the dishwasher for him.

I had forgotten, he said to himself, that my wife and Julius Caesar died at exactly the same time as Kwaznievski was born. That is to say, in the past. In the past.

He ate, as always, his toast standing up, leaning over the kitchen island so the crumbs would not fall onto his coat.

The past swallows the tragic and the trivial with equal magnanimity.

His taxi honked briefly twice.

It does not prefer the triviality of Caesar's assassination to the tragedy of Kwaznievski's birth.

The odour of innumerable occupants had been cooked into the taxi's upholstery by the diseased air exuded by the black lungs of its heating system.

Although, given the size of her head, it is not easy to imagine

Kwaznievski being born at any time, or her mother surviving the experience.

He was pleased with himself. Renewed.

Bing. Are you there?

Uh-huh.

Why do I sleep, Bing? I hate sleep. I wake up starving. Frozen. I feel like there's a head inside my head, looking behind me.

There's always Saint Sylvestry's, Lydia.

All those soupy eyes. All that yellow drool. Oh shit, let's go.

How did you make out with the Piffer?

We didn't make out. His hawk landed on my shoulder. What time is it?

The faintest.

What are the fuckles doing down there, making all that noise? Shit, Bing. Look! My rose petals, everywhere. Ah, PF. You asshole. You complete and utter. I'm not cleaning that up. Shit. Let's just get out of here, Bing.

Right. You going to answer the phone, Lydia?

Phone? What phone?

The one that's ringing.

What phone is that? The one downstairs? In my workroom? Let's go! It must be PF.

PF doesn't know the number!

How do you know? Go, go! He's a policeman, he's got the telltale eye. He picks up on the details, you don't have to twig him.

Detective Inspector PF sank back into the encompassing warmth of the taxi's rear seat and reflected that it was one of the privileges of police work that you had to deal constantly with people, like Kwaznievski, with a point of view different from your own.

While the taxi's jaded suspension rocked him spongily over the broken streets of Montreal.

Kept you from getting smug.

His cheeks began to glow.

Revealed things to you about yourself.

He uncrossed his knees to give breathing space to his stirring genitals.

Things you wouldn't otherwise see.

He saw Kwaznievski's ripe forehead, so high her hair appeared to sprout vertically from the smooth, white rind of her skull. He saw the bristled caterpillars of her eyebrows sniff each other with delicate, devoted curiosity.

He opened his mouth slightly so the taxi driver would not hear the insistence in his breathing, felt the kissing caterpillars crawl over his lips and drop onto his bristling tongue. He was deeply aroused, he changed position, looked out his window, his throat knotted, his good humour stifled by the bland melancholy of sex. He decided to speak, to sooth his gregariousness with a little human intercourse of a debonair sort.

"It's curious," he said, "how on mornings like this one, in the winter, the light seems to spread up from the ground instead of down from the sky."

"Je vous demande pardon," said the driver in his African, elegant, booming French.

"C'est curieux . . ." said PF. *"Laisse tomber."* And then, *"La vie amoureuse, ça va?"*

The driver forced a laugh. *"Vous?"*

"Non plus."

"Je ne vous aurais pas vu à la télé, vous?"

"Ça se peut."

"J'y suis. Inspecteur PF. C'est ça? Oui, oui, oui. 'Ceeteesins Arrrrehst.' J'aime beaucoup. Beaucoup. Très bon."

Detective Inspector PF considered that a prime disprivilege of police work was that taxi drivers drove you with a fastidiously law-abiding, a dreamlike slowness. He wanted to career, careen, to juke and jink, to dance down the broken field of the immediate and pressing. Not dawdle over the crumbling surface of the hot, upholstered past.

What I want, he thought, unable to rekindle his high spirits, is to fish that stockpot out of the dishwasher and throw it in the garbage.

"Hello! Wait! Don't hang up. Just a moment." The voice, over the telephone, sounded as though it were issuing from an undersea cave. Lydia heard a series of rustlings, crinklings, pops. "There," said the voice, having surfaced apparently and depressurized, "that's better. Lydia Kwannyzevski?"

"Almost."

"I'm sorry?"

"Yes, this is Lydia Kwaznievski."

"I am glad. They said you might be hard to get a hold of. That we could maybe try this number. We just let it ring, it's been ringing now for . . . I don't know how long. We just appreciate your gesture so very, very much."

Gesture? thought Lydia, irritated at how quickly her vanity was warmed by the idea, however mistaken, that something she had done merited appreciation. "I'm not sure I . . ."

"*I'm* sorry, Lydia. This is Peter deAngelis of the deAngelis Foundation. I'm Jeremy's father."

Detective Inspector PF stood in front of the newly installed, bomb-proof, metal front door of the 11th precinct police station, a stodgy, symmetrical building, constructed, according to the lintel above the door, in 1871, maintained steadily in conscientious repair but never renovated, so that no two doors were the same, bone-dry in winter, stifling in July, radiant in the spring. He touched the walls affectionately.

The temperate sky was thick and grey. His ears rattled with a wet concerto of melting snow as he considered to himself the wording of a short letter formally requesting a leave of absence.

. . . in light of the tragic — not tragic, too ubba-ubba — untimely, of the untimely — no, tragic — in light of the tragic and untimely death of my wi . . . my partner, no, not partner, marriage isn't a square dance, my life's companion, a period of reflection and reassessment of my — no, to ponder, to ponder — of reassessment to ponder my life's goals, to discontinue all investigative, investiga-tory? investigatatious?

He ran his finger down the 19th-century mortar between the perfectly adjusted stone blocks that were as blue as barn boards and that seemed to yield a dry, black sap.

To devote myself exclusively to, through television.

To move to Toronto. To Rio de January.

Broadening of the public's awareness, through televisual, through the electronic and other media, awareness of and appreciation *for*, police methodologies.

Although Bolivia was where he wanted to go. Especially La Paz. Lake Titicaca.

He had, as he placed his hand on the door handle, the bracing impression that he was about to step into an undiscovered country, as though the station, while remaining entirely familiar, had become entirely foreign.

He entered. And immediately he felt the voice leap on him like a dog, breathing its foul breath on him.

"Where the *fuck* have you been! Have you ever heard of the tele-phone? Come into my office, Inspector. I'd like to talk to you."

Lydia Kwaznievski pressed the receiver hard against her ear, trying to hear through the contained feverishness of the voice, as she might have tried to peer through a storm in order to catch sight of the bottom of a teacup.

There was considerable commotion in the background, the voice was interrupted frequently in its attempt to honour several avenues of thought at the same time, it was inspired by the outpouring of gen-erosity, daunted by the logistics, the accounting requirements alone, of staging a telethon, appreciative, deeply, of so much encouragement freely offered, ashamed, truly ashamed, to have overlooked the flowers of which Jeremy was so, so very, he loved flowers, Jeremy. The voice marvelled at the capacity of Jeremy to love and be loved, a capacity which overreached his life, overreached his death even, and which Lydia too must, must not ultimately we all, possess, given her gesture: the sanctuary, bursting with a myriad rose petals, breathtaking.

"If my forgetting the flowers induced, by some mysterious process, your gesture, than I did well to forget. Thank you," said the voice, tear-stained, on the edge equally of nobility and of hysteria. "And please, if you care to, please join us for Jeremy's funeral. We can, if you require, arrange transport for you to Saint Dunstan's Church."

Detective Inspector PF slouched in his chair, squirmed under the dog's groomed, muscular gaze.

"I have better things to do, Inspector," said the dog, "than pull your pants up for you. Apparently you were to tape an interview yesterday. With the 'head-box girl.' What was I supposed to tell them? I didn't know where you were. I don't know anything about a girl with a head where her box is supposed to be."

"Oh, she — anyway it won't be aired before June, it's not as if — she was abducted by a married couple, twisted, you must have heard of them, they clamped a wooden box onto her head before . . ."

"I'm not interested, Inspector."

"Christ, the number of times *I've* showed up and everybody else has forgotten. I can do it today."

"You can do it today." The dog drew the back of its paw across its worm-like lips. "This brings us to what I'd really like to talk about. I think, Inspector, the time has come for you to decide between television and the police. You've gone through a difficult time. We all understand. Why not take a break? To reassess your life's goals. A leave of absence."

"I'm not listening to this," said Detective Inspector PF, standing. "I have an interview to do today."

"Sit!" commanded the dog. PF did not. "You will not be doing the interview today, Inspector."

"And why not!"

"Because today you are doing the deAngelis Foundation Children of Light telethon."

Bolivia. Especially La Paz. Where his daughter's apartment overlooked the Plaza San Francisco.

Detective Inspector PF sat, straight-backed in his chair. "Christ," he sighed, "I forgot that too."

"The funeral starts, what, in a couple, three hours. Think you can find something to do till then? Here, you can run through Laliberté's daily reports. You want to drive yourself?"

"Where am I going?"

"Saint Dunstan's Church. What, is that funny?"

"No, no." The fibres of time, thought Inspector PF, his good humour restored.

6

"*Mesdames, messieurs, bonsoir.* Good evening, ladies and gentlemen."

The voice treaded light effortlessly in the luminous pool that filled the television studio.

"*Mon nom est Peter deAngelis.* I'm Jeremy's father."

A second voice made itself heard, a woman's, somewhat strained, less at ease swimming in light over its head:

"I had the impression, I remember, and I always will remember, of skinning dizzily over the tips of waves, my bones made of wood, cracking under the weight of the wind. That was the impression I had. In fact, Jeremy had broken my coccyx. Eleven pounds and an ounce he weighed. Motherhood is such a ghastly, gushy thing. Every part of you wants to come to the surface and touch. You want to stick your nose in his ears, your lips in his eyes, and your formula, your own special, right into his muscle. You want to ride your cheeks over his silvery moons and dab his big babyhood with your fingers.

You want to touch him. Not, as you believe, because he's yours. But because he's not."

The voice of deAngelis broke through the light:

"Tout ce que vous voulez, en tant que mère, nouvelle mère, c'est toucher votre enfant. Non pas, comme vous le croyez, parce qu'il est à vous. Mais parce que, justement, il n'est pas à vous. Voilà ce qu'a dit la mère de Jérémy, Alissa McBeath, que voici."

"Jeremy," said McBeath, "was one of a new generation of children."

"L'éclaireur," said deAngelis, *"d'une nouvelle génération d'enfants."*

"Jeremy was a child of light."

"Un enfant de lumière."

"He died of a heavy heart."

"Jérémy nous a quittés. Il avait le coeur gros."

A small orchestra launched an aural balloon, inflating to the point of distortion a sentimental melody that the atonal ears of Lydia Kwaznievski recognized as music only because it emerged from musical instruments. She sat at her post behind her telephone, feeling increasingly thickheaded, queasy, due in part to the ghostly invisibility of the speakers under the pouring lights, in part to their zigzagging, bilingual litany, above all to their extravagant sincerity. She had spent the day with the desperately grieving couple and their elaborate entourage, had driven with them in what was as much a parade as a funeral through the huddled and waving, the condolent streets of Montreal, from Saint Dunstan's to the Bourgie crematorium, from the crematorium to the top of Mount Royal, had witnessed the dispersing of the ashes with a thrill of revulsion mixed with envy. And she had eaten unaccustomed amounts of banquet food, damp, meatless, for which her surprised stomach, tough as it was, seemed to lack the proper enzymes.

The balloon deflated suddenly, was reabsorbed by the musical instruments.

"Ladies and gentlemen." The voice of Alissa McBeath stroked through the light now with greater confidence. "An ever increasing number of members of the scientific community, of educators, of health professionals, of just plain people, now openly embrace the notion that we have witnessed and are continuing to witness the advent of a new sort of child."

"We have witnessed," said deAngelis, sticking to English, "the coming of the children of light."

"These," said McBeath, "are highly intuitive children, creative and very strong-willed. They oscillate between a stunning assurance that disguises their vulnerability."

"And a self-critical harshness," said deAngelis, "that can make them unkind."

"They have very little requirement for company."

"But an urgent need for friendship."

Lydia Kwaznievski closed her eyes.

"They participate extemporaneously in the communion of all living things."

She wanted to flee. And would certainly have done so, would simply have stood and sidled past the other operators in her row, had not these other operators been, in many cases, already talking on their phones, noting down pledges. Lydia's telephone squatted in front of her, silent, smug.

"They do not submit their spirituality, which they accept without hesitation or discomfort, to the approval of any authority."

Lydia would not admit to being snubbed by fortuity.

"Be it time-honoured. Be it newly-invested."

"Their aura is blue."

"Their chakra the sixth."

The concerted antiphony of the voices, so different in quality, so similar in tenor, made her head reel.

"They have a dazzling sense of purpose."

"They do not accept that the future will be what it will be but what it will be made to be."

She could not help wondering if the gratitude showered upon her with relentless fervour by deAngelis expressed, as it seemed to, such deep admiration. Or indeed if the equally fervid, equally relentless gratitude of Alissa McBeath expressed such concentrated dislike.

"They are not cogs in a wheel."

And still her telephone did not flash, although even the French operators on the other side of the studio were receiving calls.

"They are the wheel."

"Children of light well know that time is of the essence."

"Not because life is so very short."

Was she to sit there all evening behind an infecund, an acarpous telephone?

"But because the future is so very, very long."

And if so, how was she to get the smirk off its face? Was she to throw it into the orchestra?

"Ladies and gentlemen, here in the studio and watching at home, you have children who are, like Jeremy, children of light."

Was she to throw it at Alissa McBeath?

"And like Jeremy, they do not necessarily make life comfortable for those whose job it is to keep the educational machine thumping along."

"Those for whom a disciplined child is nothing more than a submissive one. No. Teachers . . ."

The clear cyst on Lydia's telephone was flooded suddenly with pert, peach-coloured blood.

". . . do not necessarily find children of light imbued with creative energy."

Lydia observed the illuminated button, resisted the temptation to snatch at the receiver.

"No, they are as likely to find them hyperactive."

Her relieved cheeks too were flooded with blood, equally pert, equally peach-coloured.

"Not insatiably curious . . ."

"Hello," said Lydia.

". . . but disruptive. And teachers have the wherewithal to dim the energy of these children."

"Hello?!" said the caller.

"To darken their incandescence."

"Yes. Go ahead please."

"Who am I talking to?"

"To Lydia Kwaznievski."

"Not with angry words, not with straps and canes."

"Lydia! You're the one who makes the flowers! Where are you?"

"With medical jargon. With prescription drugs."

"Oh, there you are! I see you. Say something so I can see your lips move."

"Jeremy McBeath . . ."

"Blepharitis."

"I saw your lips move!"

". . . our son, died of a heavy heart."

"Would you like to give me your pledge now please?"

"His heart, swollen from a decade of using prescribed psychotropic drugs meant to make him more manageable, meant to thwart his natural ebullience . . ."

"I do admire you, Lydia, really, and what you did and all but I was, you know, *really* hoping . . ."

". . . his heart physically enlarged by constant amphetamine stimulation, a full third heavier than it should have been, failed twice in three days."

". . . to give my pledge to Inspector PF."

"Oh, well I'd rather speak to Inspector PF than to you too . . ."

"Jeremy was fourteen."

". . . he's answering in French. You'll have to dial the French number. He's got a caller right now."

"It is time, ladies and gentleman."

"Tell me when he hangs up. Okay? So I can dial real quick-like."

"You can't see him on your TV?"

"It is time for a new school, a school of light. Join us, and together we will build it."

"No, I can't. Maybe on the French channel. Hang on. No, it's the same picture only with sub-titles. Oop! Spoke too soon. There he is.

Oh no, he's hanging up!"

She hung up.

"We will build the structure. The children will build the school."

The orchestra launched another, a bigger balloon.

7

"Lydiak-waz-nievskilyd. Huh? Iakwa-zniev," muttered Inspector PF into his telephone in order to give the impression that he was carrying on a conversation. He had been taking pledges dutifully now for over three hours and felt he deserved a rest. He could hear, despite the fact that she herself was sitting on the other side of the studio, the finch's voice of Lydia Kwaznievski as clearly, and as unintelligibly, as if the finch were perched on his shoulder.

The telethon, modest in scope, respectful in tone, seemed to be going well. Certainly, the telephone response had been steady since the very start.

Prayer, thought Inspector PF.

For on more than one occasion during the course of the evening, Inspector PF had been delighted, moved even, by Alissa McBeath. "Children of light," she had said, "have the gift of ubiquity." Stirring.

And prayer, she was given to prayer. Not clench-faced, hand-wringing prayer, with an eye to the payoff. Just prayer.

"Let us," she had summoned, "pray." Back straight, shoulders square. "We do not accept the blindness of faith, insisting on light, then we crouch behind blinds that filter the light." Lovely. "We dismiss the prophet's ear-splitting vehemence, preferring the poet, b-da b-da b-daaah, b-poet." The idea being that we like poetry because it doesn't make so much noise that we can't talk over it.

That was how the prayer had started. And it had finished with, "The only obstacle is the task undone." But in-between. Occupied as he had been with taking pledges, and constantly distracted by the fringillid chirping on the other side of the studio, Inspector PF had only caught pieces of the rest of McBeath's prayer, and the more he attempted to reconstruct what he had missed, the more his exasperation threatened to undermine the pleasure he took in what he had retained.

He was grateful, therefore, for the distraction afforded by the orchestra leader who, his jet pilot earphones grafted onto his temples like compound eyes, was engaged in hissing, red-faced negotiation with his musicians. The orchestra had apparently already performed its entire prepared repertoire. The leader, therefore, was bent on distributing an armful of supplementary scores, which his indignant musicians, smelling bonuses, were equally bent on refusing.

DeAngelis took it upon himself to intervene. Discreet hand gesturing, head nodding. An agreement mediated, new costs incurred.

"Iakwa. Iakwa-znievskilyd."

Inspector PF was fascinated by deAngelis, by the withered ear that caused his round eyeglasses not only to cut diagonally across his noseless, nutcracker face, but also to tilt upward slightly, giving him an air of soft-eyed, cherubic ineptitude.

Captivated he was by the verbal athleticism deAngelis displayed in tumbling through sentences without the slightest trip-up or arrhythmic hesitation, by the linguistic composure with which he switched from French to English, so that the inspector could barely rid himself of the absurd feeling that the man was capable of expressing himself in any language, and always with the same, barely accented, refinement.

He approached centre stage, deAngelis did, walking with his habitual, implacable grogginess, as though he were traversing Greenland. What, thought PF, massaging his lips in order not to smile, will he come up with next? For deAngelis appeared capable of any sort of public disclosure, given that he had, earlier in the evening, depicted in arrestingly candid terms the personal hell in which he had been living before being saved by the McBeaths, Alissa and Jeremy, a personal hell characterized primarily by an addiction to heroin so overweening it had reduced him to injecting himself through the veins in his penis, which penis, much to the aghast admiration of PF, he had appeared to have been prepared to reveal given the slightest encouragement, as though it were nothing more than an ugly but disappearing scar.

No, thought the inspector to himself, inept he is not.

"Ladies and gentlemen," said deAngelis, "if you will bear with me . . ."

He observed the gracefulness with which deAngelis paused to let the studio audience gather itself.

"I'd like . . ."

A gracefulness all the more impressive in that there was, in fact, no studio audience at all except for the uninspired director shelling sunflower seeds and attempting to engage in conversation with the odd person who wandered in from other productions in other studios.

". . . while the musicians take a well-deserved break," deAngelis spun on one heel to acknowledge the orchestra, spun back, "I'd like to read you . . ." He held aloft some sheets of paper. "I used to keep a journal. It was in the form of an on-going letter to Jeremy. When you have children, your own childhood rekindles itself. You don't simply remember it, you relive it in many ways, you sort a lot of stuff out. I guess I wanted Jeremy to know, but I was too shy to tell him. The child is father to the man, and so on.

"After his first heart attack, which was not terribly severe, Jeremy was hospitalized, for observation, no one, except Jeremy, anticipated a second attack, and that night — he must not have slept a great deal — that night he wrote *me* a letter.

"I'd like to read you Jeremy's letter. If I may. It's perhaps a *bit* long, but if you'll bear with me, I think . . ."

Inspector PF had long since stopped attempting to give the impression he was talking into the receiver that he nevertheless still held to his ear. He was enthralled, he could see the white, young face.

"Dear Peter,"

The face turned, shedding its linen petals, towards Inspector PF.

"It is not without reticence that I write this letter, which is about life. Writing is an activity which adults participate in when they wish to appear highly adult. Nevertheless adults, when they participate in talking, usually wish to appear even more highly adult."

Inspector PF, unsure of himself, smiled at the face.

"You may remember our cat, Catso."

The inspector's smile increased.

"A number of years ago I put Catso in the microwave oven as he had been outside in the snow and was so cold he shook. After this experience, Catso walked in concentric circles, falling over continuously. Therefore I put him in the freezer for a short time."

Inspector PF was grinning broadly by now.

"Catso was exceedingly affectionate towards me after that, as I was not the person who had put him into the microwave and the freezer, but the person who had taken him out. To express myself otherwise, I saved him. And Catso hoped I would also save him from the fact that he was dying."

The white face looked directly at PF. It twisted itself into a roguish grimace, revealing, despite the blow-ups of Jeremy suspended from the studio flies that showed his sturdy, 14-year-old teeth, a mouth full of chromed and coiled barbed wire. The air in PF's lungs turned to frost.

"One reason I do not care for writing is that you can always delete what you have written. I say this as I would now like to delete what I have written about causing the death of Catso. The temptation is so strong, I am going to write it over again so I will not. Dear Peter, you may remember our cat, Catso."

PF was panting, his telephone was ringing.

"A number of years ago I put Catso in the microwave oven as he had been outside in the snow and was so cold he shook."

Ringing. His telephone.

"While I am relieved to have overcome the temptation, I do feel more adult now. Do you not agree that it is highly adult to do the very things you want to delete over again?"

It was four in the morning, the police wanted to talk to him. The police? said Police Lieutenant PF, his brain still stiff with the undissolved crystals of sleep, but I *am* a policeman. Yes. A young girl has been found on Graham Boulevard. On Graham? But that's nowhere near where I work, that's where I live. Yes, exactly.

"I have observed two things. One. Adults overrate life. Adults, when babies are born, cry and hug each other. Life is a miracle, life is good, thank you God, dig in. Two. Adults underrate life."

Yes exactly, thought Inspector PF, reliving, despite himself, the bleak, summer dawn, the consternation, the shame and fury, when he had had to present himself at the counter of the Mount Royal police station.

"Adults, when they get old, become highly querulous. They do not hug each other for fear of injury and only cry when no one is looking. They think life is cumbersome and ordinary and that as adults, they should be able to go on living without it."

The policewoman, imperious, tense, her shirt blatantly torn so that her brassiere looked out like an uncurious, white rodent, had ushered him into the pea-green room where sat his daughter.

"Handcuffs!" hissed Lieutenant PF, "She's only thirteen for fuck's sake!" his outrage shattered immediately however by the surge of horror that accompanied the sight of his daughter's bloodied mouth.

"She took my scissors," said the policewoman, "and tried to cut the braces off her teeth." Her arms were tightly crossed over her midriff now to close her torn shirt. There was blood on the shirt. "I'm all alone here."

"In conclusion, I feel one might compare life to a language. There is not more language in aardvark than there is in zygote just because there is a whole dictionary between them. Every word lives by its definition in its language. In the same vein, every person lives by the definition that their life gives them, although they do not always do so and are therefore not always well off. It is a good idea to use a word to understand the definition of your life."

"I wa'n't doing any'ing," garbled his daughter, "I hate the 'olice."

Her head jerked contrapuntally as the broken wires stabbed the inside of her lips, fresh blood oozed from her mouth like the centre of genteel candies.

"You just shut up!"

"I am very grateful to my father for giving me the sound of my life-word, which is 'di-PAR-cher.' But my father could not help me with the definition of my word. He took off. That was his definition. Perhaps I used to think about him often, but I do so no longer, although I am afraid he will learn of my situation and think he must come and visit me with photographs of us together when I was an infant."

Inspector PF clutched the telephone to his chest, there was a single tear stuck to the upper ridge of his cheek like an acrylic mole, the unfaltering voice of deAngelis steadied him with its bracing consolation. For daughters do grow up, they do, become perfectly competent adults with straight teeth, daughters and fathers too, grow up, though they may live in different hemispheres. And memory, while it does of course record the ear-splitting vehemence, memory preserves . . .

"I am very grateful to you, Peter, for being my spiritual father and for giving me a definition for my life-word, which is 'departure.' For many years, I was unhappy because I knew my word but I also knew I was not living by its definition. My friends and I frequently discussed suicide as a possible definition, but in my opinion, suicide was not really a departure but more like causing an accident with screaming and cars crashing."

For the policewoman had chosen to ignore her torn shirt. She had wedged the daughter's head between her midriff and breasts, had parted the damaged lips with her inelegant fingers, pointed towards a drawer with her jaw, and Police Lieutenant PF had managed, using the needle-nose pliers he had found in the drawer, to break off the projecting barbs, had wiped his daughter's teeth and gums, and covered her mouth with gauze and a broad bandage, all of which action his daughter endured with uncharacteristic passivity, although, to be fair, she had fallen fast asleep.

"I know you wish you had not given me my drugs. In the same vein, I wish I had not caused the death of Catso. But remember, Peter, Catso did not want to die. I am glad I will not get old and feel like I missed my chance to live my definition. Thank you again. The best part of my soul is happy. Jeremy."

No, thought Inspector PF, memory preserves the silence of detail.

"PS I give all my possessions to my friend Yasmina Truhl whose life-word is 'archive,' except for Catso's collar which is in my top drawer and which I would like to take with me."

Memory preserves the beefiness of a daughter's breath, the chips in the polish of a policewoman's nails, indicating a silvery-white coat applied over a blue, an odour, bitter, humid, deliciously faint, emanating from the exposed den of an uncurious, white rodent.

DeAngelis spun on one heel to cue the orchestra which atomized the solemn, tear-stained atmosphere by horning its way into a vigorous arrangement of "La Bamba."

Above all, thought PF, too moved to continue answering the telephone, humming to himself as he sidled past the other operators in his row, ". . . *se necesita una poca de gracia . . .*" touched that "La Bamba" was, if not a Bolivian, at least a South American song, above all memory preserves the silence itself between a policeman and a policewoman, bound together into a parental community by the unpolished filaments of embarrassment and duty.

He found, backstage, sitting at his jury-rigged, dusty computer, the accounting firm representative monitoring totals as the pledges were entered electronically by the telephone operators.

"*Fait chaud là-bas?*" said the representative.

"*Mets-en,*" said Inspector PF, politely admiring the representative's unimpressive equipment. "*Les pledges rentrent bien?*"

"*Ah oui, ah oui.*"

"*C'est-tu vrai qu'on va donner un prix au téléphoniste qui ramasse le plus de pledges?*"

"*Oui, c'est ça. Mille dollars.*"

"*Mille. Il est généreux, deAngelis. C'est qui qui mène?*" Inspector PF, even before he had finished asking, regretted this question, knowing not only that it could not possibly be himself, seeing as he had not been taking pledges now for some time, but also that it might very, that it was almost certainly . . .

"Van der Goo, qu'il s'appelle," said the representative.

"Pas Kwaznievski," said PF, relieved, not entirely out of small-mindedness, but because the pressure exerted on his sensibilities by the incompetent vagabond was insistent enough as it was.

"Non," said the representative, *"pas Kwaniaski."* He ran his index over the screen, brought it to a halt. *"Elle n'est pas loin derrière, par exemple."*

8

A penthouse. Mediocre furnishings, chewy carpet, all but obscured by the overgrown stand of buzzing, human guests.

Lydia Kwaznievski, the particles of innumerable telephone conversations, bits of names, fragments of addresses, still swirling in her head, sought refuge in the chilly strait, open now but formerly unnavigable due to the presence of two white-coated servers, between the tableclothed serving table and the Thermopane outer wall.

My tail between two cities, she thought.

For on the table rose a crowded downtown of empty bottles, wine, Pepsi, gin, surrounded by arrondissements of spent platters smeared with salsa and what was more likely icing than toothpaste, by suburbs of bent paper plates and overturned glasses, surrounded in turn by a wrinkled, snowbound countryside littered with crumbs and twisted napkins.

And on the other side of the glass outer wall, uncurtained, cold, streaked with condensation, the lights of Westmount rotated with sidereal slowness about the constellation of the cross on Mount Royal, beyond which ranged the invisible galaxies of Outremont, Jean-Talon, Ahuntsic.

Far below, a solitary pedestrian inched off over the snow, orange under the streetlights. A night-stalker, no doubt, who scrubbed his face with his victims' intestines. Given up for the night, going home to bed.

Always the chance, thought Lydia, that it's the ghost of Bing. Wave to Tina for me, Bing, if it's.

It was not Lydia in any case, although, from this same penthouse window, she had no doubt been observed walking through the small hours, her feet sweating in her boots, her hands clenched inside her gloves.

"Congratulations."

Lydia turned to face a man she recognized as having worked the phones earlier during the telethon, indestructible, moist, strapped into a lightweight life jacket of fat, his succulent, unblinking eyelids weighing against his insomniac eyes. She read the name tag pinned to his lapel which he pushed towards her with his thumb.

"Evert van der . . . Goo? Is that how it's pronounced?"

"It's pronounced 'how.'"

"It's pronounced how?"

"Yes."

"How?"

"Exactly." The man brightened at Lydia's confusion. "It's a Dutch name," he explained, his eyes glinting like daggers made of shiny paper. "The 'g' is pronounced 'h.' Evert van der Gouu. I finished second."

"Ah. And how many times have you regaled the company tonight with your introductory routine?"

"Lost count. Most people just keep on calling me goo. So what are you going to do with the thousand dollars?"

"Can't spend it. The police'd be all over me."

"The police? How so?"

Lydia did not answer. She wanted to say, "Topic: A woman perfectly well adapted to a life of solitary inconsequence lingers at a penetratingly vapid party in the hope that a police inspector, to whom she has no desire to speak, will speak to her. Explain." Instead she said, "Are you aware that monkeys, unlike humans, peel bananas from the bottom up?"

"Do they."

"Yes. Would you be interested in talking to the simian authority who enlightened me? Where did she get to?" Lydia surveyed the crowd squintingly.

"You," said van der Gouu, also surveying, "might be interested in the individual who informed me that it was after hearing 'La Bamba' that Bob Dylan was inspired to write 'Like a Rolling Stone.' The same person in fact, in another context, the contexts change so quickly, mentioned that it is possible, if you know what you're doing, to insert a skewer between an individual's eye and eye socket, causing no damage to the eye itself, and from there to pierce the brain, causing the individual's death. Inspector PF is the person's name."

Lydia was too weary to blush. "You really should have finished first," she said, pressing her eyelids with the pads of her fingers. "And it's really very late."

"That it is. I don't have far to go mind you. I live in this building. I admire your necklace. It's very like one I've seen around the neck of Alissa MacBeath."

"Yes. The dress is hers too. Too short of course. She added the flounce, despite yesterday's pandemonium, to hide my tuberous calves."

Van der Gouu nodded his approval. The midnight, bateau-neck dress with its grackle-blue flounce added substance and even distinction to Lydia's tall and weathered shape, reducing her high-headedness. "Very gifted, Alissa. A true polar bear."

Lydia's crinkled, wary forehead invited an explanation.

"A strong-swimming, majestic animal," explained van der Gouu, "most often spotted these days on dirty dry land, growling inanities."

"Oh. Such as?"

"Children of light. Ubiquitous. Clairsentient."

Lydia stood back from van der Gouu appraisingly, intrigued, puzzled.

"It's Peter I like," van der Gouu confided quietly, the insomnia brightening in his eyes. "And you?"

"I'm an impostor too. I took part in the telethon entirely by accident. Too busy on the phone to think about what was going on. I try not to think. That's the device on my coat of arms. 'I don't think. Therefore I am.'"

Van der Gouu emitted a mild grunt, as though he had just remembered a name long after the need to remember had passed. His life jacket straps slackened, his eyes, briefly, closed. "And what is pictured on your coat of arms?"

"Nothing. A parka with fourteen sleeves."

Van der Gouu took his keys out of his pants pocket then, removed one, handed it to Lydia.

"It's number 702. The sofa makes an excellent surface to sleep on. There's bedding in the coffee table. Leave the key on the doorstep if you don't use it. Or drop it off sometime. It's a spare."

"Thank you, I'm very tempted," said Lydia, not very tempted.

Van der Gouu, in the way of the accomplished party-goer, having displayed an altogether exceptional interest in Lydia and even achieved an unstated communion with her, moved off, their allotted time together having expired, to display an altogether exceptional interest in someone else.

And Lydia was left with the bitter-tasting idea that she was mistaken, that she had simply fallen in with a society of impostors. Of impostors, that is, who belonged. She had no business being there. And still she did not leave, she gathered the crumbs on the serving table into a small pile with the back of a knife, straightened the table-cloth, wiped the condensation off the window with a twisted napkin.

No, she said to herself gloatingly, breathing rapidly through her mouth, I'm not going to talk. Not to Bing. Not here. McBeath would love to burn me at the stake for that, wouldn't she? After stripping her dress off me. And her bra. And her snickers.

She nudged a wine bottle maliciously with her elbow. The bottle swayed, toppled over meekly, soundlessly, into an unpopulated area of the table, did not break, did not initiate a succession of falling bottles.

She seethed, close to tears, hesitated between ripping the table-cloth off the table with her two bare hands, and escaping to van der Gouu's sofa in the hope that a cloudburst of sleep would paralyze the relentless traffic of names, addresses and growling inanities. She chose the tablecloth.

No. Wait. A leaflet of a smile germinated in the parched dirt of her lips. She straightened, strode decidedly around the perimeter of the penthouse to the coat check, requested her greatcoat and boots, took out the key.

She would go down to van der Gouu's, yes, but not to sleep, to rearrange his dishes, his lamps, to hide his collection of Edwardian erotic photographs among his bathroom towels, to tie his bed sheets together and throw them out the window, so that he would search everywhere for what she had not even stolen.

"Excuse me," she said quaintly, touching the key to her lip, "I presume that 702 is on the seventh floor?"

The coat-check woman took the key, examined it, her breath rasping in her nose. The seams of her slender uniform, alert white piping on black semi-gloss, creaked with every movement of her trollish, squat body.

"Is shaped like a almond tree, the key," she said. She had a high-ranging, stony accent, Uzbek perhaps, Georgian. She handed the key back and retrieved Lydia's coat.

Lydia stepped into the corridor then, the twin doors closing behind her, threw the key high into the air, clapped her hands five times, caught the key. Free. Free. Take the elevator? Take the stairs? Threw the key up again, clapped five, spun around, caught the key, and there he was.

"Moneybags," he said, one eyebrow hooked suavely into a tilde worthy of a Spanish don. "Wait up."

9

He had his drink in his hand, tie unknotted, grey, epauletted shirt unbuttoned, he approached with a highball lilt to his step.

Look at him, thought Lydia, the democrat, airing out his chest. Like a travel agent on vacation.

PF placed his glass on the grille of a standing ashtray. "I've talked," he said, placing himself unusually close to Lydia, as though his sense of perspective had been disrupted, "to I don't know how many women tonight. Hundreds. I thought you'd never leave." He ran his finger lightly over the surface of Alissa McBeath's pearls, murmured something indecipherable, his breath suddenly drowsy, pungent with whiskey and overuse, tepid against Lydia's chin. "Too many women. So much work. Why is it so easy with you?"

It? thought Lydia. She observed unflinchingly the sedimentary striations in PF's hair, his eyelashes, sparse rays of a preschool sun wedged into the top corner of a blue fringe of sky, did not dismiss entirely the possibility of placing her hands on the back of his neck and lodging his wide head on her narrow shoulder, such, she thought, is the attraction of the adult allowing its childlike vulnerability to speak, "So much manoeuvring," he said, "so much mirth," not that it is the child within that is vulnerable, "so much work. I've had enough," but the adult crust that is, that dries out, crumbles, "kiss me."

She started as though the handle of her door had suddenly rattled.

"Kiss me," plaintive, insistent, his eyelids creaking open, raw light bursting into her room.

He wrapped his arms under her shoulder blades then, planted his lips onto hers, in the manner of a farm boy trapping a pudgy chick. And indeed, like the chick, Lydia struggled briefly before remaining perfectly still and as though listening for the real intruder. She spun around haughtily after PF released her, closed her coat tightly, said, "I thought you'd had enough manoeuvring and mirth," the ensuing silence leading her nevertheless to turn again and find him looking at her so fixedly and with such a disconcerting interplay of curiosity and challenge, that she said, "What?"

"Nothing," he said with his farm-boy leer. "I was just wondering."

"Wondering what!"

"I got my answer."

"Oh you did." Lydia blushed with humiliation. "Listen to the little man," she said, "fortified with Scotch and party admiration, a good deal more sure of his answer than he is of his question. Were you wondering if I was capable of a little warmth? Or were you wondering if you were? Do you think that because I've chosen, chosen I say, a life of solitary inconsequence, that there are no mouths in it to kiss or be kissed. Ha!"

Steadied by her own voice, Lydia sensed that she had done well. That silence was called for, hauteur. But silence was not her forte.

"There are. And that don't require fortification."

She regretted the indiscipline of this remark, attempted to return to higher terrain.

"Solitary inconsequence has its privileges, Inspector. I can kiss whomever I like, as the spirit moves me. Kiss, or . . ."

"Or?" blinked Inspector PF salaciously.

"Kiss or not kiss."

"Ah."

Angrily, Lydia clamped her hand onto Inspector PF's upper arm, herded him back through the twin doors into the penthouse, strode him around the perimeter to the serving table, took, without releasing his arm, a large handful of paper coasters from a box stowed under the table, steered him towards the centre of the room.

"Ladies and gentlemen," she called out, her finch's voice bobbing effortlessly through the fog of conversation, repelled only by a cloud bank of choristers singing French folk songs in harmony, "if you will bear with me . . ."

Inspector PF was perplexed by the gracefulness with which she paused to let the assembled guests gather themselves.

"I'd like . . ."

Alissa McBeath, recognizing her husband wearing her own dress and pearls, emitted an anticyclonic guffaw.

". . . while the musicians take a well-deserved break," Lydia spun on one heel to face the chorister cloud bank which, suddenly aware of being surrounded by open sky, broke sheepishly apart. She spun back, McBeath glaring at her with rivalrous delectation, "I would like to offer you a demonstration of the astonishing investigative ability of a modern police officer. Ladies and gentlemen, I give you Inspector PF."

The oiled applause massaged PF's face until it puffed and pinked. Lydia distributed the paper coasters quickly, returned to PF's side, scowled at his exposed chest.

"Inspector PF," she said, doing up the buttons of the epauletted shirt without interrupting her patter or even looking away from the guests, "knows where you live. He does. He knows. Where you live. Now then. I would like the people to whom I have just given a paper coaster to write down their names and addresses," she patted the shirt collar flat, "and then return the coaster to me. Pardon? Postal code? Ah . . . no. The inspector's blood-alcohol level is a little high perhaps for postal codes. Just name and street, street number if you wish, if you don't mind it being made public. Oh, thank you, that was quick. Thank you . . ."

Inspector PF, unsmiling, terrified, repulsed by the high curve of Kwaznievski's egocentric forehead, clutched nevertheless for assurance at the warm memory of her fingers doing up the buttons of his shirt.

"Alright," said Lydia, "do I have all the coasters? Yes? Now then, we're all agreed that the addresses have just been written on the coasters and that the inspector cannot have seen. Right? Right." She held up a coaster, brandished it like a gold medal that belonged to someone else, replaced it on the pile of coasters she held in her hand, read what was written. "The first name, Inspector, is Evert van der . . . Goo? Is that how it's pronounced?"

"It's pronounced 'how,'" said Inspector PF. "He lives right here in this building."

"Yes, he does! He does indeed, absolutely correct. The inspector has his first coaster." She handed him van der Gouu's coaster, held up the next one ceremoniously, replaced it on the pile in her hand, cleared her throat. "The second name . . . is Bo DiMaggio."

Inspector PF was staring at Lydia, his mouth stretched into a reluctant, pursed grin, as though he were preparing to play the bugle with an egg inserted into each cheek. His lower lids were brimming with tears. "6760," he said after a time, very softly, "Saint-Vallier."

"Eh?!" shouted DiMaggio, delighted, beaming at the faces around him as if the credit in some way belonged to him. "That's not poss'ble, eh? Not poss'ble!"

"Mr. DiMaggio's coaster, Inspector," said Lydia, handing it to him breezily. "The third name."

Inspector PF got all the addresses right. He did hesitate once or twice, but the general feeling was that he was just doing so for effect.

The enunciation of the final address was followed at first by an admirative, fair silence, and then by a foul weather of appreciation, the cloud bank reformed in concert with squalls of bravos, ovations of rain. Given the din, Lydia was obliged to motion to PF to come closer so she could say something to him. He, beaming, bent towards her.

"Kiss me," she hissed into his ear.

Cornered, he aimed in the direction of her hard cheek, a mincing osculation which Lydia caught by turning her face and planting her lips onto his, in the manner of a farm girl kissing a pudgy police officer.

The partying heavens opened.

10

Bing! Are you there? Are you? I'm out at last. Ahh, it's a dolphinium of a night! Cold, crackling. Could there, I ask you, be anything easier to be than alone? Wrong. Solitude, no matter how inconsequential, is backbreaking work. Walls to immortarize, lugs to pleak. No matter how much brew I boil, how much blue gas I emit, and I emit, Bing, I emit, from every pore, my atmosphere is constantly being breached. Look at me, my surface is pockmarked with human contact, I stagger, bla-bla drunk, barely able to distinguish a semipalmated fuckle from a three-breasted fuckledrop. Flooded I am with more orders for linen roses than I could hope to fill had I so much as a snorkelful's intention of doing so, stormed with requests to do summer camp tricks at parties, like telling people their names and addresses. The cold, the cold. At last. The cold is like love, Bing, and like love is a little deadening. Let's walk. The garbage is out here. The knack, I tell you. Garbage, you know, isn't garbage, it's the underparts of people. Their secrets, secretions, the evidence, the proof of their passing. Lift the plastic lid, Bing, with respect. Look, the bloodied Kleenex, there, under the gawnoswut, the Kleenex, was it used for a child's nose? A lover's rectum? A mother's blade? Touch it, touch their blood. Who, I ask you, who is authorized to probe such intimacy without exposing a thread of their own except for you, for me, and for God? Hmph, nothing to eat here. You can close the lid.

"Lydia?" Evert van der Gouu pushed his head into the condominium, entered, "Lydia?" calling delicately, gliding from room to darkened room, revealing, as people do when they explore their own living quarters, his latent capacity for stealth. "No," he said, turning on the lights, returning to the front door, "she's not here, Inspector."

"Where the f —" muttered PF, storming past van der Gouu. "What time is it? Six? Six." He pushed a brutal knee into the loveseat, swept aside the curtains, planted his face against the Thermopane, cupped his hands to the sides of his eyes. "Where the fuck has she got to, the fucking screwball."

Among our citizenry, Bing, the lower of the middle class, the lormicklastics, are the most imaginative, living, as they do, in a self-imposed, a rigorous delusion of abundance. Example: faced with the need to feed three, the lormicklastics prepare food for eight, gorge themselves into fatasyland, chuck the rest. Their garbage, consequently, is itself abundant, full of carrot peelings thicker than many carrots, but full of carrots too, highly nutritious, low in lipids. The lormicklastics delight in their garbage, it trumpets their capacity to not have to sweat the details. But the garbage, like the capacity, disappears, gets collected, details and all. The delusion must be reimagined, rebuilt, minute by minute, meal by meal, the lormicklastics must live.

"I thought I recognized her," said van der Gouu. "You see her sometimes, she talks. To herself."

"Not to herself. To Bing."

"Ah. She thinks she's Dorothy Lamour."

"She thinks she's Bob Hope, for all I know. She looks like him."

"Inspector. That's unfair. Not with those amphibian eyelids. I'd say she looks more like Shakespeare."

This light-hearted evocation of Kwaznievski's semi-circular, retractable eyelids not only overwhelmed Inspector PF with the realization that he had entirely overlooked a principle feature of her physiognomy, but also caused his shoulders to twitch, once, violently, releasing a shudder that fled down his spine and escaped through the tunnel of his reverberating sex.

"Got anything, Evert," he said, "to drink?"

However. You, Bing, and I, find ourselves in Westmount, sombre pale of the upprmicklastics. The garbage of the upprmicklastics is not so much abundant as it is voluminous, very, full of last week's rejected acquisitions as well as mountains of the packaging material that came with this week's acquisitions. It *contains no food. The upprmicklastics put the scant remains of their bite-sized, decorative meals into plastic containers for tomorrow's lunch. Furthermore, because their garbage reminds them that their own corporeal packaging material will end up one day getting tossed, the upprmicklastics put their refuse out on the sly, after dark, and contract its collection to firms willing to work at night. If you want to ransack it, you have to be quick and have good eyes.*

Remember, Lydia?

I beg your pardon.

Remember?

I remember shit, Bing.

Ah, Lydia.

Oh, my first all-nighter, you mean? In the car, the Pinto?

No, no.

It was like hwow! *I'm cold like to die. Couched in the pea-green Pinto I was. No gas in it. Gas is shit, Bing, hope shittier. Sheep-shanked in the back seat, starving, cold to my kidneys, working my toes in my shoes all night long, rubbing my fingers together like for hours and hours and hours. I couldn't even cry I was squeezing my bowels so hard so I wouldn't do a do-do. The fuckledrops wrecked the Pinto. Good thing. I'd grunt and puff pushing it into the sun, but ice grew out of the vinyl all the same, and the sun just hung there like a limp light bulb, sniggering.*

The first injection of dawn over the Saint Lawrence spread its bruise-coloured narcotic into the January sky of Montreal, soothing Evert van der Gouu, despite the fact that the curtains of his condominium were drawn, that he was sitting in his windowless kitchen, that his eyes were closed, and that the wide head of Inspector PF was resting forlornly on his custodial shoulder.

"Why not?" burbled the inspector, who had achieved a warm plateau of drunkenness. "You're homosexual."

"I most certainly am. But you're not. I'd rather have sex with Shakespeare frankly, even if he does look like Kwaznievski. You stink, Inspector, of heteroclivity."

"Well excuse me," said the inspector, removing his head, genuinely, if drunkenly, wounded.

"An abstract, odourless stink," said van der Gouu putting the head back, smoothing PF's hair. "The desire-sapping redolence of self-doubt. No, Inspector, I can't imagine offering you my genitalia. But I can offer you my confession. Confessions are far better than sex, when narcissism is what you need."

Remember, Lydia?

Remember! What's got into you? Oh! My first rat! Right, sure, August it was, rats are perennials, Bing, die back in winter, bloom best in filth. I'd found this dead trailer, pushed over the riverbank. Pierrefonds was it? Find of a life. Big list to starboard, no faucets, toilet gone, wires yanked out of the walls. Slept like a nail till the ratoon fell in through the roof. Too much moon maybe. The ratoon made my bladder melt, brain bring up. Chase ensued, hairy, badmouthing. Finally planted the BBQ *fork in the ratoon's neck, one eye plooped out, thorax thrashed and twanged even after the head'd disengudged. Exhausted I was, collapsed beside the corpsied ratoon, slept. By the time I woke up, rigor mortis had set in. I couldn't so much as move a muscle, my neck was killing me, the ratoon was like three feet long. Days like that, days. Nailed to the floor I was, and the dead ratoon kept growing the whole time till it was big as me. I was sure my eye was going to ploop out, sure of it, but the cats came, lucky for me, and carted the ratoon away. Lucky.*

Mmn. Remember, Lydia?

"Sleep tight, Inspector," muttered Evert van der Gouu, still stroking his pet PF affectionately behind the ears. "I hope you've more endurance as a lover than as a confessor."

"I'm not asleep," protested PF. "I've been listening to every word."

"Oh you have, have you? What did I just say then?"

"You said I've, that is you've, I've been sentenced to living happily ever after, to pushing on with my part after everyone has lost interest, trampled the popcorn into the carpet, gone home."

"Very good. And what was my crime?"

"You survived."

"What did I survive, Inspector?"

"Christ, Evert, do I have to go back to the very beginning?"

Van der Gouu's voice seemed to soften, physically, as warming cheese softens. "To the very beginning, yes."

PF sighed, sat up, scratched the back of his head vigorously, dishevelling in an instant what van der Gouu had so persistently smoothed. "Right," he said. "His name was Bernard Doxtator. The pussy was spirited."

"The pussy? Could that really have been the term I used? But go on."

"He was particularly skilful at exerting pressure on the perineal fascia."

"Good, Inspector, good." Van der Gouu was gazing ceilingward.

"Resulting in the dry ejaculation."

"Mmn." Dreamily. "The climax that yearns. Breeder love."

"Bernard Doxtator grew up in France, spoke French-French French, put on a phony British accent, sounded like Prince Charles touring Mozambique. He got on people's nerves on purpose, wrote offensive plays, performed them on the street, in bars, berated the audience — when there was an audience — with being too stupid to understand. He was, that is, happy as a pigginshit."

"Good, Inspector. Go on."

"One of his plays caught on. *Des cous et des couilles*."

"Possibly *Des couilles et des cous*."

"The actors walked on their hands, upside down, dressed up like flowers, the idea being that flowers themselves are upside down, their mouths are rooted in the ground. Their faces are their sex."

"Very good."

"Then you said that Doxtator got unhappy after *Des cous et des couilles*, possibly *Des couilles et des cous*. He couldn't go back to being cheerfully obnoxious, just genuinely obnoxious, bitter, cruel. His success seemed punier and punier, a betrayal of himself. He began to hate himself, to hate me, we spent all day doing the perineal fascia until we were ready to murder ourselves. Which is what we decided to do."

"You astonish me, Inspector. You remember every word. Did you really remember all those names and addresses?"

"Eh? No, no. It was a trick. The first paper coaster she handed me . . ."

"Never mind, Inspector, never mind. Go on, go on." Van der Gouu placed his head briefly on PF's shoulder in coquettish imitation of PF himself, returned to staring up at the ceiling, waiting for it to disperse, so he could observe the stars.

"I think I fell in love with the woman when she handed me that first paper coaster."

"Of course. It had my name on it."

"No, not your name. DiMaggio's. Your coaster was on the bottom. She knew I knew where you lived."

"Ahhh. How clever."

"God, I wanted to diddle her right then and there."

"Inspector, spare me your heteroclitorous decorum," scolded van der Gouu murmurishly. "Whatever was stopping you? But go on, go on."

"We . . ."

Inspector PF, inexplicably, remained perched on this initial word for many moments, not, apparently, because his memory had snagged on the hurrah's nest of van der Gouu's story, but simply because he had stopped functioning, fallen asleep with his eyes open. Nor did van der Gouu express the slightest impatience. He simply waited, and in time PF shuddered, just as inexplicably, and returned to wakefulness.

"We decided to commit suicide together. We were living in this very apartment at the time, we went up to the penthouse with our six-shooters, sat across from each other, counted one, two, *kpooooOooo*. And there I was, bleeding from the forehead, you can still find the scar if you know it's there, and Doxtator dying in front of me, and it struck me that what makes a face beautiful is its resistance to injury, to death, and therefore that a face must be wounded to reveal itself fully, there must be distortion, blood, and Doxtator didn't look beautiful, he looked like an imbecile, hideous, chirpy, I wondered how I could ever have loved him. My own blood dibbled off the end of my nose onto my lips, my own blue, congratulatory blood, and I've been living happily ever after ever since, playing my part after everyone has trampled the popcorn into the carpet, always in this same apartment, this loving reminder of my clean, well-vacuumed cowardice."

Remember, Lydia?
    Whatever is the matter with you, Bing? I told you, I remember shit.
    Ah, Lydia.
    Shit! I said I remember shit.

Detective Inspector PF could see the penthouse where Lydia Kwaznievski had handed him a paper coaster not more than two hours earlier. The elevator was cordoned off now, the doors locked, a team of white-coated technicians were searching for the bullet with the small clump of van der Gouu's forehead attached to it. A green garbage bag containing Doxtator slumped on the floor.

Beside PF slept Evert van der Gouu, his breathing liquid, rhythmical, punctuated by snorings and clucks, reminiscent on the whole of the dishwasher containing PF's stockpot of grief. He had fallen asleep in a position of abandonment, his face still directed ceilingward, hands dangling, pelvis forward, knees splayed. As though offering his genitalia. And what, thought PF, were he to unzip the sleeping Dutchman, what sort of wrinkled, cocktail genitalia might he find? No, were he to unzip van der Gouu, he would surely find a miniature version of van der Gouu himself, sleeping, his face directed ceilingward, which version, were he to unzip it in turn, would contain a still more miniature version and so on, and so on. And on and on.

Remember, Lydia?
  Stop it! Stop it, Bing.
  Lydia.
  Ooh! *The key! Right. I forgot about the key.*

Inspector PF crept through Evert van der Gouu's condominium, revealing, as people do when they explore the living quarters of new acquaintances, a candid, a sensual inquisitiveness. He paused to breathe in the indolent bouquet of each room, ran his fingers over the oil paintings, turned the porcelain tap in the bathroom, tested the coldness of the water, drank.

He might almost have convinced himself that the condominium was his own and that, living in it, he was able to think about something other than Lydia Kwaznievski. He explored van der Gouu's dresser, examined his Alfred Bung lotion, his hydrocortisone and Lorazepam, the magazines scattered on the massive, waist-high bed, discovered that stuffed aubergines contain 256 calories per serving, that a female anaconda may copulate with 14 males for 46 straight days, may well eat one of them, that an Albert County resident has been known to have caused a power failure by wiring the dead battery of his car directly to a transformer. He reflected, as he rescattered the magazines he had instinctively organized into a pile, that if Montreal was small enough for him to have Kwaznievski underfoot for three straight days through no effort of his own, it was certainly large enough for her to disappear in completely now that he had come to require her presence. He pushed a knee hard into the loveseat, opened the curtains slightly, was startled to find that outside the cold was blaring with broad daylight, that buildings on all sides were exhaling heavily their strenuous breath, that particulate snow was swirling along the shaded Thermopane before trailing off into the sun like surface krill.

Inspector PF closed the curtains, strode back towards the kitchen, grabbed his coat, looked in on van der Gouu who was still in position to observe the stars should they appear, and whose neck would certainly be killing him when he woke up.

"I'm off, Evert," said the inspector softly. "I don't need Kwaznievski to try the Kwaznievski solution. To hell with her. I'm going walking. I might even try talking to Bing."

"Good enough, Dorothy," said Evert van der Gouu.

Inspector PF did not realize immediately that van der Gouu, asleep as he was, could not possibly have offered this response. He recognized therefore that he must still be slightly drunk and that he was approaching his personal record for continuous hours without sleep.

Sleep, he thought, who needs it? He backed out of van der Gouu's condominium with far more circumspection than he had entered it, closed the door with infinite precaution, took out his brace of keys, chose one, inserted it, twisted delicately, his face contorted into a wincing grimace.

He relaxed, satisfied that his escape was flawless, turned, and there she was.

"No!" he said. "It can't be you. Not you. What are you doing here?" A fever of incredulity seized him. "What the fuck are you . . . is there no fucking way I can get rid of you?"

A small object navigated wobbly towards PF through the storm of his invective, sputtered, stalled, struck him inoffensively on the shoulder, and dropped onto the cushion floor with the mousiest of pings.

Inspector PF dropped to one knee, observed the object deeply, looked up.

"It's a key," he said.

"Bravo, Inspector," said Lydia Kwaznievski.

"Van der Gouu's key. He gave one to you too. He told me. You've brought it back. You threw it at me."

Lydia raised her arms in admirative surrender, overwhelmed by the astuteness of the inspector's analysis.

PF sat down squarely on the floor then, his back wedged against the door jamb. He smoothed the corrugated side-panel of his hair, remembered the saponiferous feel of van der Gouu's grooming fingers. He was not certain whether aubergine was the same as eggplant or whether it was zucchini that was. After a time he said, "Have you got Bing there with you?"

"Bing?"

"I had a secret friend once myself. Her name was Melinda." The intensity of his blush indicated that its cause was less what he had just revealed, than what he continued to withhold. "Can we go for a walk then? It's a pretty decent day out." He remembered that a female anaconda may fast for seven months before giving birth to as many as a hundred snakelets.

"It's a dolphin of a day," said Lydia Kwaznievski.

11

"It's amazing," puffed PF, "how much ground you can cover on foot. The Atwater Market already. Hungry?"

The market's clock tower stood black and depthless, backlit by the ice-bound southeastern sky.

"It was opened in 1933, the architect's name was Lebrun if I'm not mistaken." He held the door open for Lydia. "It's considered a fine example of the art deco style."

Lydia entered. "Too much perfect food here, Inspector, too many bright eyes, too many fuckles. Keep walking."

PF loosened his coat, stamped the snow from his boots, engaged the crowd openly, changing gait, yielding passage, signalling his intentions with broad movements of his arms. Lydia thudded forward like a nocturnal ice-breaker.

"The Fromagerie has hundreds of varieties of cheese. The widest selection in Montreal. The proprietor is married to a Senegalese. His name's Michou . . . what's his last name? Michou . . ."

"What," said Lydia, thudding, "a friend we have in cheeses."

"What was that?" said PF catching up, turning an apple over in his hand, searching out the apple's fleshiest cheek.

"Did you pay for that?" Lydia snatched the apple out from under the inspector's unhinged jaw, carried it righteously back to the fruit vendor. The vendor placed a square of tissue paper on his electronic scale, placed the apple on the paper, pressed the appropriate keys, wrapped the apple in the paper, brought it over to his cash.

"Cinquante-trois sous," he said. *"Autre chose?"*

"Fifty-three cents for one apple!"

"Tenez," said Inspector PF to the vendor, paying, and to Lydia, "Happy now?" crunching, tilting his head back slightly so the apple would not dribble down his chin.

Lydia pulled out her own apple then. PF glared, tugged at the flap of her coat pocket, plunged in his hand, pulled out more apples, shook his head with disgust.

"So, Lydia Kwaznievski," he said once they were outside, "you're a, an engineer is it?"

"An inventor."

"Oh yes, of course, an inventor, an inventress." His tone of voice suggested that he might have been tempted to add, "when you're not choreographing ballet." "And what, specifically, is it that you have invented?"

"Specifically I have invented hot paint."

"Ah." He blinked sceptically. "And would you mind talking a little about your invention for the benefit of the people watching at home?"

"Glad to, Inspector. What does ilmenite yield? Or rutile, for that matter."

"I don't, uh, I don't have the faintest idea."

"Titanium dioxide."

"Okay."

"And what is it that is composed principally of xylenes and boils higher than ligroin?"

"Is composed of boils higher than the groin?"

"Has a boiling point higher than that of ligroin. VM and P is the correct answer, sir."

"Veeyemenpee. Okay."

"To which, because the fuckledrops must have water-borne paint, are added, as a coupling solvent, esters of which dihydroxy alcohol?"

"Ah . . ."

"Think sugar."

"Sugar?"

"Glycol, Inspector."

"Okay."

"Now then, the vehicle."

"As in delivery vehicle?"

"As in vehicle vehicle. Polyamide resin-mobile, 1957. Metallic soap as a drier, and there you have it."

"I have it."

"Yes, you do. Paint."

"Oh. Paint."

"Yes."

"Okay. But not hot paint."

"No. No, for hot paint you need a basement. You need to be reeling with debt and swimming in mortgage. You need to have Eddy Constantine handing you cheques with one hand and pulling your snickers down with the other. You need to have a July miscarriage all over your bathroom. You need to pay, Inspector. You need to pay for the bronze powder to put in your paint, the zinc and the aluminum dust. You need to fart around with extenders and binders until you've got something that sticks to your walls. Something that will conduct electricity."

"Paint," said PF softly, "that conducts electricity." Lydia's surge of vituperation prevented her from hearing the note of apprehension in his voice, apprehension of the sort inspired by what is banal, easily explained, and yet impalpable, mysterious. By mirages for example, eclipses. By falling cities.

"You need to find additives to prevent colour flooding, anti-de-emulsifiers, anti-coagulants, you need to pee into your paint, weep into it, you need to rediscover, as if by magic, albumen. And after four years you need to paint it over an electrode taped onto the basement wall you've already painted over untold hundreds of times, and wired to a ten-bill-and-forty-seven-cent thermostat. And what happens?"

"The paint . . . no, the paint doesn't heat up."

"The paint heats up. Yes. Gradually, gradually, *petit à petit*, the paint heats up. You need to place your palm on the painted wall and feel its warmth, entirely benevolent. You need to know that the paint will not shrink this time, the pigment not turn, that you have developed a product with outstanding characteristics of adherence and durability, a product that will revolutionize the construction industry and the unknown universe. Millions, Inspector. You need to know you'll be worth millions to fully appreciate the nacreous futility of what you have been doing. You need to know that the tears running down the inside of your face are not caused by the sweet stink of success irritating your eyes, no, and that you are not even not-crying because you will at last, after years, Inspector, years upon years of fuckledropping, be able to show the fuckles what you've known all along, namely that your idea was good. No, you need to know that your tears are for a time only, a time before the folds of your brain were dripping with paint, a time when you could think about something other than your own idea. A time when you could think."

Inspector PF did not hear the last part of this tirade which was shouted defiantly at the pallid, salt-coated cars tilting through the Atwater tunnel. He was stranded, he did not know why, at the tunnel's mouth.

"Hot paint!" Lydia yelled at him, continuing to walk backwards down the passerelle. "Opportunity of a lifetime, Inspector. Want in?

Call Eddy Constantine. 642-3825."

But PF did not hear this either. He could see Lydia, pallid and coated with salt, standing on the handrail, lifting off, hovering above the tilting cars, retreating down the tunnel.

He had the impression that where he was was simply the sum total of all the places he was not.

He turned to face the market, frontlit by the winter sun which ate into the sandy brick, infiltrated every crack and imperfection so that the tower appeared to be on the verge of disintegrating into a formless powder.

He began to walk, struggling with his misappreciation of Lydia Kwaznievski. He could not imagine the set of circumstances that might have led her to an idea as singular, as sparkling, as that of hot paint. He could not bear to look at her fleshless cheeks, her creeping eyebrows and puffed skull. His amused disdain had soured, it embarrassed him now, it had turned into frank admiration, into disgust. If he was condemned to live with his thin ideas, stifling and literal, she surely should be sentenced to success, to celebration, refused access to the cell of her perversity. Moneybags. Moneybags indeed. Did chance ever tire of pouring kindnesses into her pockets?

"Inspector," she said, still flushed with mordancy, taking him from behind by the arm, "coming? You wouldn't be a hypogeodromophobe by any chance?"

He wanted to rip his arm from her grip.

"Afraid of tunnels, Inspector?"

"I was just thinking," he said rapidly, heatedly, "that criminals, of which I've known hundreds, when they're not fucking around being criminals, are completely indistinguishable from people who *never* fuck around being criminals."

Lydia's eyebrows stopped creeping, lifted their heads. "So?"

"Never mind." It was not, in any case, what he had wanted to say. He was approaching his personal record for hours without sleep. He had wanted to say, "Get away from me, please, just get away."

Nevertheless, he allowed Lydia to take his attaché case from his hand, to face him about and set him on his former course towards the Atwater tunnel.

"It's not far," she said.

"What's not far?"

"My place."

"Your place. I can't wait to see this."

12

Remember, Lydia?

Stop it, Bing. I remember shit.

Lydia. Remember?

Lydia Kwaznievski sat on her heels, her arms resting on the rim of the double-ended, roll-top bathtub which had so impressed Detective Inspector PF that he had squatted down to examine its rooty, metal feet, had taken out his pocket tape measure, stretched it from the tub's stem to its stern, five foot ten? wow, I'm only five nine, had proceeded then to take the physical dimensions of the bathroom which constituted Lydia Kwaznievski's "place," a room with a bath that is to say, originally serving the entire floor of the apartment building, with a hand basin as well as the tub, a speckled mirror behind which must have stretched a bleak and rainy unwonderland, no water, no heat, the apartments having been long since equipped with individual, private facilities, the bathroom abandoned.

Remember?

Stop it! Just stop it.

The bathroom, eight feet wide by 13 and a half long. "Measuring a room is like shaking its hand," the inspector had said. "Getting to

know it on its own terms. An investigative thing I guess. Investiga-
tory?" The heat register, lifeless, painted so often the decorative leaves
and berries of its cast were barely visible, 32 and a quarter inches
high. The window, four cemented glass blocks, a mere 16 inches
square. The disreputable hand basin, 17 inches by 22.

Ah Lydia.

She sat on her heels beside the bathtub, into which had been fitted a
cropped mattress, on top of which lay, still wearing his coat, Detective
Inspector PF, sound asleep. She was observing the inspector's face, taking
the inventory of its freckles and moles, its unshaven hairs. It struck her
that the eyelashes must be some sort of ingenious fastening system for
locking the lids shut. Nor could she help imagining speleological mites
trekking over the windfalls obstructing his cavernous nostrils.

Remember, Lydia? The Phosphallous?

The phosphallous. Lydia covered her mouth with her fingertips,
rocked gently on her heels.

   She remembered the inspector's cackle when he had first entered
the bathroom with its enormous tub. "You get the neighbours to
come and feed the silverfish do you, when you're out of town?" He
was exhausted, manic. "Have to stay awake to set my personal record
for hours without sleep. The Pope's visit in what? '82? Thirty straight
hours on duty." He had measured everything in sight including the
circumference of her head, the metal tape scorching her temples,
singeing her hair. "What time is it? Another half-hour. What can we
do now? Open my attaché case. I've got Laliberté's daily reports.
They're good for a laugh."

———

Lydia! The phosphallous! Remember?

The phosphallous. Yes, rocking on her heels.

Finally!

Spring it was, warm, stunningly so, the last remaining patches of dirty snow resembling ash. Lydia saw again the garbage collector who had surprised her at her evening meal, the sort of young man for whom garbage collecting was a relentless, a military discipline, who lifted as much and as effortlessly as possible, ran from house to house, whose musculature therefore was that of a gymnast, but whose eyes, exploring her, were liquid and uncertain, who caressed his shoulder constantly under the sleeve of his T-shirt, "Giff me garbage," he said, without either insistence or apology, his accent foreign but not French, Lydia moving away from the olive-drab plastic container, he fishing out from his hip pocket a white business card, giving it to her, "any days, six clock," spun filaments of spittle clinging to his lips, his teeth irregular, unhealthy, his breath as fetid as a child's breath. He bent for the container, backing deliberately into Lydia as he did so, straightened, his sinewy hair mere inches from her mouth.

I remember shit, Bing! I told you.

Lalibby's daily reports.

"The captain's pretty much an anglophone," PF had said, "apart from being an asshole, so Laliberté insists on writing his reports in

English, to practise. Listen to this:

'7:29 a.m. A woman attempting to climb an ormous tree with only a coat on and a bra was not there when I arrived.'

"By the way, he doesn't mean an enormous tree wearing a coat and a bra. He means an elm tree. Or this:

'10:59 a.m. Footprints discovered walking through a backyard rue Augustin-Cantin were holes made by failing snow I determined.'

"What else? Okay, this:

'5:42 p.m. A man who said he was fine just a little tired sitting on the sidewalk corner rue Ste-Cunégonde was not there when I arrived.'"

"That was you, Inspector! Sitting on the sidewalk on Ste-Cunégonde."

"The hell it was!" And then, after a time, grinning with consternation, "Do you think?"

No, no, no, Lydia. The phosphallous!

Maltex. *Gestion intégrée de matières résiduelles.* Integrated Waste Management. Boulevard Thimens. Saint-Laurent. As printed on the white business card. A fenced lagoon of asphalt over which punted the rust-eaten trucks, dyspeptic and deep blue, unloading into the clanging sheds, wheeling away empty down the boulevard in front of Lydia as she huddled at her observation post, behind the grey metal casing of an electrical installation.

If any sort of schedule or system governed the movements of the trucks, she had not established what it was. She never knew, therefore, which truck might contain her liquid, uncertain gymnast, could never predict when the sight of him clinging to the truck's rear handrail with one hand, caressing his shoulder with the other, might cause her heart to leap out of its hiding place behind the grey casing and tear off down the street after him, barking idiotically, nipping at his feet.

Any days. Six clock.

But by six o'clock, the trucks were all parked in a row, the cars had all driven off, the shoebox office building was deserted by all appearances, a black, precisely cut hole in the flamboyant, evening sky. By six o'clock, Lydia was sneaking away, irritated that the March air, so full of invigoration and beginnings, could not displace the childish, fetid breath that clogged her nose.

I don't want to remember shit, Bing. Not now.

Lydia's chin was resting on her arms which were resting on the bathtub rim. She smelled the dry, turnipy odour of PF as he slept.

"What time is it?" he had said, giggling, feverish. "What else have I got in my case? Oh yeah, a fax from the Parthenais morgue. Death advice, unidentified corpse. Some white-haired bastard bought it with a barbecue skewer in the eye. You can kill a guy that way, you know. You can slip a skewer between his eye and his eye socket, just about here, about four-thirty, and slide it right in until it punctures the brain. No blood if you leave the skewer in. Sorry! Sorry, sorry. Don't listen to me, I'm just running off at the mouth. I do that when I'm tired. Maybe I should stretch out on your mattress. Alright if I do? Christ, I'm so sleepy I could puke. Come on, there's room for both of us."

"That's okay. I'll let you puke by yourself. I'm fine on the floor."

"Remember, Lydia?"

Lydia started, her heart raced. "Remember what, Inspector?"

". . . I forgot now. Sorry."

"If you do remember, forget again. Go to sleep now."

13

"You've got twenty-seven patents, wow," said Detective Inspector PF, impressed. "How did you ever come up with such an idea, such a, an idea, as hot paint?"

"Mmn?" said Lydia. They were standing on the mattress in the bathtub, she was using PF's pocket tape measure to chart the principal geographic features of his bare back, the brown dots of the towns, the excrescent urban agglomerations, she was noting her measurements down on the back of the unidentified corpse's death advice. "Oh, it's an idea . . ." it was a broad back, the north-south equatorial strip smooth, free of vertebral protuberances ". . . that's been around for some time . . ." the northern zones characterized by a light cover of low-density, long-growing hair, the uplands to the southeast and southwest virtually unpopulated, bald, smoothly rising ". . . can't honestly claim it as my own exactly, there are other groups . . ." she was disengaging the tongue of the inspector's belt buckle ". . . around the world. Ask Eddy," pulling down the inspector's shorts in the best Eddy style, "he knows about all that." She was long about surveying the complex array of bullas and blebs that characterized the barren landscape of the inspector's ass, about raising his left foot and placing it on the outer rim of the bathtub, about measuring the foot, the calf and ham. She was particularly deliberate in mapping the back of the testicles, working with a meticulous fascination. "Remember, Bing?" she said very softly, but as distinctly as if she were addressing the inspector himself, remembering the silence of the shoebox office building at six o'clock as, having at last summoned the courage, she explored its perimeter, found an open door, entered, again with meticulous fascination, as though into a bleak and rainy unwonderland where rabbits with poisonous, black spittle might live, saw a light at the bottom of the stairs, heard the sound of running water, descended, enthralled by her own fear. "Bing, the phosphallous," she said quietly, distinctly, and still she probed delicately the inspector's testicles, descended the treaded, metal stairs, stopping halfway down.

The light came from an open doorway. A sink, water flowing from both taps. Standing before the sink a man in T-shirt and briefs, illuminated only by a flashlight placed on the adjacent sink. From her perspective on the stairs, Lydia could not see the man's head, but it was him, it was, the gymnast, without any doubt, performing a languid masturbation, holding the cake of soap in his right hand, always his right, running the cake under the taps, soaping himself everywhere, frothy dribbles clinging to the sodden T-shirt and briefs, not devoting more attention to his sex than to any other part of himself, so that his briefs seemed simply to house a normal part of his anatomy, a mid-body tusk, which, backlit by the dim flash-light, appeared as a shadowy phosphorescence inside his underwear. The phosphallous, in Bing's flippant vocabulary.

She ran her palm along the lower rim of the inspector's testicles, but she was crouched on the staircase, having been given the white business card, invited therefore, excluded, the incessant sound of run-ning water making her want to pee, nauseating her, the gymnast soaping himself, his tusk, with endless forbearance, his head and face always invisible.

"Lydia!" gasped the inspector, his right leg buckling under his weight. He collapsed onto his elbows and knees, his exhausted thigh twitched feverishly.

Until at last the gymnast let the cake of soap slip from his fin-gers, remained motionless, perched on his toes, his hand poised in the air. Motionless, utterly motionless, poised. Lydia closed her eyes, covered her head with her arms, heard him grunt shortly and crash against the sink.

Inspector PF, massaging his thigh, toppled over onto his side.

And when she looked again, the liquid, uncertain gymnast was on his knees, his head visible at last, tilted back, his chin resting on the edge of the sink, his mouth going bup bup, fishlike, his left hand attempting weakly to loosen the belt that had been tightened into a noose around his neck, his face so intensely flushed as to appear on the verge of bursting open.

The inspector rolled his thickened torso onto its back.

Lydia was touched by the redness of the inspector's ears in the icy bathroom, by the paleness of his exposed tusk, which, to her, seemed more vegetable and fibrous than carnal, less patrician than the phosphallous. So that no sooner had she engaged the tusk, than her vagina clasped it fervently, almost fraternally, startling her, "Oh," she said, "did that. . . ?" but her vagina clasped the tusk again, again, an inner valve appeared to be not functioning correctly, blue gas was flooding out of her every pore, submerging her, she was as though being crushed by the density of her own atmosphere.

Inspector PF, aghast, whimpering, struggled to get their bodies inverted, he on top, she underneath, succeeded, began working his pelvis desperately, realized that there was no point, that Lydia had already achieved a rubbery lassitude, heaved himself out of the tub, panting, wretched.

Gaunt she was, raw–boned. She looked, despite her stillness, like a pile of white, squirming eels in the bottom of a workboat.

PF turned his back to her, attempted to steady his breathing. He opened the door wide enough to put his head out, found the hallway deserted, stormed out of the bathroom, closed the door heavily.

Immediately, he felt more calm. And yet the warmth of the hallway, while it soothed his desire, nevertheless encouraged the sanguinity of his erection. He hunched over himself protectively, blew into his chilly palms. The lower part of the walls was covered with black marble, chipped in many places, cracked. The inspector straightened to observe his reflection, squashed though it was. He was not unimpressed. He recognized that he had been the source of considerable, considerable, gratification, he could not, in fact, remember having been the source of a more intense gratification. Another personal record, perhaps. He was flattered, he found himself taxiing down the hallway with majestic nonchalance, his bowsprit cutting the air superbly.

It struck him that he had no idea what time it was, what day it was even. He had fallen asleep, after breaking his other personal record, sometime after noon. But for how long had he slept? Eight hours? Fourteen? Logically, it was night, an assumption supported by the dense tranquility of the hallway. And yet, it might well have been any time, any time.

Detective Inspector PF stopped, placed his palms on his buttocks, filled his lungs. He felt a marvellous reprieve from the erosion of his life caused by the steady dripping of minutes and seconds, a disengagement from all the familiar decors into which he entered and exited with prescribed regularity.

He felt an unaccustomed vivacity, an unabashed nakedness.

A genuineness.

A door opened.

His heart leapt, he crushed himself against the wall, covering, oddly perhaps, his face with his hands.

The door closed.

PF glanced down the hallway and saw that a dark clump had been deposited outside a door. A rectangular object had been placed beside the clump. An attaché case, by all appearances.

He sighed, dropped his chin to his chest, his erection yawning, drowsy at last. He returned to Lydia's door and regarded the clump of his clothing.

The kiss-off, he thought, not without a certain regretful pride. But do I have to get dressed right away?

His feet were cold, that was true.

He put his socks on. The elasticized, black acrylic gripped his ankles with such warmth, with such routine amiability, that he felt exposed, as though he were not entirely alone, the hallway being a thoroughfare, momentarily empty perhaps, but a thoroughfare nonetheless, a public place. He felt not so much indecent as improper, his body like a wound, not a serious one, but one that should be bandaged, that people did not necessarily want to have to look at. He dressed himself quickly, eager to be on his way now, happy to be rid of the vaunting display that had seemed to him so vital only moments before.

The clump, however, did not contain his undershorts. Inspector

PF did not consider the possibility of knocking on Lydia's door to request the missing item. He arranged himself as well as he could, grabbed his attaché case, and set off, disconcerted to find that, unrestrained by underwear as he was, and the pressure exerted by his overcoat being what it was, the rhythm of walking shook, gently, his erection awake again.

14

Lydia was looking at herself in the mirror. The glass was cloudy, its mercury backing chipped and spotted. Behind the mercury fell a steady drizzle of rain. She was examining her eye, pulling down the lower lid, exposing the twiggy veins of her eyeball.

"What time is it did you say, Inspector?"

"Four-thirty."

"Four-thirty on the inside of the eye?"

"On the far side. The ear-side that is."

She pulled her lower lid further down with her left hand, touched her globular eye with the tip of her right index finger. "Here?"

"I can't see, your fingers are in the way." The inspector bobbed up and down, trying to find a line of sight. "Okay. That looks good."

"Hand me the skewer."

"It's not sterile you know," he said, handing her the skewer. Flowerets of bluish oxidation sprouted along the skewer's spine. "We should really sterilize it first, with a match."

"Whatever for? It's not blood poisoning I'm going to die from." Lydia pulled her lower lid down still further, inserted the skewer close against her eyeball.

"You're sure you don't want me to do that for you?" said the inspector, still bobbing.

"No, no, I'm fine. Oh fuck!"

"What?"

"I dropped it right in!"

"What, the skewer?"

"Yes, the skewer. What do you think!"

"How could you drop it right in? Weren't you holding on to it?"

"Get it out! Get it out of me!"

"I told you we should have sterilized it."

"Oh fuck, it's in my zooterus! I can see it. It's right there, look! Get it out! Get it out!"

"Where?"

"In my zooterus! Look! Right there!"

"Get your fingers out of the fucking way, I can't see dick-all!"

Detective Inspector PF sat, relieved, meek, in front of the desk in the office of his friend, John. It was twenty past eight, the sporting goods store was not yet open, although John, hard-birding early-worker that he was, had been only too happy to open the door for his friend.

The inspector had walked for some time after leaving Lydia's bathroom. He had then gotten onto an early morning bus. But neither the bleak crunch of his footsteps and the discipline of the cold, nor the stifling heat, the jolt and shudder of the bus, had succeeded in sedating his taunting, painful arousal. So that when he had suddenly spotted his friend's store, he had gotten quickly off the bus, had hammered frenetically on the glass front door.

The Bermuda grass carpet was richly fertilized, freshly mown. Behind the desk hung a photo mosaic of every conceivable athletic activity, glossy, lurid, the human body frozen in all manner of enthusiastic contortion, large, white, slanted letters cheering, *"La vie, c'est du sport!"*

"Thanks," said Inspector PF. He could smell the rubberiness emanating from an open carton of new, pumpkin-coloured basketballs.

John shrugged.

"How much do I owe you?" said PF.

John shrugged again. "I threw the tags out. I'll just chock it up to lost inventory."

"Seriously. How much?"

"Seriously?" John pulled a thick binder out of a drawer, found the appropriate page, read: "Carl Gauss briefs, 100% upland cotton, 240 threads per inch, zinc-washed, odour-resistant. Eighty-five dollars."

"Wow! Hear that?" beamed PF, addressing his genitals which were curled up, compliant at last, in the close-fitting nest of his new, prestigious underwear.

"Settle for my cost?" said John, leafing through the purchase orders he kept in a Black Magic chocolate box on his desk.

"Still got your old box I see," said PF, hoping to nudge an explanation for the box's existence out of his friend.

"Since day one," said John simply. "Carl Gauss. Here we go. Briefs. Ooo, eleven dollars a pair." He looked at PF with playful defiance. "They give me a special price."

"Special price my ass. I may be a cop with a degree in criminology, one in business too as a matter of fact, but I can still recognize a thief when he's looking right at me."

Why do I sleep, Bing? I hate sleep. I had this jerk-off dream about PF staring into me. I won't say where. I'm hungry.

So, Lydia, you got laid.

Don't remind me. I fucked up, eh.

Not at all, not at all. Your regina had the time of his life.

He did, didn't he. Good for him. Anything to eat? Besides apples and marmalade with moss in it? Don't say it.

Marmalade me.

I said don't say it.

Who laid you?

"Use your phone?" said PF.

"You don't have your own?"

"Would I ask?"

John turned his desk phone around to face the inspector. PF dialled.

"Laliberté. *Oui, oui, ça va. Un peu plus tard peut-être. Rien de nouveau au sujet du cadavre? Non? Bon, Lydia maintenant. Pourquoi je te parle en français? Tu es français. Écoute, Lydia prétend détenir vingt-sept patentes dans le domaine de la peinture. La peinture chauffante.* Hot paint. *Je veux que tu vérifies. Ça s'appelle* the Intellectual Property Office. *Pas à Québec, non, à Ottawa. D'accord: k, w, a, z, n, i, e, v, s, k, i.* Hot paint, *c'est ça.* Bye."

"Twenty-seven patents," said John.

"You speak French now?"

"This the lady who deposited your clothes outside her door?"

"This is her."

So, Lydia, you got laid.

Shut up, Bing.

Question: the Piffer, can he be said to have gotten laid? Phosphorize with me, Lyd.

No thank you.

If, as I think we can, we can discard the proposition that, for the male of the species, ejerkulation is the necessary culmination of the sex act, I believe we are obliged to accept that it is an essential element of the sacrament of laid-getting. At the same time, one cannot but wonder at the physical proportions of the human body which permit, indeed require, that the genital region fall so naturally, so lovingly, under the touch of the human hand, a structure so mutable it can impersonate the main copulatory organ of either sex, but with how much more investigative curiosity than the male, with how many more shades of solicitousness than the female. Indeed, the act of eating, even dead weggitables, requires a more calculated deployment of elbow and forearm than does the act of masturbing. How penetratingly human, then, of the Piffer, to slip out into the corridor to finish himself off, although it would have perhaps been more convivial, more gregarious, to have remained with us here in the tubroom, which of course brings us back to our question: can a self-laid man be said to have gotten . . .

Shut up, Bing!

Fine. Fine.

"Lydia, you said her name was? She must be pretty bright if she has all these patents."

PF blushed profoundly, squirmed in his chair. "Oh yes. Yes. Brilliant really." He looked everywhere but at his friend.

"She's brilliant," said John, "and she's interested in you?" hoping to put PF at ease with a little obvious sarcasm.

"Was interested," said PF, missing the sarcasm. He was comfortable with his friend. And yet he could find nothing more to say, and the more he struggled with his muteness, the more embarrassed he became.

"Was interested. Why was? Was she like, angry when she chucked your clothes out?"

"Not angry angry." PF rubbed his eyes with the heels of his hands. He did not know how to begin to describe Kwaznievski, who was neither incompetent nor a vagabond, not either or both, whose voice had flown into his skull and could not find a way out, not for lack of trying either, no, it flapped and banged and banged and flapped. He had told his friend about the mattress in the bathtub. His friend had laughed. That he had had sex on a mattress in a bathtub in an ice-cold bathroom. He had said all that. Why not? But he did not, now, know how to begin, was not sure, in any case, that he had not misinterpreted, misconstrued, he remained silent, rubbing his eyes, wondering just how long he had stood in the bathtub, his left foot perched on the rim, before the pain in his right leg had started to rise into his hip, into his rib cage, until his side was numb and his leg began to twitch, while Lydia caressed endlessly, endlessly the back of his testicles, muttering in her fledgling voice, to Bing, incessantly to Bing. He remembered the marine lifelessness of her white arms, her breasts draining out from under her pebbly nipples as she inserted him into herself, as though he were what? her Bing, yes, her invention. As though he were her idea. Was it that that explained his relentless, wheedling arousal, that gave him the impression that his sex, his cells, were invested with a foreign life, a contagion.

Inspector PF stood, smiling thinly, holding his coat in front of his crotch, the birdling having started to hatch in the nest of his new underwear.

"The nice thing about sports," said John, "is that a siren goes off when the game is over. So you like, know. Lydia one, PF no score. Call it a draw. Chock Miss Twenty-seven-patents up to lost inventory. Half the women in this town want your TV butt."

"Oh? Which half is that?" PF put on his coat. "Good to see you again." He adjusted his scarf. "Cold out."

So, Lydia, you got laid.

Oh stop it, stop it. Talk about something else.

Okay. Alright. Let's talk about the dung-bunny with the skewer in his eye. The unidentified corpse of PF's death advice. On the back of which you drew PF's back. Right? The unidentified corpse that you can identify.

Cannot!

Can too.

Cannot!

. . . Why didn't you just take the money to the police, Lydia?

What money?

What money! Thirty-eight gees is a whack of jack to be finding in a bag thing.

What thirty-eight gees? You weren't there. How do you know I didn't make it all up? Besides, I'm never going to claim that money. Thirty-eight gees that fell out of a corpse? I wouldn't touch money that fell out of a fuckle with a skewer in his eye.

So the fuckle had the skewer in his eye. Therefore you can identify him.

Cannot!

No? Oh. So he didn't have the skewer. Therefore he only got the skewer afterwards. Therefore the corpse wasn't a corpse when you opened the door and only became a corpse because you absconded with the bag thing.

I did not abscond! What I did do was, I took the money to the cop shop and I have no intention of ever claiming it. So I didn't abscond.

Ah. And like you said, the fuckle was dead when you opened the door.

Thank you. Fuckles, fortunately, are usually dead when they're dead.

You had just enough time to feel his pulse, stick your ear against his chest. Something! Else!

Like?

Anything.

Okay. Alright. So you got laid, Lydia.

Stop it, Bing.

Why didn't you tell PF about the thirty-eight gees? If the corpse only became a corpse because you absconded with the whack, what does that make you? Is that why you didn't tell PF?

Stop it, Bing. Stawp it! Even if he wasn't, I didn't abscond. I took the money to the police. I have a receipt for it!

And the dung-bunny with the skewer in his eye, Lyd. Tell me again it's not him. Lydia, Lydia, Lydia. Don't you ever get tired of fucking up, of having miscarriages all over everybody's bathroom? I think you should just call Eddy. 642-3825. He'll be overjoyed to hear from you.

I didn't abscond.

642-3825.

The fuckle was dead, Bing. He was.

64 . . . You had just the time to slip your pocket mirror under his nostrils, right? . . . 2-3825.

"He gave me all the patents with a resemblance to hot paint," said Laliberté on the other end of the line. "There is, like you said, quite a few. I read you one, any one, ah, 'a chlorine-free plastic sheet is applied directly upon the hot paint surface and on the plastic sheet a chlorine-free overcoat is applied and cured. Patent number 684593-76.' Is that what you're after?"

"Why not?" said PF eagerly. "Sounds good to me. As long as it's a patent granted to Lydia Kwaznievski."

"It's not."

"It's not?"

"No."

"No?"

"No patents have ever been granted to any individual, not at any time, or representing a group either, by the name of Lydia Kwaznievski."

"What do you mean, never?" The inspector's steamy breath broke against the mouthpiece of the telephone.

"Never, I think, means . . . never."

"Not ever?"

"No, sir."

"Never. Well. When you get right down to it . . ." It was five o'clock and almost dark, the entire chorus line of streetlights had apparently missed their cue to illuminate, the sewers released their stagy, January gloom. PF strained to watch a low-flying seagull. The seagull spotted a school of popcorn, veered, touched down with too much airspeed, toppled over and came to an unceremonious halt, a piece of popcorn hard by its beady eye. For an instant, the seagull thought the piece of popcorn was the skull of a goldfinch. Alarmed, it righted itself quickly and strode away as though leaving an adult seagull movie theatre, returned more nonchalantly, eyeing the popcorn steadily in case it attempted to burrow into the snow. "When you get right down to it," said PF, "that's about what I was expecting really."

Bing.
  What?
  I'm cold.
  Keep walking, Lydia.

I can't, Bing, I'm too tired. I'm hungry, I'm cold. Come with me to Saint Sylvestry's.

Nothing there but fuckledrops with faces full of eyes. Keep walking, Lydia.

I can't.

Can't? What is this noise? Suit yourself. Once a fuckle, always a fuckle. I'm not coming.

"Like I said, PF, there is a lot of patents. There is twenty-seven, like you said, that are all to one individual."

"Oh? Who's that?"

The streetlights came on suddenly, startling the seagull who took flight, startling PF who dropped the telephone, startling the telephone which bounced on the end of its cord. PF did not retrieve it. "Who, Laliberté?" he shouted.

"A somebody," Laliberté's voice trickled out of the dangling receiver, "with the name of J. E. Bing."

"Who?"

"Bing!"

"Bing, did you say?"

Detective Inspector PF was not aware that he was smiling broadly, not aware that he was jumping on the pieces of popcorn, crushing them under his boots, not aware even that Montreal had left its moorings and was drifting down the Saint Lawrence, moving under his feet.

"Bing," he said out loud, knowing he had made a discovery that would lead to a greater discovery, marvelling how the kissing caterpillars of her eyebrows, the eeliness of her arms, acquired a new and palpable cohesiveness when associated with the name of Bing.

He strode energetically through the blue snow over which floated the quiet glow of the streelights, swinging his empty attaché case as though preparing to launch it overboard. "Christ," he said, "you piss me off."

That's your problem.

He was relieved that her voice rang inside his ears now with a genuine musicality.

"So Bing's your real name. J. E. Let me guess. Jacqueline Escogriffe."
Close.

"Bing," he said, knowing he had made a discovery that would lead to a greater discovery.

"Bing." Knowing, now, how to begin.

Bing.
    What?
    Meet me after.
    After what?
    After Saint Sylvestry's.
    Pff.
    Bing.
    Whaaat?
    Meet me.
    . . . I might. Might.
    Bing.
    What?

THE OCTOBER TREE

There was a summer movie once that went huge — in Quebec anyway, the dubbed English version didn't do more than exist — about an alcoholic dog and his 10-year-old drinking companion. The kind of movie to marinate your wings in. Very sweet and very sour. I was the kid.

The story was set in the middle past, the '30s maybe. If you look closely during the blizzard scene when the dog puts his navy duffle coat around my scrubby shoulders, I have something straight sticking out of my back pocket. This is an electric toothbrush, a novelty at the time, given to me as an encouragement to keep brushing during filming, and the best thing about the whole experience. When I buzzed the sweet spot up behind my canine, on the left, just there, woo, my two eyes fairly rattled, and my ears grew.

It is true that I did a second film about an alcoholic seal and his 12-year-old drinking companion. Lessly huge, but still.

I did a number of films.

My precocious cinematic career has significance, for me, for two reasons. One is girls, twisting my pant legs around, measuring the in-seam, muttering at each other through the straight pins held between their lips, their nubby spines making me think of dinosaur chicks. Girls, blushing me, smudging me, creaming me, the buttons of their white smocks brushing the prickling edges of my closed lids. And more girls, their braces frothy with saliva, their weedy hair ablaze with sweat, their watery souls draining through their frenzied eyes as I waved at them boyly from the hip.

The other reason is that it ended.

I was arrested on Tuesday, October 20, 1970.

The October Crisis, you know about it likely. James Cross, the British Trade Minister, had been abducted by the Quebec Liberation Front on the fifth. The provincial Labour Minister, Pierre Laporte, had also been abducted by a different cell of the same group. His strangled body had been found in the trunk of a car on the 18th.

The War Measures Act had been proclaimed. Comfortable, tree-coloured soldiers, staked to their rifles, had planted themselves all over the wan pavement of Montreal, their pockets stuffed with its citizens' civil liberties.

"Daniel Painchaud. *Vous êtes en état d'arrestation.*"

I was 19. I thought it was kind of a gas.

The prison cells could not even be closed, so crammed they were with detainees vying for corners of every kind of seating apparatus hastily provided. I shared a three-legged armchair with the terrified hair of a Fredericton hitchhiker who spoke no French.

"Tell dem what dey wann''ear," I told him in my pondiest froglish. "Udderwyze, dey put like hot-red stick' in your fingurr, you know, like here? in your finnernail."

His eyes were infant fish hiding in an insufficient sea willow.

"*Mais non! Je joke!*"

The interrogation was not arduous. The interrogator's lips were waxy with exhaustion and cigarettes. He was not interested in me, only in people I had worked with, and I had nothing to offer. He did not fail to point out that his daughter thought my last film was *"poche à mort."*

Lousy, that is.

October. Colourless, no-man's month. The sky as vacant as the stare of a soldier on duty. *Mais non. Je joke.*

"Wait!" she called, in French, running after me down the police station steps. "What did they ask you? Were you in for long?" Agitated she was, asking the questions she needed to be asked herself.

"If I preferred boxer-shorts or briefs. You?"

Her breathing, rapid, strong-tempered, pushed its way up into her throat, preventing her from speaking. Her eyes darted with the randomness of light, inoffensive insects, easily squashed.

"Walk?" I said. She nodded quickly.

We had not gone far when she grabbed my arm awkwardly, dug her forehead into my shoulder, and wept. A nearby soldier, his helmet in a hairnet, looked dutifully away, amused.

She wept. And I observed the poisonous-looking fruit of an inky hedge, a surreptitious pleasure spreading up my back, certain, as I was, that she had not recognized me.

Her weeping, as we walked, was interrupted by lucid moments of anger.

"Internalize! We are too feminine in Quebec. We internalize, we eat ourselves. We kidnap a trade minister. Very well. A man of no importance, a cocktail diplomat in a big house. But the man we murder is one of our own, our best. A comedy of incompetence!"

We got on the metro at Place d'Armes, the rattle and pitch of the car shutting off her tear glands completely.

"I'm sorry for all this crying. I need to sleep. I was in jail since Sunday." She showed me a snapshot then. "The police gave me this. I'm eleven years old. The other girl in the picture was my next-door neighbour at that time. I haven't seen her in years and years. My best friend. The kind of best friend you fight with constantly. Very smart. Big personality, like a room with no carpet, no furniture, full of echo. Mmn. Mostly the echo of her own voice. The police told me she's one of Cross's kidnappers."

"Eh! She is? Her?" I searched the black-and-white splotches of the girl-in-the-picture's face for what I imagined to be early indications of a terroristic disposition, a sullen, secret mouth, a conniving eye. I did not find them. "Her?"

"You think it is not possible for a woman to be a terrorist? To subsume whatever specificity she might choose, including the handling of guns?" This last with a sharp, but strangely weightless, squeeze of my crotch.

"Sunday!" she said. "Sunday night! A knock on the door of my apartment. I open. 'Diane Dufault?' That is my name."

"Okay."

"'Yes,' I say. 'Police,' they say, 'you will come with us.' I slam the door closed. Oh-oh. *Bang!* They reslam the door open. They're excited now, they love this. They push me up against the wall and put their gun . . ." Her face started to falter again. ". . . right, right in my eyes." And again, she wept.

Exhilarated I was, swaying through the sequence of moments, years, perfectly authentic, perfectly fugitive, that had conducted the girl-in-the-picture from beside Diane Dufault, in a backyard frosted with suburban sun, into an unknown room where sat a certain Mr. Cross, dirty presumably, bound perhaps, haunted, bored. And through the separate sequence, more discreet certainly, but not, therefore, less magical, that had conducted Diane Dufault herself into the subway seat beside mine, where the surly motion of the car caused our shoulders to brush.

There was not a soldier, not a Montrealer, not one, who would not have eaten boiled rat in order to see the face of the girl-in-the-picture.

Her.

Girls, like the police, will find out where you live.

"Stop a second," I said to Diane Dufault. "That's my house."

"Where the girls are you mean?"

"Yes."

They were wearing feathers and mini-skirts, sitting on the steps in front of my door, rocking gently, hugging their cold thighs made of moulded, bloodberry cream. I changed address often, which only excited the girls' flushing instincts, and my happy vanity.

"Who are they?" said Diane.

"My fans. They've stayed away lately, but now they're back. The crisis must be over."

"You have fans?"

"You don't recognize me, do you?"

"Should I?"

"Daniel Painchaud?"

She looked at me blankly. I listed my movies. She was no further ahead.

"Come on," I said, with the chipper humiliation of a schoolboy who, having been discovered drawing obscenities, is made, not to stop, but to continue, "if we go around we can get in the backyard."

"Now that," said Diane Dufault, squeezing through the cedar hedge, "is an October tree."

An immense maple it was, its detachment of leaves wearing their dress, American-mustard uniforms. And although it stood to attention circumstantially, it could not entirely hide its anxiety over a gaping and sharp-edged tumour growing among its lower branches.

A tree house, not put together with uneven boards and bent nails, but solid, clinker-built, with a shingled roof, windows that opened, and good hardware.

"I must sleep here," said Diane Dufault, poking her head through the trap door, "here, only here, I must, I must. I'll never . . ." She collapsed onto the crumpled sleeping bag I sometimes used. "I'm too tired to sleep I think."

"Get right inside the bag," I said. "Go on. Take your shoes off first!"

"So tired, I'll never be able to get to sleep," she muttered, going to sleep.

And so I sat in the tree house and thought about girls, ogling me, crayoning me, snaffling me, and more girls, in their spinnaker dressing gowns, running bare-masted down the broadloomed corridor, as the darkening air, like quick-syrup, absorbed the face of the girl-in-the-picture looking up at me from the photo in my hands. I listened, enthralled, as I burst into the bathroom where the limp-eyed man was shaving. "Cross!" I hissed, "James Cross. You are a prisoner of the Quebec Liberation Front!" Quebec, I thought, Quebec, the most crackling name in all geography. My blood sang, sang. I thought of the summer's paling tan of Diane Dufault going greyish, revealing the craters on her cheeks made by the meteorites of childhood, and for a long time, I thought it was the October tree creaking.

But no, it was Diane. It was.

It was Diane Dufault who was creaking in her sleep.

Not enough girls in her diet, I thought, meaning fish.

It ended.

"Listen, Daniel," said my agent, also in French of course, "you've done boys up to now. And out there, they love you for it. They do. They'll feel betrayed if you do something else, jealous. You need to like, sleep for a while, spin a cocoon, re-emerge as an actor of men. We'll keep covering the rent, don't worry. We believe in you. Believe in yourself."

I did. Believe him. Despite the hot-red sticks in my finnernails.

"I could maybe try to get you something in English."

If Diane Dufault refused, categorically, and with an involuntary shying of the head, as though a powdery moth had fluttered past her ear, to ever return to the apartment where she had been arrested, she did, on the other hand, take up quarters in the tree house with disconcerting forthrightness. She sent me off to the Miracle Mart with her order, and soon enough yellow extension cords were dribbling out the windows of my house and winding themselves up the October tree in order to supply electricity to the toaster, heating unit and hot plate, as well as the mahoganoid home entertainment system out of which foamed the harps and guitars of Los Tres Sudamericanos.

And on the third morning, "I remember!" she said, bursting into my bedroom, wearing my elephant jeans and my blue-and-white oxfords, having thrown her prison wear into the garbage. "I didn't dare say so, but I couldn't remember where I worked. Weird, eh? But now I do. All of a sudden. As if I hadn't forgotten."

"Good. So where do you work?"

"At the port of Montreal. I look after the foreign sailors."

"Mmn," said I, with obligatory suggestiveness.

She made a face, not displeased.

"I take them to doctors. To dentists. On tours of the city. I organize soccer games between crews. Bye."

And more girls, pruning me, paring me, peaching me. And more still, enamelled with concentration, examining the lone hairs in their newish nipples.

Bye.

And Diane Dufault, possessed with an athleticism entirely removed from sport, her hair dry, grassy, but sturdy nonetheless, wilful, her teeth oddly misaligned, as though set in her gums by a child, Diane Dufault headed off to work each day.

While I did nothing.

It is not to be believed how, at 19, we are capable of doing nothing.

Nothing but roll around in my bedroom, like a bead of mercury in a lead pipe, breaking into bits, reassembling myself, my thoughts, all aimed squarely at the port of Montreal, ricocheting off the impenetrable walls with a metallic reverberation so persistent as to make me ill.

Nothing but turn back a corner of my curtain to confirm that the steps in front of my door were empty.

Nothing but wait for the phone to ring, despite the groaning weight of ringless days.

And for Diane Dufault to arrive with her able seamen.

Oh, they loved her, they did. And none more so than the Norwegian engineer who had survived four soundless days in the mid-Atlantic only to scream meekly when, as he was being lifted out, the water-logged flesh of his arm slipped away from the bone. Or the squat Panamanian who insisted on showing her, and me, ceremoniously, with an equal measure of pride and anxiety, not only his truss, but the wondrously enlarged testicle that it maintained in place. Or the distinguished, trembling Egyptian to whom Diane gave her arm as they stepped out into the winter sun, whose hair she touched enquiringly, while, on the other side of the closed door behind them, the dental surgeon examined the rotten bits of 12 Egyptian teeth he had just extracted, and slid them into a small incinerator.

Loved her. Sent her postcards and letters in terse, groping French, included pictures of themselves and their vessels, with pin-holes marking the portals of their cabins, and offered greetings, occasionally, to the *"vedette de cinéma"* whose name they did not remember.

For Diane Dufault, who considered all art to be exploitative, sexist, and above all, vain, who had barely seen any films much less mine, nevertheless insisted on introducing me to her men from everywhere, glowingly, and not only for the rapid enthusiasm it created, as a movie actor.

"Célebre? Ouiiii. Une star. Les filles l'adorent. Elles capotent."

Girls. With their circumflex lips, their pointed kisses, with their rooty, sour breath.

While I did nothing.

Rain, rain. The Mammameea Pizzareea. Wet they all were, in a flavoursome mood. The Basque officer offered Diane his dry shirt, exposing aristocratically the colony of black, crawling hairs that burrowed everywhere into his bare torso. Diane put the shirt on brightly, removed her damp bra with unblushing discretion, the collapsed garment appearing magically from underneath the shirt before being passed with big-eyed reverence from sailor to sailor.

So that when, amid this red-eared conviviality, Diane bit into the point of a pizza wedge only to have the topping, gluey with double cheese, come away in a piece and hang from her mouth, and when, through the alluring mirth, the Basque officer glanced at the *"vedette de cinéma"* sitting at the end of the table, he, the officer, was surprised to discover that he, I, was not enjoying himself.

No, he was in disarray, sobbing. He was on his feet, screaming insults and challenges, pushing seated sailors tauntingly in the back who, for all response, snorted festively. He was running into the bleak humidity of Montreal. He was trying not to see the fleshy pizza crust, himself in other words, deserted in a piece by its topping of girls, with their melting, meaningless eyes, girls, with their bitten, quick fingertips, and more girls, with their dry, their red and jittery mouths.

And he was deciding he was going to do something.

To do something.

Noteworthy.

And this is what I did:

I abducted Diane Dufault. Sharp, eh?

I called Marie-Jeanne Knafo, *décoratrice*, Québecfilm, acerbic and 63, explained what I needed, and it was she who was quick to suggest the mobile-home set, because she'd dismantled it just the previous week and could set it up again in my basement in less than a day, while Diane was gone. And when that was all done, I held a big party. I had no friends, fortunately, because parties always work better when you don't invite friends. I greeted the first arrivals, mingled for a while, slipped upstairs and changed. I am, or I was then, as a woman, in her late 30s, characterless, but convincing. I remingled, and when Diane showed up, I intercepted her, introduced myself brightly, and asked her if she could help me bring in a big present from my car. She reached into the back seat, I conked her, immobilized her limbs, suppressed her capacity to see or utter audible sound, and drove up to the next street where Marie-Jeanne took over the wheel. I rejoined the party, slipped upstairs, and changed back into myself. Sharp, eh? Marie-Jeanne drove out into the country for a few hours, and then returned to her point of departure where I met her, drove back to my now empty house, and lugged Diane downstairs into the mobile-home set. Naturally, I was beside myself at her disappearance, and naturally my agent was less than eager to pay the modest ransom, which I let Marie-Jeanne keep anyway. She was the one who issued the communiqués, using the pirated, untraceable phone in the October tree where, in fact, she stayed for the duration, which was really too cool. After Diane's release, the police beat the doonbocks looking for suspect mobile homes, and then they gave up. I was, of course, under close surveillance despite my airtight alibi, so I had to stay put in my house.

And do nothing.

Mais oui, je joke. I did call Knafo, to listen to her leathery, scheming, Moroccan laugh.

"*Ça va pas, Daniel?*" said Diane Dufault, generous, plaintive, an accusatory echo in her voice.

"*Ça pourrait aller mieux.*"

"Listen," she said, "this maybe isn't the right moment. Etchebarray says," Etchebarray being the Basque officer, "that you should come and work on his ship. I told him I wasn't sure it was the kind of thing you'd like to do. They're going to Cumaná. After that to Rotterdam. After that . . . If you're interested."

"Cumaná." The harps and guitars of Los Tres Sudamericanos.

It was as if the wind was in me, swirling, blowing out through my pores, lifting me bodily out of bed.

Cumaná, Cumaná, en la costa de Venezuela.

For days the wind continued, hurtling me down the streets. There was all the world's weather to get equipped for, sun hats to buy, storm pants, snow belts, slickers, Wellingtons, arctic parkas, temperate sweaters, and hot, tropical shirts.

It blew me up the woozy gangway onto the rusted deck, blew the smell of oily water into my nose, the vibrating drone of machines into my ears.

And it blew me towards Etchebarray who spoke English like a black, Spanish peacock, proud of his sleek accent, who said, "Tomorrow we leave, in the morning, at two," and whose diffident handshake sent a thrill scorching through my arm, my neck, and straight into the speech centre of my brain, so that I blurted out:

"Diane wants to come too. I know she does. Can she?"

I lifted the receiver and replaced it immediately, although I knew there was no point. The telephone does not mind. It lives only to have its chins scratched and to lick your ear. It started ringing again.

"Answer it," said Diane, who had snuck up on me. "It might be important."

The telephone does not mind. It knows that we think it is important to have our ears licked.

Diane Dufault, watching me from high aboard her departing boat, not waving, not looking away.

Diane Dufault, in the October tree, creaking in her sleep.

Diane Dufault, her breasts within easy reach, low-slung, sagacious, as though filled with flour, her nocturnal, incongruous nipples, perched high and trained, on Vega?

I didn't go to Cumaná.

"Daniel!" said my agent. "It's you they want. They just, just called me. Host of a tough new quiz show. Every week from a different high school in Quebec. Big scholarships for the top dogs. You're perfect for it, Daniel, young, you've got an enquiring mind. It gets you all over the Quebec you're always talking about, gets you into TV, a new following, older, more mature. Perfect. The perfect transition."

Diane went.

Actors, good ones, as you know, project themselves into personalities substantially more interesting than their own. I couldn't do that very well, apparently.

So I became a personality. Personalities project themselves into tight-fitting faces made of foam. They prick a matched pair of one-way eyes into the face, an odourless nose, a non-staining smile. They put considerable effort into the selection of these attributes, the number and variety of which is delightfully rich.

As a personality, I have done enormous things.

I have reviewed, at a presidential pace and in the company of flushed vice-principals, the troops of lockers in every polyvalente in Quebec.

I have owned a house in Pointe-Claire.

I have been a side-man for Chef Julien Batata, have read the thousands of ingredients you will need into the lenitive, cleansing silence.

I have, and this is perfectly true, advertised plastic wrap, one, to conserve food, two, to insulate windows and three, to bind the entire body as a weight-reducing technique. I have done this at different times in my life, having signed different contracts with different production companies hired by different manufacturers, and yet the plastic wrap in every instance was exactly the same, as demonstrated during the course of a consumer hearing at which I, in fact, testified.

I have met Catherine Deneuve.

It appears to me, now, that I was ahead of my time, and that the times, surprisingly, have caught up. I am, at last, *chez moi*. Everyone's buzzing their sweet spots now. Personalities are everywhere, every-where. They have no shrill principles, no vital, cross-membered scaffolding to belt themselves to. They offer conciliation, mystery, a fluid, well-spoken self-reliance, and no, thankfully, no invitation to chip off the foam face in order to visit the limp-eyed life under-neath. Dirty presumably. Bound perhaps. Haunted. Bored.

Jasper Cross the Trade Minister? They found him eventually. You know that. His defeated abductors were shipped off instantly to Cuba, their demands ignored. I never knew if the girl-in-the-picture was one of them. Could be.

All something of a what, a whang and a bimper thing.

But you know that, too.

THE CHOCOLATE DICK

In a washroom in the basement of Saint Mathieu Hospital, stood on a toilet seat, Superintendent PF. Breathed through his mouth silently. Drew his wide head into the nest of his hunched shoulders. Waited, hidden in his stall, for the unseen other occupant of the washroom to finish running water into the sink, and leave. Felt, despite the dewy-eyed melancholia of his lingering mononucleosis, an inner excitement, an exuberance that squirmed inside his body, as though his upper vertebrae had been replaced by new ones that swivelled with liquid precision, but that were meant, surely, for a much larger man.

Up four storeys and over and down a corridor and to the right, in the continuing care wing of the same Saint Mathieu Hospital, lay Superintendent PF's mother, her stricken brain repairing itself half-heartedly, her speech centre apparently fried forever. She no longer recognized her son except, oddly enough, when she saw him on television. Superintendent PF appeared frequently on television. Not three hours earlier in fact, he had taken part in the afternoon taping of a talk show hosted by a man who had an engaging capacity to make his guests squirm, and whose name was Daniel Painchaud.

The hiss of running water ceased abruptly, was followed by the throaty gargle of the basement drain, and then by silence.

Was it a good idea? he asked his mother to himself, seeing again her corned-beef tongue wedged into its usual resting place at the corner of her lips, a thread of drool running from its tip to a drop of clear, epoxy spittle on her chin.

The window screen rattled. The washroom door had, therefore, been opened. Superintendent PF waited until the screen calmed itself, accorded the ensuing stillness a further period of grace before accepting, for lack of all evidence to the contrary, that he was alone.

He got down quickly, let go the pants he had been holding up, and refitted his buttocks into the egg-shaped hole of the toilet seat, certain, as he was, or almost, that he would not again be interrupted.

His mother's eyes stared at him with an eerie, unwavering, emptiness.

"What's the point?" he said.

"She's your mother," answered the nurse, wheeling the television stand into place at the end of the bed, "she'd love to see you on TV."

"She doesn't recognize me in real life. She's not going to recognize me on TV."

"You don't know for sure she doesn't recognize you," said the nurse, feeding the cassette into the slot in the VCR.

No sooner did Superintendent PF's image appear on the TV screen than his mother struggled in her bed, plucked at his sleeve with her one functional hand and pointed his arm weakly at the set. She gooed soundlessly, radiantly, while the nurse said, "That's your son alright," made playful spikes in his mother's hair and smoothed them out again.

His bowels began to move.

"Is it possible," said Superintendent PF, "that the stroke also knocked out the part of her brain responsible for unhappiness?"

"They're often like that," said the nurse. She handed him back the cassette. "So was it a good idea?" She was pleased with herself.

He held his breath, the melancholia of fatigue pressing his eyes against his closed lids, his pulse thudding in his neck, and voided.

An almost painful relief flooded his body, retreated, drained out through a funnel in his spine. Was it a good idea, he thought, to have my mother recognize me on TV, proving conclusively thereby that she does not recognize me in real life?

And then Superintendent PF, as he always did, and always had, ever since his very early childhood, got down off the toilet seat and examined his stool.

Whitefriar he was. He drew back the hood of his tunic and turned to face his students.

"Remember," he said sententiously, "it is not by looking into their eyes that you will discover your patients' true nature. It is by observing their excrement. Melinda di Savoy, advance. Man or woman, say Melinda."

"A trick question. Female excreta cannot be distinguished from male."

"Very good. Young or old?"

"Not young. I believe the subject occupies a position of some authority."

"Mmn. Single, married, or otherwise?"

"I can't say."

"No. A widower in fact."

"Ah."

"Chuck Quinty, advance. Pathological appraisal, say."

"Robust, well-formed, spinach notes, and chocolate. The subject enjoys good health and happitude. An assassin perhaps."

"Really. Melinda?"

"Mr. Quinty forgets that in cyclothymic cases, it is not the lively but the depressive intervals that are characterized by the laying down of fine stools such as these. See how they do not tear when held lightly in the fingers thus. I suggest the subject is melancholic."

Superintendent Whitefriar PF shook the water off his hands and sat down again on the toilet seat, amused by his game, reassured. He felt in his pocket the crinkling cellophane wrapper of the Luer syringe, the plump vial of morphine. An assassin perhaps. His heart raced at the idea.

He reflected that his mother, who had never tired of telling how he used to plunge his hands into the flushing water to save his drowning turds, could not have suspected that so many years later, he would still be at it. Small revenge, seeing as she now only recognized him on television.

He tipped his head back, studied the crystalline formations of dust in the fan above his head, and remembered.

"My next guest," said Daniel Painchaud, orange sun-lamp tan, patent leather hair attached behind his head, "has an intimidating number of accomplishments . . ." The makeup made the hair on the back of Superintendent PF's hands tingle ". . . certified paramedic, Master of Criminotology, what'd I say? Criminology, thank you, M.B.A., I got that one right, acting director, computer crime . . ." he could smell the fabric of his dress uniform, warmed by the lights ". . . award-winning host of the popular television series *Citizen's Arrest* . . ." a gentle hand placed itself in the small of his back and pushed him forward ". . . put your hands together and welcome . . ." he advanced over the studio floor ". . . now in its how-manieth season? Seventh?" He nodded affirmatively and took his seat, feeling, now that he thought of it, not unlike water draining through the enamelled faces and gargling applause of a washroom sink, wanting only to be in Saint Mathieu Hospital, skulking the basement corridors, eating the vending machine hotdogs made of doughy wieners and fleshy buns, four storeys below his mother where she lay.

"I hear your mother's not well."

"No . . . no."

"That's a shame. You've been ill yourself?"

"Oh, a little run-in with mononucleosis. It tends to drag on. Self-diagnosed by the way."

"*Self*-diagnosed."

"With the help of the Internet. My doctor had me ticketed with leukemia and death."

"Wow," said Painchaud. "So you can even solve the crimes of your own body."

Beside Superintendent PF slouched defiantly Faïp, lead singer, La viande rose, a rock band, her face padlocked behind various metal rings, links, and cotter pins.

"You've been a cop, you don't mind being called a cop? for what, thirty years?"

"Thirty's good."

Faïp pulled her bare shoulders slightly away from, turned her face slightly towards, him.

"Okay. In that period," said Painchaud, reading from the letter-sized cards that served him both as property and prop, "urban community police have laid charges one thousand, ten thousand, one hundred thousand, or five hundred thousand times?"

Of course, had he thought about it, but it is not easy to think on television and Painchaud, in any case, was sure of his effect.

"A hundred thousand?" said Painchaud gleefully. "Nope. Actually, it's a trick question. The answer is none of the above. Two *million* times is the real answer, Superintendent. Believe that? Two million. Hey, at that rate somebody here has *got* to have been charged. Fess up. All you baddies raise your hands. Nobody? No break and enters? No fake money passers? Not one? I don't believe you."

Superintendent PF believed them. The manner of Daniel Painchaud, elusive, deprecatory, made him uneasy. Nor could he prevent himself from feeling that the entire 30 years and two million charges, enormous though they were, would fit on the end of a pin.

"And you," said Faïp.

"Me?" he said.

"You." She nodded, not unlike an impatient horse, towards Painchaud.

"Me what?" said Painchaud.

"You have been in jail sometime, I'm sure of it. No?"

The audience howled. Superintendent PF laced his fingers behind his neck, breathed deeply the resonant calm of the washroom, saw again, as she pushed open the door of his LeSabre, the shiny and as though poisonous metal bead that orbited Faïp's navel, the memory competing weakly however with the voice of Daniel Painchaud, reading from his cards, quickly resuming Superintendent PF's brief stint in homicide, saying with stunningly amicable presumption, ". . . and then, as I understand it, you blew everyone away by solving the case of the bit nipple . . ." the voice tailing away deftly, leaving Superintendent PF no alternative but to fill in the ensuing silence with a murmured description of the case for the benefit of the slavering audience.

"Yes," he said softly, "I did in a way. It was . . . an unpleasant homicide, bestial, the victim's left nipple was bitten completely off. The only hope of proving the undoubted guilt of the prime suspect lay in demonstrating that it was he who had done the biting, and yet the plaster cast made of his mouth simply did not fit the clearly defined teeth marks of the wound. It simply did not." Superintendent PF did not mention the blow-up of the bloodied nipple tacked to his cork-board for weeks, until it appeared to be made of stone, an asteroid, in eclipse. Nor did he mention that when the appallingly obvious solution occurred to him, he did not immediately accept it himself, a part of him preferring an artificial and theoretic doubt to a humiliating certainty.

"Because the investigators," he said, more softly still, "had let themselves become mesmerized by the assumption that the biting had taken place during intercourse, whereas it was only necessary to turn the cast around and the fit was perfect. The suspect, you see, had been standing or . . . at the victim's head."

The hot-cheeked audience cheered his acuity, whistled.

"Incredible," said Daniel Painchaud, shaking his head with vested admiration. "How many dead bodies have you had to look at? Don't answer that. Anything *funny* ever happen in homicide?"

Superintendent PF, who had agreed to prepare an answer to this question, and who had never had to look at any dead bodies, except in photographs, trotted out a story about arriving at the scene of a gruesome slaying, stepping over the yellow tape, and noticing that it was printed with the words, "Slippery when wet."

The audience re-howled, Superintendent PF dropped his chin to his chest and imagined the pipes running down the ceiling of the basement corridors of Saint Mathieu Hospital, disappearing through the walls, running up four storeys and over and down a corridor and to the right.

"Piaf backwards," said Faïp, minuscule in his LeSabre.

"Oh of course," he said, "Edith Piaf, 'La Vie en Rose,'" resisting the desire to say more, to talk endlessly to Faïp, so circumscribed within her obligatory, blatant sexuality. They had driven, apart from the directions she had given, in silence. She had opened the car door.

"That was funny," she said, her gnawed fingers resting on the door handle, "about the 'slippery when wet.' You told it like you've told it before, and like it wasn't true."

"No, no, it's true. It didn't happen to me though."

"I knew it."

"Did I tell any other lies?"

"Not more than me."

He did not dare say that her face, so riddled with metal decorations, appeared stoic, closed.

"Okay," said Daniel Painchaud, reading from his cards, "We have the unfortunate habit of waiting for special occasions, anniversaries and the like, to express our affection for those we love. Right? Now then, Superintendent, I'm sure there's someone you'd like to express affection for. Say it now, go ahead, you're among friends. Don't wait for the special occasion."

No, said Superintendent PF to himself, soothed, in a strange way, by his own discomfiture, it is not easy to think on television.

"Well alright," he had said, hadn't he, looking deeply into the palms of his hands, "I'd just like to say then, that, mmn, you were one brave customer, one fine mother. I'm so sorry you passed away."

The audience howled, howled, while Superintendent PF, red to the roots of his hair and attempting to gather around him the distinguished career which had fallen off the end of its pin, felt the hand of Faïp place itself briefly on his own, looked at her, grasped immediately the unintended humour in his response.

"But I thought that was what he *wanted*," he said, as she held open the door of his LeSabre. "Say it now. Don't wait for the funeral."

"Oh no," she said, "he didn't want you to get more laughs than him."

He listened to the steady trickle of water in the cistern, remembered Faïp's breasts, no less smooth under her top, no less adolescent, though she must have been close to 30, than Pizza Pockets. He closed his wet eyes.

The washroom stall disengaged with a clang.

"Shit," said Whitefriar. "Quinty! Chuck. Get in, hurry. Di Savoy, Melinda. Quick, quick, quick. Are you in? Good. Meet Ip, Fa."

"Hello," said Faïp.

"Hi," said Quinty, breathless, latching the stall door even as the stall itself began to descend with perfect smoothness. The passengers could hear the gurgle of groundwater, the murmur of the inner earth working, could see, through the metal walls, the meaty stone. Faster they went down, faster, the pressure squeezing the creamy oil out of Whitefriar's pores, his heart thickening with each beat, the rings in Faïp's eyebrows bursting open into stinging barbels, the metal partitions of the stall becoming thinner and thinner, coming away in large flakes, the earth bulging through the partitions, as red and glowing as tongue, the stall thudding to a halt at its point of departure, jolting Superintendent PF awake, nauseated. "So," said Daniel Painchaud, aligning the edges of his cards. His ears whining. "We're going to play 'Which would you druther.' Know how it goes?" His lungs dilating and constricting with a pronounced regularity seemingly disassociated from breathing itself, the evasive bonhomie of Painchaud and the smell of the warm dye of his uniform making him queasy. "Okay, which would you druthrer: make love to a woman knowing she is thinking of someone else, or know of a woman making love to someone else while thinking of you?" The audience intrigued, he scrutinizing every syllable for duplicitous meaning, hesitant, flushed, "I think it would be, the second one, if I understand correctly, flattering, very much so."

"Bye," said Faïp, having closed the door to his LeSabre, "Think of me. I'll think of you."

"Which," said Painchaud, "would you druther: be the blind guy who relieves himself," the audience snorting, "hey, I'm just reading what it says here on the card!" guffawing, "the blind guy who relieves himself out a second-storey window, or the sighted guy who convinces him the window's a urinal?" "Neither one!" said Superintendent PF too quickly, the audience grumbling, disappointed. "Or both maybe," the audience brightening.

"Which . . ." said Painchaud.

No, thought Superintendent PF, no more, I'm ill. He stood abruptly, did up his pants, pulled on the flush lever, the torrent bursting into the evening silence. He fumbled with the latch of the stall door.

"Which would you druther . . ."

And again he saw the eight-ounce Dairy Milk chocolate bar that he had placed beside him on his battered wooden desk, he heard the vituperative clamour of the prostitutes being herded down the stairs, the clanging of the cell door latches opening in front of them, closing behind.

"Be slapped by a woman you love . . ."

A gasp heaved itself into the throat of Superintendent PF, he felt again the intense glare of the television lights, the hand of Faïp on his own.

He smelled the air strong with chewing gum and gin, with perfumed makeup, smoke. He listened as the irate babble of the women yielded little by little to resignation, to weariness, until, through the ashy, black silence sprouted a green sprig of snoring, another and another, a new field of somnolent breathing.

"How can anyone sleep in this racket?" said a voice from the darkness of the cells.

"They are sleeping," said Constable PF, sleepy himself, sitting at his wooden desk, having designated seventeen minutes past three as the hour at which he would eat his chocolate bar.

"What time is it?"

"It's, uh, getting close to three."

"I haven't eaten like, in fourteen hours. Food, I mean."

"There are vending machines upstairs. I can get you something."

"Would you? It's just that I'm allergic to so much stuff. There's only like, three things I can eat. Potato's one, if it's mashed, but there wouldn't be any of that."

"No," said Constable PF, put on edge by the steady trickling of the woman's voice over her lips.

"I can drink buttermilk, but you . . ."

"No, no."

"That only leaves Dairy Milk chocolate, as long as it's the eight-ounce size. Otherwise I get these . . ."

Constable PF cursed under his breath at the woman's elaborate subterfuge, was genuinely angry, knew that had she simply asked he might well have responded that it was against regulations, padded, therefore, over to the voice dutifully and surrendered his chocolate bar. He heard the tearing of silver paper, the gluttonous slurping. He felt unseen, giggling hands pin him to the bars and seep under his uniform, was instantly aroused, terrified, struggled mutely, helplessly, against the undoing of his pants, felt the warm, chocolate slime coat his turgid person. He could not, for days after that, resist slipping into the men's room to observe himself, the florid bruises on his hips, the chocolate stains disappearing from the high-smelling sex he dared not touch, much less clean. Inspired he was, humbled by the capacity for life of his own body, having ejaculated with such intensity that he had lost consciousness, had been unable, when he came to, even to stand on his trembling thighs, had felt certain that he had harmed himself permanently.

"Or kissed," said Daniel Painchaud, "by a woman you dislike?"

"Fess up!" shouted Superintendent PF into the fading hiss of the flushing toilet. "Fess up. How many of you have ever come so hard you passed right out? Nobody? Not one? I knew it."

In a canteen in the basement of Saint Mathieu Hospital, sat on a plastic chair Superintendent PF. Ingested a limp hot dog no stubbier than a field mouse. Felt, despite the deep, nocturnal stillness, and despite his lingering mononucleosis, an inner excitement, an exuberance that drained the strength from his arms, so that simply holding the hot dog as he chewed left him breathless.

"Faïp," he said out loud, "I need your opinion."

He saw her again as she had sat, minuscule in his LeSabre, her hand resting on the open door. The desire to tear out the metal cyst growing in the fold of her chin made his hands perspire.

"You do?" she had said, raising her eyebrows in doubt. "You like my tattoo? I'm not so crazy about yours. The one inside your head."

"I thought," he said, smiling, expansive despite his better judgement, "it would be a good idea, when I was young, very young, to be a policeman. Because, I thought, if I fought crime really hard, then by the time I got to be forty, forty-five maybe, there wouldn't be any more crime."

Faïp shifted her gaze from the dashboard directly in front of her, to the dashboard somewhat closer to Superintendent PF. The electric brightness of the vending machines in the dim basement made his eyes ache.

"It's true your mother is sick?" she said.

"She had a stroke. Massive. She wouldn't recognize herself now. Except on TV."

"When I was young," said Faïp, her gaze moving over the dashboard, "I thought I was a stern."

"A stern? Like of a boat?"

"No, a bird. It's white, you see them at the sea. It's not stern?"

"Tern, tern."

"Ah. I thought I was a *tern*. I had arms and legs, I *looked* like a girl, but I *was* a tern. One day, I was tired of being schizo. I didn't care if people knew who I was. I climbed up on the fridge and I flew off. One problem, I really *was* a lobster."

Superintendent PF put his hands over his ears.

"I need to ask your opinion, Faïp," he said, as openly as if she were sitting on a plastic chair beside him, not having had the courage to ask in his LeSabre. "I want to commit a crime. The very idea fills me with the strangest excitement." He felt again the Luer syringe in its cellophane wrapper, the vial of morphine. "I want to put an end to my mother's life."

A draft, humid, smelling faintly of linen, lifted a splinter from the stony lump of his hair.

"Suffering? No. She's as happy as a pigginshit. The nurse says they're often like that. It's a question of dignity. I wouldn't *want* her to recognize me. And certainly not herself. The real crime has already been committed by her own body. Thank you, Daniel Painchaud. I'm just an accessory, after the fact."

He could feel the black air operating delicate changes in his tissue, heightening his eyesight and the quickness of his mind.

"Essentially, Faïp, I am a broker for human degenerateness. People fuck up, they always will, and I take my cut. Two million charges. So Painchaud says, and he must be right.

"For years, Faïp, years, I've been scrutinizing every woman's face hoping to recognize the one face that gave me the chocolate job of a lifetime. Not because I want another, no, no, a hundred times no. I just want to say, 'There she is! Her! That's her!' Ridiculous? I agree.

"I'm a dick. A chocolate dick. Laugh. Go ahead. I'm tired of being schizo. I mean which would you druther: have them all hover around your bed impatiently, wanting you just to get on with it so they can tip you out and destroy the sheets? Or climb up onto the fridge, and try again? Which?"

He strode through the canteen, exalted, brave.

"I'm going to do this, Faïp. I'm going to give new life to my mother. Laugh if you like. I'm going to be my mother's mum. Ha! I am."

Through the half-lit continuing care wing of Saint Mathieu Hospital, crept in his stocking feet Superintendent PF. Held, so they would not rattle in the pocket of his dress uniform jacket, the Luer syringe in its cellophane wrapper, and the plump vial of morphine.

Felt, despite the opiatic hospital air and his lingering mononucleosis, a predacious, vibrant intensity.

He stopped, nodded at Quinty, Faïp, and di Savoy, indicating they were to follow him closely, circumvented the illuminated central bay where the night nurses sat murmuring, and entered a long corridor. A light emanated softly from his mother's private room. A beacon, beckoning. A consecration.

Never had he felt so rarefied, essential, so almost ghostly.

He reached the edge of the open, glowing door, closed his eyes, impressed by the singing vigour of his pulse. He entered, pushed the door closed with stylish precaution, and was surprised to discover his mother was not in her bed.

"Mother!" he hissed, "Mother!"

She was not in the room.

Christ, he thought, she hasn't died on me!

She had not died. She was in the washroom, on the floor. She had fallen off the toilet seat.

He looked at her, helpless, forgotten. He had the impression that her flesh had melted, run down into bulging pools, and then cooled again. He was infuriated by her ostentatious bovinity, her sluggishness in this room which was, for him, the preserve of boyhood, of high thoughts, silliness, of inventive regret.

How long has she been like this? he raged. Five hours? Six? He fingered the cellophane wrapper, his resolve disintegrating.

"I'm not," he muttered, "a veterinarian."

He went back to the bed, found the call button and pressed it hard.

His mother bleated in the washroom. He was perspiring, stifling in his uniform. His mother bleated, and no steps approached.

He cursed under his breath, returned to the washroom, took his mother under the armpits, was appalled by her clammy sponginess, hoisted her onto his shoulders, dumped her onto the mattress and arranged her limbs.

He slumped then into the leatherette armchair which sighed as it absorbed his weight. Overwrought he was, exhausted, his arms were trembling, empty. He listened to his mother's breathing, to the concerted, hospital drone. He listened, aware of another sound, inside the room, a percussive, dry sound. Sitting up straight, he saw a lobster, of all things, marching stiffly by, its swimmerets ticking methodically against the floor. The lobster watched Superintendent PF with its shiny and as though poisonous metal eyes.

"My kid," said the lobster, "is in your pocket."

"What?" said Superintendent PF, astounded. He reached into his pocket, pulled out a transparent, gooey crustacean, dropped it with a thrill of revulsion. The crustacean rattled across the floor, waking Superintendent PF who hurried after his vial of morphine and was relieved to find it undamaged.

He had not slept for more than a matter of minutes, and yet he was utterly refreshed, alert, reassured by his dream.

"Quinty," he whispered, "Melinda, give me a hand."

They wheeled the television stand into place at the end of the bed. Superintendent PF turned on the set, took out the videocassette from the generous inner pocket of his dress uniform jacket, fed it into the slot in the VCR, fast-forwarded, reversed, pressed 'play.'

"My next guest," said Daniel Painchaud, orange sun-lamp tan, patent leather hair attached behind his head, "has an intimidating number of accomplishments . . ."

He put the TV on 'mute,' watched himself advance over the studio floor. His mother struggled in her bed, made awkward, good-natured sounds in her throat, like those a young seal might make. The audience applauded noiselessly.

He stood next to his mother, next to her right arm. They watched together for a time. Faïp was sitting beside him, he was using his teeth to tear open the cellophane wrapper of the Luer syringe.

"I can never," he said to Faïp, "give an injection without thinking of the palm trees in Santa Monica." He tapped his mother's vermiculate, black brachial.

"Too much drugs," said Faïp, "when you were a hippie."

"Hippie? Me?" He inserted the needle, supporting the artery with his left thumb. "Actually, Santa Monica was where I did my paramedic training way back when. Where I learned to do this." He glanced up at the television. Faïp nodded, not unlike an impatient horse, towards Painchaud. "Insulin would be quicker, and just as painless. But I feel more comfortable with the morphine."

Faïp put her hand onto the hand of Superintendent PF's mother. "Fly," she said, squeezing. "Fly hard."

Superintenent PF drew the syringe out sharply, applied pressure to the artery with his thumb, bent the arm over. He observed the back of his mother's hand, was struck by how much the skin resembled phyllo pastry. He felt no remorse, no, and no release. No shame certainly. And no joy. He felt almost as if he had done nothing at all.

Like, he thought, an assassin perhaps.

The audience howled.